When The Tik-Tik Sings

When The Tik-Tik Sings

Doug Lamoreux

Published 2015 by Creativia
Paperback design by Creativia (www.creativia.org)
ISBN: 978-1516815654
Cover art by http://www.thecovercollection.com/
Edited by D. S. Williams

This book is for
Barbara Anderson
in case she has nothing to read

Acknowledgments

Thank you, Eduardo Bagtas, for sharing a terrible moment with me so long ago.

Thank you, Gar Lamoreux, for loaning me a spooky notion.

Thank you, Jenny, always.

Contents

One	1
Two	7
Three	15
Four	24
Five	33
Six	42
Seven	48
Eight	56
Nine	62
Ten	68
Eleven	76
Twelve	82
Thirteen	88

Fourteen 93

Fifteen 98

Sixteen 102

Seventeen 107

Eighteen 114

Nineteen 119

Twenty 125

Twenty – One 132

Twenty – Two 140

Twenty – Three 149

Twenty – Four 154

Twenty – Five 165

Twenty – Six 174

Twenty – Seven 179

Twenty – Eight 186

Twenty – Nine 192

Thirty 198

Thirty – One 203

Thirty – Two 208

Thirty – Three 213

Thirty – Four 219

Thirty – Five 225

Thirty – Six 234

Thirty – Seven 239

Thirty – Eight 246

Thirty – Nine 254

One

You hold in your hand the record of a nightmare. It began as many nightmares do, in the deceptive tranquility of the dark. It began with an early morning jog.

Since her college days, when she was known on campus as 'that runnin' broad', every day of Erin's life started with a pre-dawn jog, to work the muscles, and get the blood flowing. A workout to ready the body for work with just enough pain to feel alive. She puffed her way up from the lower tier, her fourth and last time around, three miles, climbing back to the famous *point* of Eagle Point Park. Every morning without fail, summer, autumn, winter (more a slog; the point was never plowed), and spring. Especially spring when the cool forties of night ushered in glorious days in the mid-sixties.

This was a spring morning in late April just before Easter. *Tik-tik. Tik-tik.*

Erin reached the top of the upper circle, left the poorly-lit drive for the unlit footpath and, in gloom, headed for the bluff peak. *Tik-tik. Tik-tik.*

She halved the distance and was passing the Julian Duncan Memorial, a twenty-five-foot-high tower crowned with cornices like a medieval castle; burial site of the city's founder.

Tik-tik, Tik-tik, tik, tik, tik...

When the dark thing jumped – out and up, Erin darted left, lost her balance, landed on her backside on the wet grass. Gasping, from the run or the fright she wasn't sure, she brought her hands up in defense. But from what? Whatever it was, a big bird, or a bat – she didn't know – burst from the top of the tower flapping like billowing canvas, with a high-pitched ticking sound, eerily musical like bird song from Hell. *Did they have birds in Hell?* Erin wondered. It didn't matter; the sound had gone. The dark thing, whatever it was, had gone too and without her getting a look at it. She stared into a sky the poets' (or Churchill, or someone) had said was darker just before the dawn. Dark but empty.

It had been there, hadn't it? Something had leaped out – well, up, at least – from the top of the tower. Maybe a kite, lodged in the stone parapet, had come loose and flapped away? But it hadn't flapped or flitted like an aimless moth. It had launched itself like an owl from the barn rafters, taken to the air with speed and force, with size and the sound of powerful wings, and an awful ticking noise. It frightened her out of a year's growth and Erin wasn't easily frightened. But where was it? She stared, searching the skies overhead, but there was nothing. She laughed nervously, then spoke aloud. "Enough." Erin forced her thoughts back to the here and now.

She caught her breath, rose to her runners, and dusted her rear. She groaned and pulled a face. Her sweats were soaked and stuck to her tush. It had rained the night before (and would probably rain again that night). But she'd gone for a run, not a sit, and not a soak. The breeze came up, the clammy cold set in, and her sweat turned to a chill.

On a normal morning, she'd have reached the point and would be cooling down, gauging her pulse and respirations. Thanks to darting shadows, there was little point in checking them now. Still, she had her other tradition and even flying phantoms couldn't stop it. She followed the path to the peak, leaned on the retaining fence, and took in the view. For Erin, her breathing evening out, it was the one great moment of the day when the city of Duncan and all the river valley below came awake.

The night sky had begun its change to deep blue with pink, crowning the Mississippi River to the north. Across the river, southwestern Wisconsin remained in country dark and East Duncan, Illinois was aglitter with pinpoints of light. Barges slept in line from the lock and dam below, past the island, the bridge, and the Port District to the south.

A first glance made Duncan look shabby with its rusting barges and dusty industrial plants hugging the river north of the port. But a look beyond, to the glitz of the greyhound race track, the convention center, water park and river museum or, on this side of the port and into the city, to the nineteenth century charm of carriage rides, Bed and Breakfast houses, and the quaint beauty (if not the historical importance) of the river town, showed so much more. Erin turned to the west end of Fourth Street where the cars of the funicular rail elevator rested on steep tracks. The sight would vanish in three weeks when the budding trees shrouded the bluff. She looked east to the town clock at the old city center, two blocks further to the golden dome of the City Hall, and back again to the port. The water was quiet. The steam dredger rested in her moorings, awaiting museum guests. The casino bided its time for tourists as well. Despite dark things, real or imagined, that burst into her life, created chaos, then vanished, all appeared right with the city she'd sworn to protect. There was nowhere else on earth Erin would rather be.

She made her way back to the path and past the tower. Free of leaping shadows, it looked harmless. She entered the upper lot where her cruiser sat alone. Erin Vanderjagt was a cop, a sergeant, and the city's Police Training Officer. Her run was finished and her day about to begin. She had no idea it would be the first day of a week she would remember with fear for the rest of her life.

She pulled from the lot and followed the twisting Memorial Lane along the bluff, into the dense trees and out again where the lane became a 'Y'. Southern Gate Road forked back into the park on her left. It passed under the log cabin, available to rent for family gatherings beside the playground, then the wading pool. Erin eased the squad car to the right, starting down Eagle Point Drive between the tennis courts and the rock-tiered (and currently empty) koi fish ponds, and out of the park. She passed the private residences bordering the bluff and the river above Mississippi Pool 11, then switch backed onto Shiras Avenue looking down into town.

Erin had her mind on a million things. The job, yes, and the day ahead. There were always those and they were important. Law enforcement was her passion but there were other things in life. Her mother, lately feeling ill, had been a nagging monster. *Why do you have to be a police officer? Why must you carry a gun?* (The cyclical argument.) *When will you find a man? When will I be a grandma?* (The sickening argument.) *Why can't you be like Phyllis' daughter? Her favorite straw man!* Then there was Tony, her brother, with business trouble again. Poor Tony, at twenty-three, two years her junior but always the baby of the family. Who didn't have trouble keeping afloat nowadays? But none of it mattered, not her mother, not Tony, not really. What mattered at that moment was… him. Outside of policing there was another passion. So far, to govern stress, a secret passion. *He* was on her mind again.

But only for a fleeting, bittersweet second. One second later, she saw a black Lexus tearing down Orchard Drive. Erin hit her brakes, controlling a slide on the wet pavement and bringing her squad to a stop, fortunately, as the Lexus crossed into the empty oncoming lane at the Orchard – Shiras merge. The Lexus clipped the 'Stop' sign in front of her and the sign cracked his windshield, cartwheeled over her squad (yes, she ducked), and disappeared into the weeds on the road shoulder. The car, with a maniac driver and a spidered windshield, kept going, careening across the lanes, headed for town.

Erin's day had truly begun. She took a deep breath, flipped a switch lighting the bluff in blue and red, and squashed the accelerator. On the move, she grabbed her radio mic, and using enough 10-codes to give scanner geeks orgasms, told dispatch she'd witnessed a hit and run by a possibly drunk driver. "In pursuit, south on Shiras; a black Lexus missing its rear license plate."

Her quarry was all over the road past the front entrance to the park. From there it was a race and the Lexus had a lead. Shiras had only two bends the whole way to Ham House at the edge of downtown. At that speed, they were there in no time and, of course, the runaway driver blew the light. He shot across Lincoln without slowing and crossed Rhomberg as if neither existed. Then, to Erin's disbelieving eyes and ears, he laid a patch of rubber with a cringe-inducing screech. The luxury car fishtailed, somehow avoided flipping, and when the driver regained control (with a turn signal, no less), eased onto Garfield Street.

Erin hit her brakes, without his slide, and turned after him. Amazingly the car sat parked at the right-hand curb, the lone occupant quietly waiting behind the wheel. She pulled up behind, told dispatch the vehicle was stopped, and studied the situation. It had gone from a high-speed chase to a peaceful traffic stop in seconds; it was too odd. Without a plate, no progress would be made until she discovered the operator's main malfunction, checked his registration, insurance, and for wants and warrants. Then she'd see. Without taking her eyes off the driver, Erin lifted the mic to tell dispatch she'd be out of her vehicle.

Of course, that would have been too easy. The driver's door was opened.

Erin swore. She flipped the squad's Public Address on and said, "Stay in your vehicle." Ignoring her, the driver stuck out a leg. Erin was out of the car quickly, hand to her hip, only to realize she was still in sweats and not wearing her service belt. Her gun, her uniform, and probably her brain was in the trunk. "Sir," she shouted, "Stay in the vehicle."

It took a moment but the leg was retracted and the door closed. Erin breathed a sigh of relief, and would have thanked a lucky star but the sky-full had vanished with the rising sun. Her luck vanished too. The driver, who for a moment seemed co-operative, lowered his window, poked out a bad toupee and, unable to turn a full 180 degrees, demanded of the sky, "Who the hell do you think y'are?"

Great. Erin wasn't on the clock, wasn't in uniform, hadn't even had coffee. But she had her first loudmouth of the day, giving the world a hard time. She slipped her flak jacket on. She doubted she'd need it, but the vest would identify her as an officer once she stepped away from her car.

It was forbidden, and darned stupid, to approach a vehicle without your side-arm. But Erin wasn't about to embarrass herself by digging it out of the trunk and strapping it over her jogging outfit. She already looked the fool. Luckily, this guy had proven himself the bigger fool by far. She approached the Lexus down the blind alley behind his left shoulder, hearing him mumble abuse as she neared. She reached his window and interrupted his tirade to ask for documents. He demanded she repeat herself. But Erin wasn't listening anymore. Her attention had been diverted. *Tik-tik. Tik-tik.*

Though farther away, it was the same sound she'd heard on her jog. Erin was certain. She listened, and though she had no idea what it was, knew what it wasn't. It wasn't wood or metal scraping. It was not mechanical. It was a natural sound; unnaturally natural, if that made any sense. It was a song from some living creature, eerie as cricket song or the call of a Mourning Dove. It came from nothingness, a chilling *Tik-tik. Tik-tik. Tik. Tik. Tik...*

Then Erin heard the unmistakable shatter of glass and afterwards, from somewhere nearby, an all-too-familiar sound in her line of work... somebody screamed in terror.

Whether the screamer was male or female, Erin couldn't tell. She shushed the drunk, but by the time he quieted, found the scream had stopped. She studied the houses in gloom, looking for movement or light, listening for anything. A chill ran up her back. The driver mumbled something. Erin shushed him again and grabbed the keys from his ignition.

"Hey! Give those back! This is 'merica, sugar tits. You can't—"

"Shut up!"

Silence. Then, from the right, came another scream. The drunk froze. Standing over him Erin saw the hairs rise on the back of his neck. She was paralyzed too, but from frustration, not fear. Erin wanted to get her gun. She wanted to run to the screams. She was trying to pick which one to act on first, when a two-story house, yellow with black trim, three houses down on the right, suddenly exploded.

Two

In the wake of the explosion came fire and a chaos alien to the residential area of the laid-back tourist town. The source house, the fourth of seven on the right side of the street, was gone; just gone. Those parts of the walls, ceilings, floors, furnishings and contents not obliterated by the concussion had taken to the sky in flaming shards and were already dropping back as scorched hail, or drifting back as blackened confetti. What was left collapsed into the basement which burned like the sixth circle of Hell. An exception was the front door frame. The door was gone but the frame still stood over the three-step stoop, over the flaming pit, like a grave marker. The front third of the roof had blown off in one chunk. It cleared the sidewalk, Erin, the drunk, and his Lexus and landed in the street in one burning piece. Having dropped to the pavement and covered her head, Erin did not see it land. But she heard it, tons of burning wood, ripped shingle, torn flashing, landing ten feet away with a crack and crunch that rattled her teeth. Hot embers pelted her and the Lexus like shrapnel. Finally, the hot rain stopped and Erin's world was deathly quiet.

"Sugar tits, what the fuck was that?"

The Fire Department was there in no time, attempting to deal with the catastrophe. 'Attempting' because, despite their best efforts, the man-power from the city's four stations wasn't enough to do the job. The roof burning in the street, the yards peppered with fiery shrapnel, were merely their first discoveries. In minutes, they found that thanks to radiated heat, the houses on either side of the pit were ablaze, along with a four-stall garage facing the street behind. If that wasn't enough, the explosion, or the fires, or perhaps the flying roof had cut a neutral line in front of the blast house. This electrical *short* crossed the street and set two residences there on fire. That threatened an auto body shop on the corner. It was a beautiful start to everyone's day. 'A' Shift wasted no time calling the chief. The chief wasted no time calling the troops; every firefighter in the city.

Among these was the Station 2, 'B' Shift gang, firefighters, paramedics, friends, and department rejects all. Stationed together in the low-rent district because each was considered a trouble-maker, they arrived as a gang, in their personal vehicles, loaded down with gear. Benjamin Court and Nestor Pena led the way with Ben riding shotgun in the New Mexican's SUV. Josh Tucker and Dewey Arbuckle, massive truckies, weightlifters and beer lifters both, were behind in Tuck's van, with their little sister, rookie paramedic Kristina Pierce. All found their progress arrested by, considering the hour, an impressive crowd of rubber-neckers at the Garfield – Shiras intersection. It was as close as they were going to get. They piled out wearing helmets, bunker pants and boots, carrying coats and gear, and hoofed it through the cars and crowd to the scene a half block north.

Erin's squad, now crossways on the street, kept the crowd back. But Erin, Ben noted, was nowhere around. Five-inch hydrant lines from both ends of the block fed two engines, going opposite directions, fighting a ridiculous number of fires. Part of a roof lay smoldering in the street. One house was a door and a burning basement. The gang saw immediately they were joining a cluster.

Then came Erin, wearing a flak jacket and a stylish jogging ensemble, running down Garfield toward them. A Fire Department ambulance, Station 1's 1-Boy-16, followed her with lights flashing, apparently with a patient on board, headed out.

"Who they got?" Tuck shouted. "A taxpayer? Or one of those dumb asses from 'A' shift?"

"Citizen." Erin backed up her squad to clear the way for the ambulance. She leaned out the open window. "He was inside the house when it went."

"Balls!"

"Both balls," Nestor agreed.

"And a big cock," Pierce added. Ben smirked, looking from Pierce to Erin, and shook his head. The gang broke up laughing. Not at a burned man, but at the pain life dished out and at the way their rookie had quickly learned to deal with it; the way they all dealt with it every day. 1-Boy-16 sounded its siren and eased through the crowd. Erin pulled her squad forward, closing the street back off.

It was then the 'B' Shift gang noticed the dark Lexus at the curb. A man inside, handcuffed to the steering wheel, gave Nestor a new reason to laugh. "Should we ask?"

Erin shook her head. "Just another day at the office."

The gang moved past Engine 4, with three lines pulled, two from the bed, one from a side mount, charged, and snaking to three separate structures. "What a fucking circus!" Tuck said.

It was that, Ben thought, taking it in. A circus with five rings. Only the Calliope music was missing.

Without an air pack, face-piece dangling from his neck, Ben moved through an open overhead door into the burning garage, eating heat and dragging a charged 2½ line on his shoulder. The fire was floor to rafters in the back wall. He opened the playpipe nozzle and unloaded seventy-five gallons a minute across the base of the flames. Wet on red, that was the name of the game. Everything was pie until he saw movement on the right. Three hunched Duncan Rural firefighters had entered the opposite end of the garage through a walk-in door. Blue lighters! It wasn't that pro firefighters had anything against volunteers; they were well trained, energetic guys. But they faced the monster for love instead of money. How screwed up was that?

The band of men, three in a conga line, wore full air packs and gear but gave themselves away in black turnout with white reflective tape, as opposed to the yellow and orange of Duncan city. That and the sad fact that between them, they carried one red 1¼ grass hose that made them look like the Three Stooges taking a garter snake for a walk. And they were messing with his fire.

In the movies, this would have been the instant when an angel appeared on Ben's right shoulder to say, *Don't do it,* followed by a devil on his left sneering, *Go ahead, let 'em have it.* But this was real life, where firefighters and incorrigible rogues made split-second decisions. Before his conscience stopped him, Ben pivoted the nozzle blasting the fire, heat, and smoke across the garage and at the volunteers. The trio had no choice but to retreat.

Ben heard a guffaw and turned to see Nestor, portable radio in hand, leaning on the overhead frame laughing his keister off. "Nice," Nester said. "Now… if you're done harassing the whistle pricks?"

"Maybe." Ben shut down his line and lowered the nozzle. Gray smoke swirled around him. "Why?"

Nestor waved his radio and pointed at Ben's. "You forgot to turn yours on."

"Yeah. Let's go with that. I forgot."

Nestor smiled impishly. "Ethridge is politely requesting our presence."

The day when 'A' Shift's commanding officer, Captain Booker Ethridge, politely requested anything would be one chilly day in Hell. Both knew it. Even if it had been true, it wasn't by the time the pair arrived at the Incident Command Center. Ethridge was a good guy, but tactless. The grizzled captain, talking to Art Blackmore, his engine driver, when Ben and Nestor walked up, growled, "Grab 1-Boy-18 and get over to the 800 block of High Street. 1-Boy-16 has been in an accident."

Nestor moaned. "This is the best fire I've had in years."

"Sorry to ruin your good time, Pena."

"Can't you send a couple of rookies?"

"I can," Ethridge barked. "But I'm not going to."

"How bad is it?" Ben asked.

Blackmore butted in. "We're not there, Court, are we? What do we look like? Swamis?"

Ben smiled. Blackmore was an ass – which was his problem – but he was also their Union president, which was theirs. Blackmore liked himself a lot. Neither Ben nor Nestor shared his opinion. The result was rancor and a perpetual verbal shoving match. "The man I was addressing looks like a captain," Ben told him. "You, Art, look like what you always look like, a penis with ears."

"Enough," Ethridge barked. Five fires and he had to play referee? Goddam firefighters and their nonsense; like psychotic kids. "Can we get back to work? I don't know how bad, Ben. They were hit by another vehicle. They're out of service and their burn patient needs to get to the hospital. When you get there, you'll know. Then you can tell me."

Ben lost the coin toss on the way to the rig. Nestor got to drive and he was stuck with patient care. There were a hundred places on earth Ben would rather have been.

Being hit by a taxpayer while operating an emergency vehicle was worse than traumatic, it was embarrassing. And a screw up a city employee couldn't live down. It was a shame because it was rarely the firefighter's fault. Nine times out of ten, the blame lay with the citizen. Despite blazing red, bright white, or electric green paint, despite sirens and pulsing phasers, despite reflective tape and the yellow, red, white, and blue flashing lights from stem to stern, one day a citizen was going to slam into your fire engine, truck, or ambulance and claim they 'Didn't see you' and 'Didn't hear you'. That was the situation 'A' Shift paramedics Bennehoff and Cooper were in when Ben and Nestor rolled up. A Caddy had blown a red light and broadsided 1-Boy-16 in an intersection.

"Take Roger Ramjet, will you?" Ben asked Nestor. "I'll check the patient and crew."

Nestor eased past a cop directing traffic and parked 1-Boy-18. Ben tossed their jump kit into his vacated seat, for Nestor, then headed for the wrecked ambulance. Nestor started for the Cadillac.

It took the New Mexican a minute to track down the driver, who was out of his steaming vehicle roaming, and several more to get him to stand still. He denied injury and angrily refused to be touched. As he had no acute distress, Nestor called another ambulance, from one of the volunteer Mutual Aid groups, to let them argue with the guy.

1-Boy-16's patient compartment had been stoved in. The same could be said of the pride of the ambulance driver, Shug Bennehoff. Ben found him unhurt but genuinely pissed. "The chief's head is going to explode."

Unable to disagree, Ben offered the only salve available. "It'll be an improvement."

Sandy Cooper, the paramedic treating the patient when the accident occurred, was sporting what looked to be a broken arm. Ben could barely hear her moans because the burn patient on the cot was screaming his head off. "Has he been like this since the accident?"

Cooper shook her head. "Before. Been screaming since we left the fire. I don't blame him."

"Me neither. What's his name?"

"No idea," Cooper said, wincing as she held her arm.

Ben and Nestor transferred their empty cot to 1-Boy-16 and moved the patient, and Cooper, into their ambulance. Bennehoff, opting to remain with his crippled rig, refused to join them. They took off for the hospital.

In the back, Cooper treated herself, tying her arm in a sling while Ben busied himself over the burn patient. Sadly, there was little he could do. Cooper, estimating second and third-degree burns over eighty percent of his body, had established an IV and oxygen at the scene before they'd run. All that remained was to keep the wounds clean and the patient cool without sending him into hypothermic shock. To that end, Ben covered him with a sterile sheet and poured saline on the burns. The patient screamed non-stop. But no doctor, Ben knew, would authorize painkillers in the field for burns that severe. There was no point asking. The patient continued to scream while Ben radioed an 'inbound' report to the hospital. Ears ringing, he cradled the mic, silently wishing Nestor would get them there.

Up front, Nestor was in paramedic heaven. Legal speeding, carefully weaving through the maze of downtown one-way streets, without the stress of patient care. He alternated their emergency tones with a switch in the steering wheel. An ear-splitting 'siren' for the straight-aways, a flick to 'wail' for the intersections, and the god-awful 'phaser' reserved for assholes who ignored the others. He gave some phaser to a soccer mom making love to her cell phone. "Curb right for sirens and lights!"

Northeast Iowa wasn't New York but it wasn't a desert island either. There were plenty of folks in need of medical attention, and in Duncan, they got it at the 300 bed Duncan Memorial Hospital on the edge of the Port District. It had an ER, an Intensive Care Unit, a Psychiatric Unit, and its own Burn Unit; music to the paramedics' ears. In Ben's case, make that the paramedic's numb ears. The patient was still screaming. The intensity of his shouts had lessened since Ben had applied the saline, and what seemed to be a word or two were finding their way out between the shouts. But, if they were words, they were foreign and meant only more noise to Ben. "Any idea what language he's speaking?"

"Nope," Cooper answered with a frown. "Don't know that either."

Though his burned rags had been cut away, the patient still wore a set of dog tags. Ben examined those, found them as foreign as the patient, and returned them having learned nothing. In a way, it made things easier. His inability to decipher the man's cries isolated Ben from the pain. Thankfully he would soon be handing the problem off.

Nestor took the curving drive to the Emergency Room and backed into a stall. Ben abandoned ship and helped Cooper down. He released the cot and he and Nestor rolled it out. They dropped the wheels to the carport pavement and pushed through the sliding doors as the patient perfectly summed up the trip by screaming at the top of his lungs.

Three

Scrub suits and lab coats came out of the woodwork as the paramedics rolled their cot into the exam room. The patient screamed on, pain peppered with, apparently, his three or four favorite words in a language nobody spoke. And he'd added a new trick, struggling to get off the cot. "Aswan," he cried, or something like it. Then a scream. "Mennon! Gal!" Then another scream. And then, God knew why – Ben certainly didn't – the patient shouted, "Tick. Tick!" as if he were a clock. It wasn't funny; the guy was hurting. Still it was hard not to laugh as he started over. He had the attention of all assembled; pharmacy tech, lab tech, respiratory therapist, two nurses, and the ER unit clerk. "Aswan!"

"Whoa!" one of the techs said, covering her ears.

Ben caught the O2 bottle trying to jump the cot rail. "You should have been in the rig."

"Mennon! Gal! Tick tick! Tick tick!"

The charge nurse shushed the patient, with little result, and rolled the bed sheet in her hands. "One. Two. Three." The patient was lifted to the bed. The hospital staff moved up. The doctor entered, looking grim.

"Sorry, Doc," Ben said, "I treated the burns, but failed in rendering psychological aid."

The doctor slipped between an x-ray and a lab tech, took one look, and told a nurse, "Start another Ringers, wide bore. What's his name?"

"No idea," Ben said. The patient screamed again. "That's been his whole conversation."

"Any notion what he's saying? What language it is?"

Ben shook his head and looked at his partner.

Nestor shrugged. "Some of it's sort of familiar, but it's mostly gibberish. Don't think it's either language I speak. Not sure – I got a C in Spanish."

"He's wearing dog tags," Ben said. "But I'm not certain what army they're from."

"If they're from an army," Nestor put in. "Lot of people wear those as decorations."

Snapping on a glove, the charge nurse lifted the tags. "The surname is… impossible to pronounce. The first name looks like Soomnalung." She let it roll off her tongue. "Soom-na-lung? Asian? Korean? Filipino? Do we have an Asian translator?"

Nestor snorted. "There's no such thing as an *Asian* language. Asia is fifty different countries."

Ben stared in amazement.

"What?" Nestor asked defensively. "I can know things." Stray laughs were cut off when the patient screamed again. Nestor pointed. "That one word he keeps shouting, Aswan or whatever, that's familiar for some reason. My wife is from Manila." He stole a look at the tags over the nurse's shoulder. "Yeah," he said. "The letters look Filipino."

"Can you read it?"

Nestor shook his head. "Recognize it; seen their money. They speak over a hundred languages on the islands. Mostly Tagalog. And English. And something my wife calls Taglish." The New Mexican smiled. "It's all Greek to me."

The nurse frowned, giving up on Nestor, and turned to the doctor. "Should we see if there's a Philippine translator in the hospital?"

"No. Let's worry about keeping him alive first." The doctor eased the buds of his stethoscope into his ears. "Make soothing noises to him now. We'll talk to him when and if we get him stabilized."

Ben and Nestor filled out paperwork in the conference room while their patient screamed in his room across the hall. It remained the same, agonized squawks, repeated gibberish, and the tick, tick of a spastic clock. Finally, with an infusion of morphine, it had gone from toe-curling to just annoying. Still, the paramedics were ready for someone to change the record.

Cooper wandered in, her iced arm supported by a nifty new sling, and took a chair.

"Broken?" Ben asked.

"No break, thankfully." Her relaxed smile suggested the burned man wasn't the only patient with a pain killer on board. "How's our Garfield guy?"

"His name's Soomnalung. He's just like you found him," Ben said. "Well done and screaming."

"He wasn't."

"Wasn't what?"

"He wasn't screaming when we found him. He wasn't doing anything." Cooper adjusted her arm. "He crawled out of that basement like something slithering up out of Hell, then he just sat down on the stoop. That's how we found him. House exploded, basement burning, and him quietly sitting there like he was waiting for the mail. He didn't start screaming until we loaded him up."

"Must have been the shock," Ben said. "Before his mind got the message he'd burned his ass off."

Across the hall, Soomnalung shrieked again. "He's making up for lost time."

"Well, I've had enough," Nestor said. He turned to Ben. "Ready to get out of here?" Then to Cooper. "We're going to see if they left any fire for us. Want a ride?"

Cooper eased back into the plush chair. "I'm going to sit here and enjoy the meds for a while."

On the way to the exit, cot piled with replacement equipment, Ben felt a tug on the gurney. The New Mexican had stopped and was staring into the waiting room at a middle-aged man, checking the coin returns of the vending machines. Nestor whispered, "It's Rickie."

Before Ben Court or Nestor Pena were thought of, Richard Savage III had been a Duncan mainstay. Called 'Rickie' by the locals, even transplanted locals like Ben and Nestor, he was as recognizable as any tourist attraction in town. Every day, without fail, Rickie could be seen riding his bike, delivering newspapers, collecting bottles, and checking the coin returns of every pay phone, soda box and candy machine from one end of town to the other. For thirty years he was the 'slow' guy or the 'retarded' man. Then the city's mental health professionals cheered themselves by labeling him, first, 'emotionally and educationally challenged', then, 'developmentally disabled'. Rickie didn't know the difference and couldn't have cared less. None of the titles changed his life a bit. He was sixty-ish; with the mind of a twelve-year-old. His ever-present crew cut had gone gray. His stomach had grown round. But after half a century of riding the Mississippi bluffs, Ben guessed, the guy probably had the legs of a Greek god.

"Rickie," Nestor repeated, this time to Rick Savage himself. "How you doing?"

Ben sighed. "Don't pick on him."

"Who's picking? Did you ever talk to this guy?"

Only once, Ben thought, remembering the incident too vividly. He'd talked to him as a patient and the child-like Rickie was deathly afraid of ambulances. It had been no treat.

Nestor was going on. "He's smart as hell. If he played his cards right he could be the next fire chief. Hey, Rickie!"

Stooped and about his work, Rickie answered without looking up. "Hi."

"Find anything?"

Rickie stood, empty-handed, but not disappointed. He picked up a cold can from the table beside him. "Got a pop. Want to buy it?"

"Nah. You keep it. Hey, Rickie, there's a big fire across town."

"Six fires," Rickie said, correcting him. "Five houses, one garage."

"Oh, you know about it?"

"Yes."

"Aren't you going to go watch?"

"Did. Can't get near."

"Those mean firemen keeping you away?"

"No. Police."

"Yeah. You gotta watch those cops, Rickie."

Rickie tilted his head and stared. Apparently there were a few paramedics he thought needed watching as well. He gave up on Nestor and lifted the can toward Ben. "Want to buy it?"

"How much?"

"Dollar."

"I can get it for a dollar from the machine." Rickie just smiled. "No, you keep it. You found it."

Outside, Rickie tucked his soda into a heaped plastic bag in the front basket on his bike, climbed aboard, and pedaled happily away. Ben and Nestor, reloading 1-Boy-18, watched the old guy go.

"Tough life, huh?" Nestor asked.

"What do you mean?"

"Being challenged like that."

"Don't you have any challenges? From my little experience, life seems pretty tough for everybody."

"Yeah, but how would you like to survive by checking pop machines for change?"

"I wouldn't. But maybe it works for him."

"Nobody would choose that life."

"Nestor, you're a snob. You've got everything in life; a beautiful wife, a child on the way, an incredible house, a decent job that lets you sit on your ass all day. So you pity Rickie. Why? Because he wasn't lucky enough to be born you? Then you give yourself points for compassion. And none of it helps Rickie a bit. Outside of the fact he hates ambulance rides, I don't know a thing about him. Could be you're right. Could be Rickie's miserable and I should be ashamed; or maybe he's happy. Maybe he gets laid three times a week. Maybe he's rich as Caesar. For all I know, he fingers pop machines because he's kinky. Maybe he's trying to do the best he can with what life's handed him, like the rest of us who weren't lucky enough to be born you. All I know is... I don't know."

Nestor eased the ambulance through a larger crowd on their return to Garfield Street. Judging by the remote vans, lights, and notepads in evidence, most of the increase came from the media. Ben spotted Mark Forester, whose picture and by-line he'd seen in many an edition of the Eagle Dispatch, Duncan's paper of record. At Forester's elbow was his rival in news gathering, Jamie Watts, a reporter for the local television station, WKLD. Each looked exactly as you'd expect; Forester with uncombed hair in an unkempt suit, Watts conservative, but camera-hot. There were others, plenty, Ben knew by sight if not by name, all eager for a taste of blood.

Erin's squad remained in place but another officer, a recent Police Training graduate named Parker Traer, manned the post. Now a full-fledged flat-foot, rumor had it Traer might make a good cop, if he didn't take house explosions as welcome parties and let it go to his head. Erin was nowhere to be seen.

Never one to let dogs lay, Nestor (unwisely, Ben thought) asked, "Where's the prisoner?"

Traer didn't seem to understand. That was all right, Nestor frequently had diarrhea of the mouth. Unfortunately, Forester overheard. As reporters care about everything until they ask enough questions to discover they don't, he shouted to Ben, "What does that mean? Hey, what's your partner talking about? What prisoner?"

"No idea," Ben said with a shrug. "Must be an inside joke." He hurried Nestor away from the reporter, the crowd, and the cop, whispering under his breath, "One of these days you're going to get your tit in a wringer. Yours or someone else's."

The charged lines had been pulled from the houses on the far side of the street. Ben's garage was extinguished. Activities around ground zero were reduced to hanging smoke ejectors and chasing hot spots. At the Incident Command Center, Fire Chief Anthony Castronovo, his white helmet shining like a coin in a beggar's cup, led a huddle of department bugles thinking great thoughts. Near Quint 2 some kind soul had laid out coffee and donuts. Several firefighters were there, refilling their personal tanks.

"Want a donut?" Nestor asked. "Or should we report our return?"

Ben didn't feel like a donut. Neither did he feel like visiting the bugles. "I'm going to take a look at 'A' Shift's basement. Do me a favor and report for us; Castronovo hates my guts."

"Take things too personally. He hates everybody's guts." Nestor laughed. "If he doesn't saddle me with a crap duty, meet up with you in a few minutes."

Nestor went while Ben turned slowly in a circle. The few still at it were overhauling, without shifting evidence more than necessary. Ben headed for the pit of debris that earlier had been a basement. He studied what he saw, and as his fire scene 'sixth sense' kicked in, he got a feeling.

Making an effort to avoid attention, Ben lifted a scuttle hole ladder from the nearest engine, dropped it to his side, and strolled toward a rear corner of the pit. He wore his bunkers, with gloves in one of the thigh pockets, but otherwise only his uniform shirt. His coat and helmet were in the ambulance. Going near a fire without gear was against every rule and not very smart. But donning turnout, while everyone else was standing down, would make the reporters and bugles howl questions. He didn't have answers, just a feeling from an item he'd spotted below and wanted a closer look at. *Phffftt* to the rules. As nonchalantly as he was able, Ben snapped the ladder open, lowered it into the basement, and started down. He'd barely reached the scorched floor when—

"See something?"

"Geez! Don't do that!" Nestor stared down at him, laughing. "I think so. I wanted a better look."

"Here. Before you catch hell." Nestor tossed his coat down. He followed it with his helmet and truck belt, then moved for a better look and to block the view of officers and press behind him. "Don't do anything stupid down there. My name's on the coat; they'll think you're me."

"If they think I'm you, they'll expect me to do something stupid." Ben carefully moved through the steaming, smoking mess scanning the mounds and spaces for the object. He found it and pointed.

"Is that plastic?"

"Looks like." Ben moved a toppled ceiling joist from its resting place. He grabbed a bright red melted hunk on the floor, struggled to get it up, and pulled it free. "A gas can."

"Okay. Not a good idea to store gas beside the water heater. But a lot of folks probably do."

Ben directed his partner's attention to another red melted blob. "Another." He pointed again. "And another." He shoved the remains of a wooden box aside. "There's another one."

Nestor whistled. "I'm convinced. Obsessive lawn mower or not, that's a lot of gas."

Ben reached the least damaged corner of the cellar, protected by another collapse, grabbed a handful of fallen floor, and pulled. The wreckage fell exposing shelving and a waist-high metal cabinet. The cabinet door bulged at the top. Using Nestor's spanner, he pried it open, then pushed the helmet back on his head, staring in wonder. Inside were four gray metal boxes with GRENADES stenciled in black on their sides. "Get a load of this," Ben called up, backing off. "Hand grenades."

Every firefighter Ben had ever met was a pyromaniac who thought explosive ordinance great fun under the right conditions. Unexploded munitions discovered at a fire scene, on the other hand, meant get away. It also meant keep it quiet, as the reporters would love it.

"Pena! What's going on?"

The bellow was unmistakable, Tony Castronovo on the stomp. Before Nestor could answer, the chief was beside him and glowering at Ben in the basement. "Well? What are you clowns doing?"

"I'm watching Ben discover evidence of arson," Nestor said.

"I'm discovering evidence of arson," Ben added. He pointed. "There. There. There. And there."

"Gas cans," Nestor explained. "As far as the eye can see. And that ain't all."

"Yeah?" Castronovo demanded. "What else?"

Still backing away, Ben tripped and fell over more tented debris. He rolled to his hands and knees facing the steaming pile on the floor. "You all right?" Nestor shouted.

"Yeah," Ben replied, staring into the debris.

"Well?" the chief shouted. "What else did you find?"

Though they'd been a top priority a moment before, the boxed grenades were no longer on Ben's mind. Instead, he pointed into the steam and smoke beneath him to a thin object protruding from the rubble. Nestor and Castronovo, following his gaze, saw it too. One of them, Ben wasn't sure which, swore. He agreed. The object was a burned and blackened human foot.

Four

It had been one heck of a day off, fighting fire, doctoring, finding contraband weapons and a corpse, exposing certain arson and probable murder, with plenty of report writing on the side, not to mention the day-ending impromptu meeting with brass and bugles where the order, "Keep your mouth shut" was repeated until his head swam. Ben was all in. And he was staying in.

Ben lived in the old Port District in a closed brewery being renovated into apartments. His was the only unit so far and he the only tenant. The building was said to be haunted and, he had to admit, there were nights when it got spooky. There were always sounds of 'settling' and odds bits of light sometimes flashed in the corners of his eyes. But he believed it was mostly his imagination. He'd met no ghosts; just creaks, and groans, and 'what's-that' noises that were probably nothing at all. As sociable as a ghost himself, one sound Ben rarely heard was his own doorbell. When it rang that night, he opened the door with guarded curiosity.

On the other side, lit by a single bulb in the unfinished hall, stood a cop, Sergeant Erin Vanderjagt. Ben raised a brow. "Good evening, officer."

"Good evening. Could I have a word?"

He stepped back and waved her in. "Please."

Erin stepped in; Ben closed the door. He took her in his arms. She wrapped hers around his neck. They melted together, sagged against the door, and disappeared in a kiss. The rotten day vanished.

Sometime later the doodads on Erin's gun belt stabbed Ben and they came up for air. He began the work necessary to secretly love a lady cop. He took the belt, all twenty-two pounds with holster and gun, re-loaders, pepper spray, handcuffs, and radio holster (sans radio), by the front and with Herculean effort undid the double buckle. The belt slid off Erin's slim hips and onto the nearest chair.

"No, no," she said. She grabbed the belt, folded it, and carried it to his kitchen cupboard. "Safety first," she added, returning to his arms. The uniform shirt came next, hastily unbuttoned and peeled away to expose a Kevlar bulletproof vest. Ben sighed, Erin laughed. Determined, he eventually found the slim blonde beneath but not before the mood had been seriously disrupted. Both were laughing.

"Artichokes and onions are a cinch compared to you."

"Yes," she said. "But I'm better eating."

Ben would have agreed but he didn't get the chance. The cop spun out of his arms and was peeling off the armor. "Oh, what a day from Hell. I blame you for it."

"Me?" he asked innocently. "Why me? I didn't buy your speeder a drink. I didn't blow up a house. I'm so far down the chain of command, I barely register as a peasant. What the heck did I do?"

"I can handle the drunks. I can even handle the explosions. But then you came along…" she looked around and dropped her voice to a whisper, "…and found hand grenades and a body."

"And reported them like a good little brown shirt."

"That's the problem. You should have buried them again."

Ben laughed. "Lead to a little red tape, did they?"

"You couldn't have caused more excitement if you'd thrown a slut over a prison wall. Your chief wants them for the fire marshal. My chief wants them for the feds. They argued in whispers so the press didn't hear it. Being brothers-in-law, they'd probably still be fighting it out, but who sneaks in to add politics to the legal nightmare? Jerry Light."

"What's the mayor got to do with it?"

"You are kidding, right? That little tin god? He ordered them both to shut their mouths. They are to offer no information on the corpse, which is fine because there isn't any information on the corpse, and to pretend the munitions don't exist until he can decide what to do about them."

"Where's he get the authority?"

"From the back of his lap. But, since the police chief and fire chief are both appointed by the mayor, he who works beneath the gold dome makes the rules. And because the burn victim, I mean the live one, the survivor, is some kind of foreigner... You knew that?"

Ben rolled his eyes. "Oh, did I know that. A loud foreigner."

"Mayor Light is certain any nod to a higher authority is going to introduce the word 'terrorism' into the conversation. He can already feel the tourist dollars slipping from his fingers. For the moment, the grenades have been locked up in the police station and nobody knows nothing about nothing. If you haven't been told to shut up, you will be."

"Oh, I've been told. I didn't know it was special. Castronovo rarely says anything to me but 'Shut up'. Come to think of it... " Ben reached for her. "You'd better keep me quiet."

They kissed again. But Erin pulled away before either lost their heads. "That must wait," she said. "I'm filthy. I'm disgusting."

"Don't believe all those hurtful things people say."

She hit him, playfully, but with force. "I mean I'm grungy; dirty." She started away. "You've already washed this horrible day away. I'm covered in it and, I'm afraid, coitus is interruptus until I borrow your shower." She headed for the hall, doffing t-shirt and panties as she went while Ben took the opportunity to notice she was firm and straight, and soft and round, in all the right places. She grabbed a towel from his hall cubby hole. He followed her glorious rear end to the bathroom, teasing her on the way. "All you did was direct a little traffic. How dirty could you have gotten?"

"For hours," she said, starting the water running. "In the heat and smoke. Dealing with the public and the media so you heroes didn't have to. And dealing with that drunk."

"What did you do with him anyway?"

She disappeared behind the curtain. "I let him go. By the time the fires were extinguished he was sober. Of course, he started all the usual BS about suing for false arrest."

Her silhouette undulated in the steam. With effort, Ben kept his head. "How'd you calm him down?"

"With a counter offer. I said I'd shoot him and claim self-defense. That got his attention." She shook a bottle, squeezed out its dregs and, with it, a sound you never hear on television. "Have you been using my body wash?"

"It's my shower. Besides, men don't use body wash. They use bar soap."

"Uh-huh." She was unconvinced. "Anyway, I told him I probably saved his life. I reminded him he'd served his sentence in a Lexus, so it could have been worse. I said I was ready to press a dozen charges on top of the DUI. We agreed to call it even and promised to both be better people."

"So that was your morning. How'd the rest of the day go?"

"Crap. We're low on detectives. Judey Taylor just retired and, unlike the movies, they don't call retired detectives back for tough cases. Tankard is fishing somewhere in Canada. And everything is landing on Peter Chandler's desk. He's swamped."

"Did I miss something? How did we get on to detectives?"

She poked her soapy head through the curtain, said, "I'm telling you," and vanished back inside. "My point was; your discoveries gave the department lots of new things to detect. I thought I might get kicked up. They moved Shane up instead."

On his side of the curtain, Ben grimaced. Horatio Shane had far less time on the force than Erin. In fact, she'd trained him. Any reply now would need to be carefully worded. Thankfully, Erin saved him.

"I admit it," she said. "I'm jealous."

"Why?"

"Why am I jealous?"

"Why Shane? You have more time. You're more qualified. I know for a fact you're Chandler's pet. There's no way he chose Shane over you."

"He didn't choose. Peter wasn't asked. Chief Musselwhite said detectives were just detectives. That I was too valuable training patrol officers. End of story."

It was also the end of the shower. Erin turned off the water. Ben handed in her towel. "Being valued by your chief isn't the worst thing in the world. Mine doesn't think I'm worth a damn."

She stepped out, drying her lovely body. "He couldn't be more wrong." The exhausted civil servants' kissed; the weary firefighter longing, the hard cop now all soap and softness.

"Do you want a drink?" he asked.

"No. I want you."

They made love. If you've ever been passionately involved, and had to keep the affair a secret, you know the tidal wave of feelings, pleasures, fears, and thrills at work. No play by play would carry you to those heights. If you haven't known the situation you can't know the feelings. Afterward, they lay side by side, Ben stroking Erin from her muscled thigh to her velvety right breast and back again; Erin watching the stars through the bedside window and drifting at the edge of sleep.

Then a face appeared outside and pressed against the glass.

"Hell," Erin shouted. She dove to the floor, taking the sheet with her, grabbed one of Ben's shoes as she rolled to her feet. Naked as the day she was born Erin hurled the shoe. The face retreated. The window shattered.

"What?" Ben shouted, bolting up as he came awake.

Outside, there came in quick succession a shout, a scream, a thump, and a groan.

Erin used the sheet to improvise a toga. "Someone was peeping through the window."

"What?" Ben rolled to his knees on the bed, still not getting it.

"Someone was peeping!" Erin snapped the light on and pointed at the busted window.

"That's crazy. We're on the second floor. There's no fire escape. Who the hell would shinny… You're barefoot. Watch the glass." Ben threw a blanket over the splinters, then threw their pillows on top. Erin turned the light off again; the better to see out. They came together at the window.

As their eyes adjusted, they saw Nestor Pena, flat on his back in the yard below, alternating between drunken laughter and groans of pain. His wife, Angelina, dark, lovely, and exceedingly pregnant, stood nearby. Her arms were folded over her ample belly and the poor woman looked anything but amused.

"For the love of Pete," Ben yelled down. "Is he dead?"

Angelina studied her husband for a moment, then looked up, and in her clipped Philippine accent replied, "Only from the neck up."

"I can't believe this," Erin whispered.

"What?" Ben asked innocently. Then he shouted out, "You broke my window!"

"The cop broke your window," Nestor cried. "I broke my ass."

"Angelina, if that idiot you married isn't paralyzed, bring him up. I'll unlock the door."

Ben's and Erin's search for their clothes was hindered. Neither was fully awake. The clothes were scattered from the bedroom to the front door. Erin wanted something to wear instead of her uniform. And she was furious. When Ben asked why she went off. "Our seeing each other was supposed to be a secret. Why is Nestor here? How does he know? And what the hell is he doing scaling the building to look in the window?"

"Good questions. But why are you mad at me?"

"He's your best friend. You must have told him."

"I didn't tell him. I haven't told a soul despite the fact I want to shout it from a mountaintop. Like we agreed; no complications, no intrusions in our work, not a word to anyone until we're sure. Which, of course, means until you're sure." Ben pulled on his pants. "What about you?

You and Angelina are close. You didn't mention to her we're seeing each other?"

"Well, of course I did. Angelina is my best friend in the world."

"So it's all right to tell her. But you're mad because you think I told Nestor; even though I didn't?"

"Girls share those kinds of things. Men aren't supposed to!"

"I didn't!" Ben sighed a ton. "But if it's okay for girls to share, how do you know Angelina didn't share it with Nestor?"

"They're married."

Ben stared, thought of ten things to say, but said none.

"Besides," Erin said, going on. "The way Nestor's been lately. Angelina isn't telling him anything."

"What's that supposed to mean?" The doorbell rang. "How's Nestor been lately?"

"See. You're such great friends and you don't even know. They've been having trouble. Arguing, Nestor drinking too much, arguing about Nestor drinking too much. He thinks Angelina's at the hospital too much, that she shouldn't be playing nurse when the baby is so near. That's what he called her career, 'playing nurse'. What do you think of that?"

Ben raised his hands in surrender.

"They've been having a bad time of it. Fights, stress, and threatening behavior."

"Nestor is not abusive."

"I didn't use that word. I'm not ready to, yet. But, after this, don't expect me to be all sweetness."

"I expect nothing. I take things as they come." The bell rang again with zeal. "They're here."

Ben opened the door in an atmosphere worlds' apart from what it had been only minutes before. He was annoyed and trying to hide it. Erin was equally annoyed and wary. Angelina entered, marvelously pregnant, but looking tired and embarrassed. Nestor brought up the rear, limping, holding his butt but giddy and oblivious to the others' gloom. Ben tilted his head to stare at his best friend. "What the hell are you doing outside my window?"

The New Mexican pointed. "Knew 'bout you two. Told Angie 'bout you two. Told her you were getting some like the big people. She said I was full of crap. But I wasn't full of crap." He grinned. "I wanted to see how it was done."

"Your wife's pregnant, you ass," Ben said with a laugh. "Don't you know how it's done?"

"Who told you about us?" Erin asked, not laughing. "Ben didn't let it slip?"

"Ben didn't say a thing. Didn't need to. We've been partners forever and friends longer. Know all there is to know about Ben Court. For instance: Ben picks on everybody. No one is safe from his rapier wit. But you; he don't say a thing to you, just smiles. So Nestor asks himself, 'How come my old buddy, Ben, don't pick on the lady copper?' "

Erin nodded, though she didn't believe it. "We would appreciate it if you didn't spread this around."

"I couldn't agree more," Nestor said, rubbing his aching rear. "Your sex life is your business and my window peeking is mine. You're not the only one with a rep to protect."

"We'll just file it away with your other perversions," Ben said. "Do you need a drink?"

Angelina frowned. "He needs ice for his bottom."

"I'll get the drink," Ben said. "He can take care of his own bottom."

Nestor followed him to the liquor. "Sure, that's what you say when the girls are around."

Erin and Angelina watched them go. "They're both morons," Erin said.

"I know," Angelina replied. "And we give them our bodies. What is wrong with us?"

Nestor served the girls then returned to the bar for his own. He found Ben slacking off. Instead of pouring, his partner was staring out the window at something in the nighttime distance. "What's up?" he asked. "What are you looking at?"

Ben turned as if emerging from a dream. "I thought I saw something. In the harbor."

Nestor glanced out. "How could you see something that far away? You taking vitamins?" He gulped his drink, turned with a groan, and limped back to the girls.

Ben, hesitating, took a second look. He saw only what he always saw, the dimly lit street below and the tourist attractions of the Port District in the distance; the casino, the museum, and the black outline of the old dredger at her harbor moorings. He could have sworn he'd seen something on her deck. Then he heard Erin laugh and shook off the notion. At that time of night, what could he have seen?

Five

Sirens woke Ben the next morning. Sirens and the buzz of a helicopter. While neither were alien, they were not usual morning sounds for a quiet Iowa tourist town. With apologies to Dickens, he peeled his eyes open experiencing the best of times and the worst of times. The best because of memories of Erin the night before. The worst because her place beside him in bed was empty. The best because, though it was a 'B' Shift day and the sirens were those of his gang, he'd taken the day off and could hear them from bed. The worst because Erin's place beside him was empty. Come to think, now he was awake and thinking, why was her place empty?

Atop the coffee maker, Ben found a note from Erin. Seeing it recalled the warm memory. Reading it ruined his morning. She'd forgotten to tell him, owing to the explosion, the body, and the evidence of arson he'd discovered, her day off had been canceled. Meaning, she'd had to sneak out to her own apartment without waking him. His vacation day had been Erin's suggestion, now he'd spend it alone.

Hope you have a quiet day, she'd written. Then added beneath, *Come to think, hope I do too.*

Ben grumbled as he picked up broken glass in his bedroom, dirty glasses in the living room. His mood grew darker as he recalled yesterday's events and Erin's comments about Nestor the night before. Strange things were happening. More, he paused at the window to stare in daylight at the port and, in particular, at the old dredger in the distance. He tried to envision the figure he'd seen but couldn't. Had it been his imagination?

One of the sirens that morning belonged to Erin. She killed it, but left her light bar flashing, and stepped from her squad to stare up at the historic Grand Opera House. She covered her eyes against the sun, heard the *whoop whoop whoop* above, and finally spotted the Duncan-by-Air helicopter hovering over the roof. The pilot and owner of the airborne tour company had called it in. *It* being a report of a woman's body lying on the opera house roof.

Engine 2 roared past Erin and pulled to the curb. The air brakes hissed and its growl eased to a purr. Ben's co-workers stepped down from the rig; the massive muscled Tucker, his gold front tooth glinting in the sun; Arbuckle, his Caucasian twin without the fabulous dental work; and their morose lieutenant, Maximo Pontius, looking put-upon as usual. The ambulance pulled up behind the engine's tailboard. Nestor and Pierce, Ben's replacement for the day, hopped out.

The Fire Department personnel, from bugles to rookie, were still pulling on their gear. The opera house lived downtown, at the juncture of West Eighth and East Eighth streets, between Main and Iowa, putting this 'Unknown Medical' call a half block away from Fire Station 2 around the corner. It would have been faster to walk and there'd been no time to don their accoutrement. Erin was grateful cops carried all their toys on one belt.

"Hey guys." Erin considered adding a casual, 'Where's Ben?'. She wasn't supposed to know, and wouldn't she wonder? She vetoed the notion, feeling silly. The relationship was wonderful, but the secret part of it was becoming a drag. Maybe they ought to knock it off and be a couple.

Tucker, in bunker pants, suspenders, and a uniform T-shirt, tried the front doors and reported from the top step with a shout, "Nobody home. Locked tighter than a nun's box." He did a take in Erin's direction and grinned. "Sorry."

"No worries," she replied. "I'm a Baptist."

Nestor eyeballed the hovering helicopter. "What have we got?"

"Not exactly sure. Tourist flight called it in. There's supposedly a woman lying on the roof. Hasn't moved a muscle since he first spotted her and looks 10-79."

"Easy," Arbuckle muttered. "Poor dumb firemen here. Ten – who?"

"Dead," Erin said. "Of course, the pilot can't be certain. I've called for the key holder. That puts the decision of whether or not we wait on your shoulders."

Tucker aimed his gaze at Nestor. "What say you, Doctor Kildare? We gonna wait for the key?"

The New Mexican twisted his lips. "No. I don't know why she's there. But if she's alive she needs help." He turned to Pontius. "Your call, lieutenant. Break a lock? Break a window? Call in a ladder?"

Pontius considered the question in silence. Or maybe he was thinking of his retirement? Either way, he stared at the sidewalk without a word.

Tuck sighed. "We could just go back and pretend she ain't up there."

The lieutenant looked up. "I guess... We don't really have a choice. Better force the door. But do it carefully." Tuck smiled and headed back up. Arbuckle followed, raising the daddy of all pry bars like a magician about to do a trick.

"Don't, please!" The high-pitched squeak interrupted the assault. "Please, please! Don't!"

Elliott Manwaring, the opera house manager, was a pale skeleton in a shabby bathrobe. Hairless white stick-legs, black socks, and black Florsheims completed the ensemble. He was ancient, but spurred by panic, took the steps two at a time. "My God," he said, ogling Arbuckle's wrecking bar. "My God! This is a historic building. You can't... just..."

"Do you have the key?" Erin asked.

Despite having the truckies as stretcher bearers, it was no small feat getting the cot and equipment to the top. The handicapped elevator in front went only to the second floor; the freight elevator in the rear only to third-floor storage behind the Ballet Academy rehearsal hall. That meant four floors of stairs with tight turns on every level. But the gang, even without Ben, were goers. Led by the manager, they soon arrived above the empty 700 seat auditorium, the offices, dressing rooms, rehearsal spaces, fly spaces; above the ghosts of one hundred and thirty years of operas, silent movies, vaudeville shows, sound movies, stage plays, and live wrestling matches. The group crammed up the final set of rarely used stairs, the Grand Opera about to debut its first corpse.

Five firefighters and a cot, a cop, and a key holder, pinched like beef in a tamale, found the dusty door to the roof chained and padlocked. Manwaring, gasping from the climb, searched his ring, realized the key was not there, and breathlessly asked to run to his basement office to look for it.

"Forget it," Nestor said, easing him out of the way. Manwaring squawked, but the paramedic growled him down. "What is it? A historic padlock or something?" He nodded at the truckies.

Arbuckle put his bar through the lock like a hot knife through butter. Tuck shoved the door. Dust danced in daylight as the morning breeze bathed the rescuers in the stairwell. They stared out, first to the helicopter beating the air above, then to the rag doll on the tar and gravel twenty feet away.

"Oh my," Manwaring groaned.

"Hold it." Erin slipped through the group. She stepped onto the roof and drew her weapon making sure the area was secure. "All right. Come up and out, but stay by the door."

The gang followed instructions, maneuvering the equipment-heavy cot onto the roof.

"Nestor," Erin said. "Just you. Disturb as little as you have to."

The patient, a dyed redhead, wore a red skirt and matching blouse, the blouse ripped down the middle, white lace bra beneath yanked aside exposing her left breast. Her left sleeve hung by threads above the elbow. Neither nylons nor socks were evident. Her left shoe was a red leather pump. Her right shoe was missing. Nestor approached and crouched. Her face, neck, left arm, and stomach were covered in contusions, scratches, and several deep lacerations. Her pale skin gleamed beneath the dried blood. No doubt she'd put up a fight. Nestor paused and took in air as he noted what looked to be a gunshot five inches above her navel. He laid gloved fingertips to her carotid artery. An EMT cannot legally pronounce death, but they can decide whether or not to treat. Nestor had no trouble deciding. She wasn't a patient; she was a corpse.

Erin made a survey of the roof, with special attention to the blind spots behind the air conditioning unit, several old brick chimneys, beyond the short wall running the building's width, and of the eave. They were alone, the sergeant was satisfied. She was mystified as well. With no fire escape, no second access from inside, and no connection to another building, how had the woman and her attacker gotten there? How had her attacker flown the coop?

From the door, Pierce called out, "What do you need, Nestor?"

The paramedic peeled off his gloves. "She can't use a thing."

Erin radioed for backup, the homicide detectives, and the coroner, and told Manwaring to return to the lobby and escort them up when they arrived. She asked the firefighters if they wanted to wait there and wasn't displeased when Nestor replied they were stuck until the coroner took over.

Giving the body a wide birth, Erin crossed the roof. Gaining speed, she jumped the short wall and disappeared beyond the painted ironwork supporting the air conditioner. There, in a corner behind an old brick chimney, with all the privacy afforded an open rooftop by a hovering helicopter, Erin threw up. It wasn't much. She'd skipped breakfast, tip-toeing from Ben's apartment, and grabbed a coffee on the way to the station. There was little in her belly. But she violently surrendered all she had to the dirty tar and gravel of the roof. So much for historic. Panting and pale, she stared over the edge, four stories down to the rear door of the Style Store across the alley. Yeah, Erin thought, catching her breath, I've got style, all right. She drew a handkerchief, dabbed her eyes, and wiped her lips.

"Erin? You all right?"

She spun around, covering her mouth with the handkerchief, startling Nestor almost as much as he'd startled her. "I'm fine."

"Sorry. Wasn't spying. Saw you head this way and thought you might need help. God knows I can't help the corpse." Erin nodded. Nestor fidgeted. "It's okay," he said. "Not going to tattle. Dead bodies aren't for everyone; much less murder victims. My first got to me."

"This isn't my first," Erin said, spitting the taste out. "I've seen homicides. And shootings, and stabbings, and assaults. It isn't the body at all."

"Oh. Okay. Didn't think you had a weak... I mean... Just saw you puking there and I—"

"Nestor, please, shut up."

Across the rooftop, Manwaring escorted the newly-arrived detectives onto the roof. Peter Chandler was all a fiction writer could put into a heroic cop, forty, handsome, calm and collected. He nodded hellos to the civil servants then turned his steel gray gaze on the scene. Hugging the wall behind, with no eagerness to venture further, was Chandler's new junior partner, Horatio Shane. He was African-American so he could hardly be described as pale, still three steps made it plain the young man hated heights.

"You broke the chain to get up here?" Chandler asked the lieutenant.

Pontius thought about it longer than need be. "Had to. No other way up from the inside."

"Fire escape?"

"No. Not for years. We didn't know the condition of the patient, so we couldn't wait for a ladder."

"No criticism intended," Chandler said. "Just getting the lay of the land." He started for the body. Halfway there, he turned back to see Shane still at the wall. Chandler lifted a questioning brow. Shane took a deep breath, and walking a tightrope, joined his senior.

Chandler greeted Nestor, then Erin, by the body. The paramedic was a formality but Erin was clearly a favorite. Chandler made no attempt to hide it as he asked what she had.

"No signs of a perpetrator," Erin replied. "No indication of a struggle. No identification. Who she is, how she got here, how she died; it's a locked door mystery."

Shane whistled. Erin and the lead detective turned to find him over the body. "The wound on the stomach," Shane called out. "That's just like the one on the crispy critter, ain't it?"

Chandler asked Nestor to excuse them. When the New Mexican joined his gang by the door, the detective glowered at his junior. "I applaud your initiative and deplore your thinking out loud."

"No. It's just that this wound is—"

"Forget the wound, Horatio."

"Huh?"

"Stop talking, Detective." Shane scowled. Chandler didn't care. "As my tight-assed British father would say, damn blast it to hell, what do you think you're playing at? You do not refer to fire fatalities as 'crispy critters' in public. That's a term left in the squad room. As to the wound, you are not qualified to determine what it is. That's what the coroner is for. You are correct in noting its appearance. But that is what you do, note it, quietly, for possible future use. Point it out, quietly, to the coroner. When and if he establishes a medical fact, it becomes our secret to cherish. You don't blab it from a rooftop."

"I thought we were all on the same team," Shane said.

"Homicide isn't a game."

"Right. I got that, but these guys are the Fire Department."

"Which is not the Police Department."

"No. I was just explaining. You chewed me out—"

"Detective Shane."

"Yes, sir."

"Stop talking. You are in training, learn something. While you work for me, you are never to have a conversation with anyone for any reason wherein you divulge more than you learn. Now, observe the scene, write copious notes, and be quiet."

Two simultaneous events ended the lesson. First, Stanley Pickles, the jovial coroner arrived. Second, an odd report came over Erin's portable radio. Pickles was a 'kind of' sort of guy; kind of middle-aged, kind of overweight, kind of disheveled, and kind of goofy. He had a cherubic face, a Saint Nick laugh, and an unsettling habit while shaking hands of stretching two fingers to feel your pulse. He whistled a hello to the firefighters and made a splayfooted beeline for the body. Meanwhile, over Erin's portable, Officer Traer's tinny voice reported. "There's signs of a struggle down here."

Erin and Chandler moved to the roof's edge. (Shane held his place, and balance, beside the coroner.) At the eave, the cops peered down to see Traer, four stories below in the alley separating the Opera House from an insurance company to the west, looking up at them. He waved a purse in his free hand. "Five-two. One hundred and fifteen. Red hair. Green eyes," Traer said. "Ring a bell? Her money is still here. More than eighty bucks."

"It sounds like her," Erin said to Chandler. "But it doesn't sound like a robbery. Why chuck the purse off the roof if you haven't bothered to rifle it?"

Detective Chandler's eyes were daggers, his jaw set, as he nodded. "Good question. Tell him, please, to put the purse back where he found it."

She did and, below, Traer did as instructed. A moment later, the humbled patrol officer was back on the air. "There's eh… There is a red high-heel by the corner of the building at the mouth of the alley. Eh, nobody touched it."

"Better and better," Chandler muttered.

Erin's radio squawked again. "There's blood beside the dumpster." The young officer pointed, first at one spot, then at another. Soon he was indicating dried splotches all over the gray asphalt. Erin's radio clicked. "Looks like it rained blood."

Chandler looked from the alley below to the body behind them, and back again. He disappeared deep in thought and, when he returned, said only, "Maybe it did."

"Hold further reports," Erin was telling her radio. "I'll be en route." She looked to Chandler. "There are too many scanners in Duncan."

"I agree," he said, nodding his approval.

"This doesn't make any sense," she went on with a sigh. "The purse, the shoe, blood, and signs of a fight, all down there. The body up here, covered in defensive wounds, but with no signs of struggle anywhere around. How did it get up here?"

"That," Chandler said, "is the question."

Pickles ogled a meat thermometer and scribbled a note. Shane, with stilted steps and tape in hand, measured the body's relationship to its surroundings. The 'B' Shift gang hovered, waiting to be let go. All perfectly normal activities at a scene that was anything but normal. Erin felt something in the air – more than death, something darker.

Six

After a morning of sitting home alone, Ben was so sick of his own company he'd have been glad to talk to anyone up to and including his chief. When his cell phone finally rang, and he saw it was Erin calling, he grew giddy as a school boy. "Hey there. I almost didn't answer. Couldn't read the name on the screen. It can't be right, can it?"

"Why?" she asked, sounding far away and tired. "What's wrong with my name?"

"It's too long."

"Erin is too long?"

"No. I saved your name and number before we were an item. Vanderjagt? I see it every time you call and… I don't know. You say it and barely get past the 'r' before you're exhausted. You should consider changing it."

"Uh-huh. Any suggestions?"

"Anything would be an improvement. How about Court?"

"Ooohhh, I don't know."

"It's dignified. It makes a statement. It's short."

"It's more brusque than short. And it's deceptive. Listen to it. Court. Makes a lot of promises it can't keep, don't you think?"

"Wow. That's harsh."

"You started it. My daddy worked hard to give me that name."

"You're right. I apologize."

"Yeah, until the next time. What are you doing?"

Ben plopped into his sagging couch. "Completely wasting the vacation day you told me to take. But you didn't call to hear me whine, so I'll change that to, I'm enjoying a relaxing day off."

"Glad to hear it."

"Yeah. Hey, what are you doing tonight? Want to hook up? Get something to eat?"

"You must not have heard the news. We've got our second suspicious death of the week. And this one's stranger than the last."

"What happened?"

"I'm not allowed to say beyond the publicly issued 'A body has been found. An investigation is ongoing'. If you want saucy details, talk to Nestor. He can tell you what I can't. Anyway, I called to tell you, if nothing else happens, I'll be doing paperwork until midnight. Then I'm going home to crash."

They commiserated several minutes more, then Erin returned to work and Ben returned to sulking. Misery might love company, but Ben wasn't loving anything about his day. Not long after hanging up, his phone rang again. This time, he would have been delighted to read 'Vanderjagt' but it wasn't in the cards. The screen said 'Fire Station 2'.

The long unusually hot day became an unseasonably cool night and a thick and rolling fog moved in from the river. In that pea soup, the blue door of Room 101 of the Quality Stay Motel jerked open. A young blonde, her blouse torn open, was propelled across the broken sidewalk and onto her scrawny behind in the lot. Her handbag sailed after her, missed her head by inches, and slid across the pavement. A torn jacket and shoe, matching the one she wore, came after, thrown with passion. The pitcher appeared in the doorway, a sculpted black mass backlit by the light of a bedside lamp and the flickering blue of a television. "What's the matter with you, bitch? I gotta get up outta my bed; be called down here? 'Cause you don't know how to treat yo' damned customers?"

The girl, pinching her blouse together with one hand, collecting her scattered belongings, fighting not to cry, dropped it all again at her feet. "He's a pig!" she screamed. "I'm not doing that with a pig!"

"He's a payin' pig. S'all that matters. Who the hell you think y' are?"

A second shadow, short and grossly fat, appeared behind the first. "Who you calling a pig?"

"I didn't call anyone a pig, bitch. Shut up and back up. I ain't talkin' to you. I'm talkin' to my lady."

"She ain't a lady. She ain't nothing. She sure ain't what I paid for. She won't—"

The big shadow turned on the fat one. "Why the hell you think I'm here? Shut the fuck up."

"I'm the customer. I'm the one that's paying!"

"Yeah, man, I know. You'll get what you paid for. Just go back inside."

The fat shadow disappeared. The big one stepped out onto the sidewalk. No longer backlit, he became just an average pimp. He pointed at a parked Lincoln like a manager calling to the bullpen. "Alice!" A meaty brunette hopped out, and eying the blonde with contempt, hurried to her man's side. "Get in there. Shut that son of a bitch up." Alice obeyed while the pimp returned his attention to the blonde. "Hit the bricks, tramp. Don't come crawlin' back here."

The blonde shrieked, grabbed the loose shoe, and ran at him. He retreated and slammed the door. Screaming acid, she beat the door until she ran out of breath, and the room number and the heel of her shoe came off at the same time. Red-eyed and exhausted, she turned away. She covered her breasts as best she could with the torn material and two remaining buttons and scooped up her belongings. With nothing but anger and humiliation for fuel, she picked a direction, and crying again, headed out. Her name, if you care, was Crystal Evers. She felt certain not a soul on earth gave a damn.

The quickest direction away from the motel would have been to head down the hill to Dodge Street, the main thoroughfare for traffic coming from Illinois across the Grant Bridge. There, by shaking her ass or maybe just undoing one of the remaining buttons on the blouse, she could get a ride, some cash, or if she wanted, a place to sleep. Then again, Crystal had had it with creeps for the day. Weren't all men creeps? She didn't want to hook up. She didn't want to hear another word. She didn't feel like telling another lie, not that night.

Her mom's place was some ways away, ten or fifteen blocks. But they were dark, quiet – and tonight – foggy blocks where she could walk alone and be alone. Yeah, her mom was a selfish old cunt and they didn't get along. But by this time of night she'd be drunk and ready for bed. Snagging a sandwich and a corner of the couch would be no biggie. Maybe there'd even be a beer left.

Crystal took in the long Hill Street drive that served as the motel entrance but decided against it. For the rest of the night, it would be nothing but shortcuts for her. She pulled off her remaining shoe and started barefoot through the bushes to the north, headed up toward the intimidating Duncan Memorial Hospital. She crossed the open field and the painted pad where the medical helicopters landed. She crossed Williams Park into the hospital's lot and to the opposite side. She crossed Langworthy Street and cleared the hospital property. She paused, stared up the bluff, and sighed. Some short cut. Like the rest of her life, it was all uphill. Crystal wiped at her tears and started walking.

She'd only been at it a few minutes when a cab eased to the curb and a drunk leaned out with a slurred proposition. Crystal continued walking without a glance. The drunk called her a name and rolled the window back up. The cab disappeared into the fog.

Crystal was too tired to wonder what else the night concealed. Had she, she could never have guessed that ahead on the bluff, on a limb midway up in an ancient oak tree, on the grounds of the nearly-as-old nursing home, the dark thing perched, watching her heading its way.

It wouldn't be a chance meeting. Moments before it had landed atop the oblong sign of the Quality Stay Motel. It grabbed the metal frame of the wooden billboard with a barely audible snick and scratch of its claws and folded in its leathery wings. It aimed piercing green eyes below and inhaled, sniffing for a particular scent despite the heavy air of the Mississippi fog. Then the door to Room 101 jerked open, the young whore was tossed out, and the dark thing's senses came alive. Oh, the smells; the booze, the smoke, the sweat, the old sex doused in lilac perfume; deeper odors yet, scents the world could neither sense nor relish. It watched the violent drama play out. Then, when the girl walked away, it unfurled its wings and took to the air. It circled the lot. It climbed and swooped, loving the darkness. It trailed her to the bluff. Now, from the oak tree standing sentinel at the old nursing home, a place rife with pungent odors of its own, the dark thing watched the girl approach.

Barefoot, Crystal's step was silent as the night around her. *Tik-tik, Tik-tik, tik, tik, tik...*

Crystal heard it, a strange fast song from a bird maybe, or an insect – she didn't know. Other than crickets, what insects did she know? One of a thousand, a billion, creatures of the night. Crystal knew it was creepy, and that in the thick wet air, finding the singer would be impossible. She didn't want to try.

North, that's where Crystal was headed. Uphill, straight up James Street. Until she stopped. *Tik, Tik.* Until she thought she'd change her mind. *Tik, Tik.* It wasn't the night. It wasn't even the weird noise, *Tik, Tik, tik, tik, tik...* though the noise continued and was creeping her out. It wasn't that; it was her route. If she took Burch, she'd have to pass the old folks' home, the place where her Gran had died. The only person in the world, her Gran, who had ever treated her like a human instead of a punching bag or a cum dump. She loved to visit when Gran was alive but now the place freaked her out. She couldn't stand the sight of the building, the memories. She jogged right at Third, avoiding both, and yeah, if she could, avoiding the weird sound.

She stayed on Third an extra block, then headed north again on Summit. Okay, not a short cut, Crystal knew, but what the hell, memories were real. A block later she reached Fenelon, the street her mom lived on, and headed up the bluff again. *Tik, tik. Tik, tik. Tik, tik, tik, tik, tik...*

The sound again. Something more; something behind her. No, she suddenly realized, something above her. Bed sheets on a clothes line billowed by the wind? That was it. But that was silly. Where in the street could…? *Tik, tik. Tik, tik. Tik, tik, tik, tik, tik…*

Crystal turned, searching downhill, but saw nothing. The flapping grew louder. A hair-raising shriek split the air. Crystal looked up, screamed, and took off up the bluff. Running for her life.

Seven

Crystal Evers raced through the shadows up the bluff, up Fenelon Street, in terror. She heard the leathery flap of wings and the shriek again. This time, she didn't look back. In the night and fog there was nothing to see. She just ran.

A glow appeared on the left, a street lamp taking shape, and behind it the outline of the Thatcher House. The beautiful Bed and Breakfast had always been a palace in the mind of the little girl inside of Crystal. She'd grown up catty-corner from it on the quiet intersection. She knew her mother's house was there somewhere, lost in the gray swirl. She couldn't go home, you'd need a home for that, and she'd never be safe. But she was almost at her mother's and it had a door. But the flapping, the shrieking, and now a guttural growl, were right over her shoulder.

The wet concrete made the sidewalk slippery. Her bare feet and mostly naked chest were all-but numb with cold as she reached her mother's unkempt yard. She hit the steps running and dove for the porch. On her knees, she threw the screen door open. It banged and echoed in the thick air as she grabbed the inner knob. Panicked, she tried to turn it and nearly broke her wrist. Why was it locked? Why in God's name was her mother's door locked? This night of all nights? The bitch hadn't locked a door at night, hadn't done anything responsible, in twenty years. Crystal balled her fists and banged. "Helen! Helen, open the door!" Something *thumped* heavily on the porch roof. "Helen, open the door!"

The heavy something scraped the shingles creeping to the roof's edge. The eave was a black line, the world beyond a gloomy gray in the street lamp's nimbus. The gray was broken, Crystal's eyes grew wide, as a thin hand with clawed fingers reached down and grabbed the gutter. The scraping again. Something flitted behind the hand. It took a moment for Crystal to recognize the tip of a huge wing. She screamed. She darted a glance to the door and realized it was useless. There was no answer, never would be. When had there ever been safety with her mother?

She heard a hiss. Something more – a head she decided – followed the hand over the edge. Backlit, it showed no features, just a black head with stringy tresses hanging down and swaying as it undulated. It opened two almond-shaped eyes, bright green in the dark. More of the wing presented itself, fluttering. The dark thing hissed again and reached for her.

Crystal screamed and ducked. She bolted around the outstretched claw and off the porch. She slid to a stop in the street, terrified and unsure where to run. Then it came to her, a hope for shelter. The focus of everyone on the bluff in that silly tourist town, the elevator!

There in Mayberry, Crystal knew, to the goobers on the bluff, the elevator had always been the tits. At 296 feet long, angled from the top of the 190-foot bluff, the Fourth Street Elevator was the shortest, steepest railroad in the world, a funicular railway, listed in the National Register of Historic Places. It had two cars; one atop the bluff, one at the base. Connected by cables, they counterbalanced each other and passed one another at the mid-point. Each car was a solid box with a sliding door. She could hide, she hoped, in the car at the top. Crystal raced for the Fourth Street Elevator.

The frantic flapping of the horrible wings sounded behind her, coming on. Despite being barefoot on slippery pavement, Crystal ran with all her speed. She jumped the turn-style at the entrance and juked the zig-zag path to the tourist attraction. The top car appeared out of the fog ahead but, with less than ten feet to go, the creature was upon her. Shrieking, its wings whipping the air, the dark thing grabbed for her. Crystal slapped at the grasping claws. Razor nails slashed her arms, bit the flesh of her wrists, dug into her hair. Screaming, hysterical, Crystal blindly lashed out, punching scaly flesh, hard muscle, coarse body hair. She yanked the hair dangling from its head. The dark thing retreated, flapping madly to regain elevation. Crystal, feeling no victory, used the pause to dive into the tram.

The flying thing would not be denied. Behind her, it hit the door with a crack, folded its wings, and used its arms to swing through. Crystal spun, falling onto the wood bench, and threw her feet up. She kicked and screamed at the top of her lungs. Hissing and shrieking, unable to get hold, the creature leapt out of the car and into the fog. An indescribable silence followed. Torn and bleeding, her blouse in tatters, crying and trying to catch her breath, Crystal eased herself up on the bench. Fog curled into the car. *Tik, tik. Tik, tik.*

Crystal gasped. The strange noise again and the frenetic flapping of leather. Weight and substance hit the roof. The tram shook violently. Crystal screamed until she thought she'd lose her mind. The car stopped shaking and she caught her breath. Silence again and wet gray fog. The thing was gone.

Sniffling and wiping at her swollen eyes, Crystal stood. She scanned the fog, straining to see, to hear. Then again, a noise outside of the car. Distant but nearing. She held her breath to take it in. A low growl and the same evil song. *Tik, tik. Tik, tik. Tik, tik, tik.*

The car rocked. Crystal yelped and grabbed for the bench. There came a snap and a metallic twang. The car jolted as something lashed the rear wall like a bullwhip. Crystal jumped as the car lurched. She screamed as the bottom fell out of her stomach and her world. The tram rattled on its tracks as it plunged down the bluff.

An alarm tone sounded. "City Fire, Station One. Engine and ambulance needed, Cable Car Square, for a reported explosion. Engine and ambulance needed for a reported explosion, Cable Car Square. Time out – 21:36 hours." A radio crackled and, over the air, the voice of 'B' Shift's Captain Rosenka dispatched Engines 1 and 2, and 1-Boy-16. (A temporarily rented 1-Boy-16 standing in for the smashed original.) In the ambulance, in the fog, blocks away from the station, Ben reached for the radio mic.

Yes, Ben Court. No, you haven't missed a chapter. You knew Ben took a day off, at Erin's request, to spend with Erin. That, due to uncontrollable circumstances, she'd been called to work leaving Ben with no plans. Bad, but it got worse. Without mentioning Erin, Nestor let slip news of Ben's tanked day off and the rookie got an idea. Pierce called Ben, and as his day was a bust, asked if he'd cover her shift for a few hours. With no reason to refuse, Ben was now filling in on the ambulance with his own partner on his vacation day without pay. As the Looney Tunes would have it, it was a revolting situation. He and Nestor were returning from an uneventful non-emergency when dispatch reported… what they'd reported.

"Explosion?" Nestor asked in disbelief. "Another explosion?"

"That's what the lady said." Ben acknowledged the call.

"What the hell?" Nestor lit the lights. "What is there in Cable Car Square to explode?"

Ben killed the siren. Nestor maneuvered 1-Boy-16 across Bluff Street and into the square where both paramedics peered through the night and the swirling fog at the answer to Nestor's question. As if scripted, the same phrase escaped their mouths in unison: "Holy shit!"

The Fourth Street Elevator had been one of Duncan's most charming tourist attractions. It was built in 1882, believe it or not, to shorten lunch breaks. With the business district below, and most residences on the bluffs above, it took working men a half hour by horse and buggy to travel one way; morning, noon, and night. Add in lunch and it was two and a half hours a day, with no business conducted, for the worker to travel 200 feet as the crow flies. A funicular railway – 'the elevator' as the locals called it – was the answer. As the auto gained popularity the elevator became less a necessity and more a unique attraction, a symbol of the city. That's what it had been; now it was a pile of wreckage.

Somehow the steel cable had snapped. The top car had dropped the length of the track and crushed the bottom one. Like dominoes, the wreckage of the conjoined cars smashed into the motor house at the track base. The devastation was eerily visible in the fog because the motor house was on fire.

A police squad was already there, and before Nestor could park the rig, the officer – whose forearm was bleeding – hustled over to report a female victim (cops never say patient, it's always subject or victim) in the wreckage. He'd tried, but had been unable to get to her.

Engine 1 arrived and backed in. Engine 2, right behind, parked outside the square. Captain Rosenka had his boys, from the clean side of town, pull a line and head for the fire. Tuck and Arbuckle joined Ben and Nestor at the wrecked cars. Lieutenant Pontius stared.

Ben climbed the bottom tram to peek into the folded car on top. Flames licked at his rear and he sent up a grateful prayer for fireproof clothing. Still it was hot as Hell. "She's here." Ben jumped down to give the truckies room. To a chorus of loud cracks, Tuck and Arbuckle peeled the tram wall back.

Nestor shouted, "Don't stay too long!"

Ben slipped through the fissure. His partner's advice had been sound. The heat inside the car was oppressive. Only a few feet away the motor house was totally involved and the lower tram catching. The engine crew, ready to douse the fire, were waiting for him to get the patient out.

Ben found the girl upended, her head on the floor, her legs pinched by the collapsed roof. He lifted with his shoulder and freed her legs. Then he felt for her carotid. Her face was soaked in blood but that meant little. The head teemed with blood vessels and the smallest injury could bleed buckets. But there was no pulse. From the unnatural twist of her head, it was obvious she was gone. But he wasn't going to leave her to the flames. Ben lifted her through the hole as the superheated air in the building flashed over. The wreckage erupted.

Engine 1 revved. Her team opened the nozzle on their attack line and went to work.

Clear of the fire, Ben laid the girl in the lot. She was torn and bleeding from top to bottom. Her feet were bare and her top shredded, the buttons gone. He tried without success to cover her.

"I'll get the jump kit," Nestor shouted, starting away.

"Forget it," Ben said. "Her neck is broken. Just get a sheet."

The girl at their feet was now merely a body, one hundred and five pounds of decaying meat. As only Jesus and Hollywood could revive a corpse there was nothing for them to do but call the coroner. Ben radioed dispatch. Then he stared again at what had been Crystal Evers, another Jane Doe to him. She'd had a hell of a tussle with someone. She also had track marks on her arms betraying a heroin addiction. She'd apparently had a hell of a tussle with life, too.

Nestor covered her. "Another one."

"Another what?"

"Another murder. Another gunshot." He lifted the sheet and pointed to a round red puncture on her stomach. "The same wound the Keddy woman had."

Still distracted, Ben asked, "Keddy woman?"

"The D.O.A. Pierce and I had this morning. On the opera house roof. They found her purse in the alley; name was Linnea Keddy." Nestor grinned. "Erin was there."

"Yeah, yeah. Get to the wound."

"I'm just saying it's the same or a lot like it. The roof lady had it."

Ben examined the small deep wound about four inches above her navel.

"Cops think it's a gunshot," Nestor said. "Looks like it. But it's a hell of a way to commit serial murder. Shooting people in the stomach?"

"Serial murder?"

"Yeah. He might have been talking crap," Nestor said, "but Shane, the detective, said there was another. He must have been talking about the Garfield Street Jane Doe because he said it was on the 'crispy critter'. The same wound as the roof lady. The other dick, what's his name…?"

"Chandler."

"That's him. Shane must have given away a state secret or something because Chandler told me to scram, then chewed on Shane's bootie."

Ben exposed the wound again. "What do you think, Paco, is it the same?"

"I know nothing from nothing, pal, you know that. Looks the same. But who shoots women in the stomach? And, if it's not a gunshot, what makes a puncture like that? The others had it, so it's not from the tram. It's too big for an ice pick or an awl. It's too round for a knife or bayonet. There was no room on the roof or inside the tram for a horse, so she wasn't jousting."

"Be serious."

"I am."

"Are you sure the first body, the house fire fatality, had the same mark?"

"Am I sure? No. I told you I was eavesdropping. I'm no better at that than I am at window peeping. I think that's what Shane said. But maybe he's delusional. I don't know the guy. What difference all this?"

"Three victims. Three identical wounds. Two explosions. There's something we're not seeing."

"There is," Nestor agreed. "If you look at the patch on your shoulder, you'll *see* Fire Department. Sleeping with a cop don't make you one."

"Goddammit, stop bringing that up. Do you know what 'Keep your mouth shut' means?"

Ben felt like an ass before he'd finished shouting. Nestor threw his hands up in surrender. Their mutual looks of apology were lost in darkness as a cloud of steam joined the rolling fog and the inferno that once had been a set of historic tram cars went out. *What the hell else,* Ben wondered, *can go wrong with this day?* He froze as the foggy night answered his question. From the top of the bluff and the height of the destroyed railroad came a high-pitched, terrified scream.

Eight

Ben and Nestor were half-way up the bluff when the call came: ambulance needed at 600 Fenelon Place, atop the destroyed Fourth Street Elevator. Rosenka dispatched his Station 1 ambulance. Nestor, at Ben's suggestion, countermanded the captain's order. "1-Boy-16, City Fire. We're 10-8 and en route. We'll take that call." The captain barked, but thanks to scanners everywhere, had to choke off a tirade. They arrived up top a few minutes later to find nearly as much chaos as below.

The fog had thinned slightly. The flashing reds and blues of their ambulance matched the muted auras from the patrol vehicles already there. Ben slid the rig between two squads to the right and an unmarked sedan with a dashboard light to the left, and eased it near the Thatcher House overlooking the tram. Nestor slipped into the rear compartment for their jump bag.

Detective Chandler was there, Johnny-on-the-spot, interviewing a disheveled, middle-aged woman. Several uniformed officers looked on. Shane met the medics. "What's happening below?"

"Fire's under control. Occupant's D.O.A." Ben pointed at the woman. "Is she the screamer?"

Shane nodded. "We thought we'd need you. Now I don't know. She's Mrs. Helen Playford."

"Playford?" Nestor asked, scribbling on his clipboard.

"Yes. The victim below is tentatively identified as Crystal Evers, her daughter. Mrs. Playford saw the incident from up here. Or as much as she could have seen in this fog. Like I said, it's tentative but likely. It's about as sad a deal as can be. She's a hungover mess; belligerent, defensive, and a drama queen. I think the screams are for attention, not her daughter. Says she can't breathe."

Few, Ben knew, were at their best at a scene of violence. Allowing for that, and the familial trauma she'd endured, the woman was still no treat. She was thin, gray, moving with the stilted half-speed of an inebriate, holding a bloody handkerchief to her cheek, with a cigarette bobbing in her mouth. Ben greeted Chandler with a nod and the patient with a muted smile. "Mrs. Playford? We're with the Fire Department. We're here to help. You cut your cheek?"

"I fell down," she replied in a voice made of gravel.

Ben nodded. "I understand you're having a little trouble breathing?" He plucked the cigarette from her lips, dropped it to the pavement, and crushed it out.

"Hey! I just lit that. Those are expensive."

"They are. But you're having trouble breathing and you can't smoke around oxygen." Ben gently took her wrist and moved the hanky to examine her face. Her cheek had a lovely case of road rash. Nestor cracked the seal on an O2 bottle and was opening a nasal cannula.

"I don't need that," Mrs. Playford insisted. "I'm just upset."

"You wanted help," Chandler reminded her. "Let these guys help you."

They did, across the sidewalk and onto a chair on the wrap-around porch of the Bed & Breakfast. Ben assessed her vitals, Nestor applied the oxygen. In the same tone used to ask if the morning paper had arrived, or if the dog had finished its business in the yard, Helen Playford asked, "She dead?"

"Yes," Ben said. "I'm sorry."

"Dead," she repeated blankly. "Crystal never was nothing but trouble."

Ben nodded an acknowledgment, sorry he'd wasted the apology.

"Can you tell us what happened?" Chandler asked. "How you discovered there was trouble?"

"Heard banging on the door." She pointed. "Heard banging, shouting. Didn't know what it was, who was banging. I hadn't seen anyone come up to the house."

"Were you looking?"

"No. I was out of it."

"You were sleeping?"

"I was out of it. I didn't know it was Crystal 'til I seen her going. Don't know how she got here. Where she come from. She's a night person. I just don't… The banging woke me up. Time I got to the door… When I looked, I saw Crystal across the way, running for the elevator. Then she disappeared in the fog. Something… something disappeared after her."

"Something?" the detective asked. "Do you mean someone?"

She ignored the question; perhaps she hadn't heard it. She stared blankly. The cop frowned, flipped his notebook closed, and shrugged. Ben touched her arm. "Mrs. Playford? Mrs. Playford?"

Her eyes slowly focused. "Crystal? She left before I could open the door. She ran…" She pointed to the top of the tracks. "Ran like she was being chased. I ran after them. I ran… crossed the street." From wherever she'd gone, Helen reported in a dull monotone. "Got to the far corner of the Thatcher House and looked down. Crystal was there, hard to see in the fog, screaming, and scratching, ducking back into the cable car. He was going in after her. Jumped right in after her. Right on top of… my baby girl."

"Who was it? What did he look like?"

Helen shook her head. "He was dark. It was dark and the fog was so… He had long black hair… and a big black cape." She turned first to Chandler, then to Ben, staring past both. "He was flying. He was jumping and flying and Crystal… she backed into the elevator. Screaming."

She continued the incoherent nonsense, and Ben, Nestor, Chandler and Shane listened; hogwash, all of it, lubricated with alcohol. Any one of them might have told her so had Helen Playford not started to cry again. But this bout was different. For the first time, Ben believed she really was crying for her daughter. "Couldn't see," she went on. "The dark. The fog. Her screams were so loud. Crystal! It was a man flapping around in a cape. Then it wasn't a man at all. It was a woman. Then it was nothing at all, just a dark thing made of shadows. Big wings made of shadows. But it couldn't have been that." She touched her cheek, tears racing over the wound, then looked at Ben, pleading in a drunken haze, pleading in terror. "Who was it? What was it? Followed Crystal into the car?"

"Mrs. Playford," Chandler said. "What happened after Crystal climbed into the car?"

"The car was rocking," Mrs. Playford said. "I heard Crystal screaming. I ran as fast as I could. I slipped and fell. It wasn't my fault. I have arthritis. The doctor says I need a knee… It jumped out of the car. The cape flapped all around and the shadows and the fog. Everything was spinning. I felt so sick."

Chandler scowled. Mrs. Playford was again the center of attention. The perp had gone full circle from a shadow, to a man, to a woman, to a shadow again. Not very helpful. Her speech grew more slurred, whether from her swollen face or the effects of alcohol, Chandler didn't know.

"The car dropped. It started forward and down by itself with Crystal inside. I don't know how that could happen. That's not supposed to happen, is it? The car disappeared down into the fog. And the sound when it hit…"

"The man," Chandler said. "Where did the man go?"

She stared silently past him into the sky.

Ben told Helen she needed stitches, a tetanus shot, and x-rays and tried to talk her into going to the hospital. She seemed not to hear him at first, and when she did, refused to go.

"If you won't have the ambulance, Mrs. Playford," Chandler said. "You'll have to go with these officers. We're moving your daughter. The medical examiner will need you to identify her. It's the law. Maybe, if you feel more like it then, someone can take a look at you."

Without argument, Helen Playford went with the cops. With a "Thanks, guys," Chandler returned to his work.

With an "Oh, Shit," Nestor spotted a red and white 4x4, with flashing lights, appear out of the fog and park near their ambulance. It was Fire Chief Castronovo, wearing his white bell cap and his ever-present scowl. He waddled past a growing number of on-lookers, including Mark Forester, the newspaper reporter who apparently never slept, and straight toward his paramedics.

Nestor sang under his breath, "We're going to catch he-ell."

"What else is ne-ew," Ben sang back, before switching to a whisper. "I better get to church. When you worry what the chief thinks, it is clearly a sign of the apocalypse."

Castronovo was on them, barking like a junkyard dog. "Who do you think you are, countermanding your captain's order? Why did you leave your patient below?"

"The girl below is dead," Ben said. "Rosenka's right there. She's surrounded by cops and firefighters waiting for the coroner. When we heard screaming up here, as far as I was concerned, our duty below was discharged. We can do more for a screamer than we can for a corpse."

"It wasn't your choice to make."

"I'm the senior paramedic," Ben said, refusing to retreat. "The captain's sitting on his ass in the Engine 1 cab. It was my call. If you have a problem with that, chief, you have remedies through the Civil Service Commission. Howling at me in the street is not one of them."

Castronovo sneered. "You think you're so smart, Court. Well, hear this; this station house lawyer routine of yours is wearing thin. But keep it up. Every time you pull it, you're one step closer to looking for work. You have no idea what's hanging over your head." Castronovo stormed away, grumbling.

None of them had any notion what was over their heads. Helen Playford had been mistaken. The dark thing had not gone. It hung above them, on a branch in the top of a tree, watching the commotion through the slowly thinning fog. It watched the engine company put out the fire. It watched Coroner Pickles, with the firefighters' help, zip Crystal Evers earthly remains into a vinyl bag. It watched the fire chief leave in a huff and Ben Court and Nestor Pena pack their gear wearing grins of minor victory in their skirmish with the powers that be. It watched the neighbors, passers-by, and media sluts end their rubber-necking and call it a night. It relished the taste in its tongue, and lusting for more, sniffed the thick air for that special scent.

The odor it wanted was no longer present. The humans below no longer interesting. Unseen, the dark thing took to the air; searching.

Nine

"To vacation days," Ben muttered. "And romance." Smiling wearily, he drank his toast alone.

What had been intended as a relaxing day of laughter, good food, and great sex had ended up one long trudge through Hell. Thank God it was over. Thank God for fermented grain. While he was at it, thank the furniture makers for his comfy bar stool.

The Well, a watering hole on the fringe of the Port District, had once been his home away from home. When he'd started seeing Erin, that changed. They'd never gone together. It was in public, after all, and Erin despised the place, called it a dive. Ben liked it for precisely the same reason.

In his civvies, relieved by the returned Pierce, off duty and back on vacation, Ben was in The Well aboard his stool, guiding a lime sliver with a cocktail straw around a submerged olive and through a gauntlet of ice cubes in a tall gin and tonic, when Mark Forester slid uninvited onto the stool beside him. Ben didn't say hello, and when Forester did, didn't reply. Forester, an old hand at Public Relations, put it down to preoccupation with the day. Why else would anyone be so rude to a harmless newspaper reporter? He struck a bargain with the bartender for a scotch and soda and, after a gulp, a cough, and a second gulp, asked Ben, "Heck of a day, huh?"

Ben sipped his gin, sighed, and sipped again.

"Yes, sir," Forester repeated. "Heck of a day." He looked at Ben. "What do you figure? Three women killed, in three undeniably bizarre accidents, in just two days? Two explosions? One man burned beyond recognition? Which must be a treat when you're still alive. Inexplicable? In the little town of Duncan? Yes? No? Is there an explanation? They were accidents, right?"

Ben stared into his glass, envying the olive. God loved a gin-soaked olive. God didn't love him, Ben realized. God sent him reporters.

"You know," Forester said, going on. "I could have started with a 'Gee, strange meeting you here,' or a 'What a coincidence.' You know, a little bull crap to grease the way. But, like you, I'm not much of a lube pro. And it isn't a coincidence. I saw you leave Station 2 and followed you; first to your apartment, then here."

"Whoa. That's kind of creepy."

"It would be if I was a stalker. But I'm a reporter, so it's just annoying for you and boring for me." Both drank their drinks. "So what do you figure?" Forester said, starting again. "These deaths?"

"Just what you said. They're inexplicable."

"Come on, Ben, you were there. At least for the first and the last. A house explodes. The elevator explodes. There's a connection, isn't there? That connection leads somewhere?"

"Forester, I can't talk about it. If I could, that doesn't mean I would. Or that I'd have anything intelligent to say if I did. Or that you'd be able or willing to get it right."

"Try me."

"City Hall is full of bugles, badges, and offices with lettering on the doors," Ben said, lifting his glass. "Why don't *you* go try them."

"How can I convince you I'm on your side, Ben?"

"Who said I have a side? And who told you to call me Ben, Forester? We're not buddies."

"All right, Mr. Court. I can keep it professional. As one pro to another, these aren't ordinary deaths. There is something strange about them. That wasn't your average house fire either. Give me a hand, can't you?"

"Against the rules. My job is frequently in jeopardy. I don't need your help."

"The deaths are a matter of public record."

"Unquestionably. But the details are not. They're a matter for police and fire investigation."

"All right." Forester dug into his jacket pocket, pulled out a ringed notepad, and consulted a page. "Let me ask you something specific. What can you tell me about this... severely burned man from the Garfield Street fire, Soom-na-..."

"Soom-na-lung," Ben said, finishing it for him. "I can tell you nothing more than what you told me. He is a severely burned male patient."

"No one will release any more information about him. The hospital isn't allowing visitors."

"That is not a mystery, Sherlock. No severely burned patient gets visitors. Their skin is gone. They have no way to fend off infection. As to specific information about that patient..." Ben shrugged. He caught the bartender's eye and pointed to his empty glass.

"I'll have another too," Forester told him before he got away. "Did he cause the fire, this patient, this Soomnalung? Did he kill the burned woman? Or is he a victim too?"

The barman returned with their drinks. "Who's got the honors?"

"I've got mine," Ben said.

Forester shook his head and waved a bill. "I've got both."

"Where does a reporter get money?"

"*Meh.* Phony expense vouchers but there's no story in that." The bartender left. Forester leaned toward Ben, lowering his voice but heightening his plea. "This woman on the roof, eh, Linnea Keddy. They wouldn't let me up there."

"It was a crime scene."

"Right, I agree. My point is I soon realized I didn't want to go up. The murder story was in the alley. I've seen crime scenes, and the way they were going over that alley, it *was* a crime scene. Why, I asked myself? Why, when the body was over fifty feet above? That question led to another. And another. Suddenly it's a story like I've never seen. But

I'm an idiot because everybody with a badge keeps telling me there is no story. It stinks, Ben. It stinks grand. Now, I'm a level-headed guy; I'm not a conspiracy nut. Elvis is dead. Nine-eleven was a terrorist attack. Oswald did it. Okay? But, damn, what happened in that alley? How did the victim end up on the roof? And if I am full of cheese regarding recent events in this city, if exploding houses and bodies on rooftops are normal, okay, I'm full of it. So, tell me, what happened tonight? What about the girl, whose name is being withheld, but who is certainly Crystal Evers, twenty-six, of 600 Fenelon Place? How was she killed? Why was she on a tourist ride not in operation? What happened to the ride? What snapped that cable and dropped that car? Who was the unnamed Crystal's mysterious attacker, the man in a cape?

"You've heard all the whispers."

"I didn't need whispers. The neighbors up and down Fenelon Place want their fifteen minutes of fame like everybody else and they're babbling like brooks. I listen. I hear. I'm not one of those reporters who goes to an interview with the story already written. I want to know what happened. I'm not an angel and don't pretend to be. I'm in the business like the rest. If it bleeds it leads. But that does not mean I want it to bleed. When it does, I'll be there to get my headline. But I also want to know why it's bleeding. And how you guys stop the bleeding. And I want to know and say what the community can do to help."

"My, oh my, I had no idea what a decent fellow you were."

"I am. But I suffer for it. My name's mud at the paper. The editor hates me. The janitor thinks I'm a slob. The old man that runs the press would like to break my neck. I'm tolerated because I'm a damned good reporter. Everything I've heard and seen says the same for you. I'm not looking to get you in a bind. I don't want sensation. I want facts, whatever they are, and a chance to present those facts to my readers." Forester emptied his glass. "I told you I look and listen. I've noticed your relationship with department authority. Love/hate doesn't begin to describe it. You're a passionate firefighter and a fine paramedic, but you don't follow orders and you say the wrong things to the wrong people. Every one of them from your lieutenant to that rat bastard mayor would like nothing better than to assign you to a dark basement where you could spend the rest of your career picking gnat shit out of pepper."

"It's none of your business, Mark!"

"I never said it was. I said I saw. Thank you for calling me Mark."

"What do you want?"

"I need a friend downtown."

Storm clouds roiled in Ben's eyes. "I ought to knock you off that goddamned stool."

"I don't want a spy. I don't care about fire house gossip. I'm asking for help getting beyond political bull on matters of importance to this community. I need a friend in the Fire Department and I haven't wasted time denying it. Return the favor and admit you could use a friend at the paper."

"I have no intention of giving you dirt on my brothers and sisters in the fire service."

"See? You're lofty too. I didn't ask it; I wouldn't. But if you're trying to convince me you're one big happy family with common goals, I'm calling bull crap. You're as far on the outs as I am and you're a pain in everyone's ass. Your chief despises you. There is no love lost between you and your lieutenant. And you and your union president?" Forester whistled. "Oil and water. They tolerate you because you're a fire eater and an excellent paramedic. In fact, if the department didn't have you they'd need to invent you. But they hate you. They live for the day they can make you go away because you won't stroke their egos and play their games. When they do finally put the screws to you, it wouldn't hurt a bit for the paper to remind the public you only eat the babies that deserve it."

Ben sighed, sick of the day. "Fine. You're Mark and I'm Ben. We're bosom buddies. Now what?"

"Now give me something, a hint, on what's going on in this town. What do you say?"

"I say, I don't have anything for you. I agree there are weird things happening but I have no inside track. If you want to know about these deaths, ask the police."

"I did," Forester said with a sigh of his own. "Peter Chandler is in charge of the investigations. Have you ever spoken to Chandler? The guy is a clam – and not a happy one."

"From what I've seen, he strikes me as a damned fine cop; well thought of in the department."

"I can't tell you how that excites me as a taxpayer. But as a reporter, I'll pass. The guy can disappear off the face of the earth any time without upsetting my digestion."

It was lubricated talk, nothing against Detective Chandler. But, for a man who lived off words, Forester was sometimes free with them. He would come to regret those last few.

Ten

Two nights later, a block off of Duncan's historic Town Clock Square, a bone-weary Peter Chandler climbed from his unmarked car outside of a Stopwatch Hamburger joint. Though he knew the answer, manners forced him to lean back in and ask his partner if he cared for anything.

"Don't suppose I could talk you into a bottle of water?"

"Outside of a drought," Chandler growled. "I don't suppose you could either." Even tired, the senior detective slid effortlessly into a Jesus speech. "America has the cleanest drinking water in the world, Horatio. Why, in the name of all you millennials call healthy, anyone buys bottled water, is beyond me." Shane nodded like a bobble-head but wasn't listening. Chandler sighed. "I'm talking about food."

"Nothing in there my body recognizes as food." Shane pointed to the Fitness Center on the corner.

The older cop grunted. "The way this investigation is going?" He pointed the opposite direction, to the Senior Employment Center. "That's more likely; for me at least." Chandler went for his burger. On the way, he tried not to think about the case but failed miserably.

Two full days had passed since the destruction of the Fourth Street Elevator and the discovery of Crystal Evers body. Two days since the Opera House and finding Linnea Keddy dead. Three days since the arson explosion on Garfield Street, the hospitalization of the Unknown Foreign Object, Soomnalung, and the discovery of Jane Doe in the burned basement. Plus, munitions, for the moment hidden at the station, unmentioned in any report. The reports! Dozens of interviews with family, friends, and enemies of every victim with nothing to show. An avalanche of reports. But who or what had set it off? What in God's name had any to do with one another? The one common factor, an inexplicable stomach wound, thought to be a gunshot at first but now known to be something else entirely. A wound so unique that, despite the different scenes, the crimes had to be connected.

Tensions were high in the police and fire departments, and more so, in City Hall. Most off-duty law enforcement personnel were working double shifts. All vacations had been canceled. The bus station, airport, and train station were being monitored, though for what, no one knew. Spot checks were being conducted on vehicles crossing the Illinois and Wisconsin bridges, but again, the feeling was all they had to go on. Anyone acting oddly was questioned. And, oh, how many odd people there were. The city map on the pin board in his office was filling with gory crime scene photos, but to what end? Forget means, motive, and opportunity. They hadn't even a clue to weapon or suspect. Three bodies, one burn victim who wasn't talking, in any language, and a lot of unanswered questions. The case offered no tunnel to look down, let alone light at the end. Neither he nor Shane would be going home soon.

He hadn't eaten all day and it was well into the night. Despite Shane's assumptions, Chandler didn't like junk food. He simply needed fuel. Stopwatch Burgers it was.

The detective did not know the young family ahead of him in line. He'd never seen Catherine Herrera before, or the girl (two-ish) in her stroller or the lad (perhaps five) pouting against mom's leg. But, always a detective, he couldn't help but detect while he waited to order. The packages in mom's arms, under, and atop the stroller told of shopping the stores off the Square. The giggles said the girl was having a grand night. The boy was tired and showing it. Mom too, had had enough and Chandler couldn't blame her. Atop her present load, the woman was very pregnant.

It took a few minutes for the woman to place her order, but Chandler didn't mind. Glad for the break, he used the time making faces at her son. At first, the lad hid behind his mother, but he soon forgot his pout and gave the detective as good as he was getting. Despite his British ancestry, Chandler enjoyed children, their energy, their honesty, and curiosity; they were natural detectives. That's what he needed in a partner, a detective with childlike curiosity. Childish was, so far, all Shane had shown. Erin Vanderjagt was suddenly on his mind again. Not in a romantic way, nothing like. She was an attractive woman, no doubt, but that had never been his focus. He was impressed with Erin, had been since the day he'd met her. Given the chance, she'd make a fine detective. She was being wasted. He'd give anything for Erin to be working these cases.

With only coffee and chicken sandwiches (one for Shane whether he'd eat it or not), Chandler's order was ready first. Offering the young mother a parting smile, the detective was suddenly struck by an idea. The wounds were not the only common factor in the recent deaths; there was another. It had been in Pickles' autopsy reports all along. He'd failed to make the connection. It might mean nothing, Chandler knew, could be merely a coincidence. But he needed a starting place. Coincidences made good ones.

He stepped from the Stopwatch, reassessing the case in light of his revelation. He took in a breath of air, but was thinking too hard to take in the night or his surroundings. So involved were his thoughts, Chandler was unaware of the thing perched behind him atop the dark restaurant roof. He remained oblivious as it slowly, quietly, unfurled its wings.

Chandler reached the squad and his bored-looking partner as Catherine Herrera left the restaurant with her children. The detective heard the oddest sounds, a leathery flap like the main sail of a Galleon caught in a typhoon, and then a scream. He dropped the sandwiches and coffee.

It took the detective several seconds to wrap his mind around what he saw; a completely alien flying creature with massive wings beating the air, bobbing above the mother and her kids. He couldn't get a good look. The light was dim, the shadows stark, and the creature facing the opposite direction. It darted at the mother like an angry bee. Catherine was the target, but the children were in danger all the same. The boy cried out and fell, slapped by the creature's left wing. The other broomed the stroller aside. Chandler ran toward the scene. Shane jumped from the vehicle, pulled his gun, and following the rising and falling target, started firing.

Half-way back to the restaurant, Chandler turned and shouted, "No!" Yes, the thing needed to be stopped. That didn't justify discharging his weapon in the heart of the city, in the direction of a victim, and an occupied restaurant, over his head! His complaint was academic. In the time it had taken to form the thought, Shane's gun was already empty.

A restaurant window had shattered, hit either by a stray bullet or one that had passed through the flying thing. Glass shards littered the walk. Chandler, near enough to make out a head of wild black hair and human-like hands tearing at the mother, could also see several entry wounds in the creature's back. They oozed a dark fluid, unlike any blood he'd seen. The children were crying. The mother, torn and bleeding, looked to be unconscious. Chandler dove under the hovering thing to cover the woman. The creature shrieked.

Shane saw the thing dive on Chandler. Gobsmacked, trying to reload, the junior detective shook so badly he dropped the fresh cartridge. With no choice but to take his eyes off of the attack, Shane swore and dropped to retrieve the ammunition. He didn't hear the *Tik-tik, Tik-tik, Tik, tik, tik…* above his head. He found the cartridge, slid it home, and looked up into a flurry of black and red. He saw bright, slitted eyes and a flash of talons. *Tik. Tik. Tik, tik, tik…* A razor-edged vise clutched his throat, another his face. His weapon clattered to the pavement, smoke rising from the hot barrel. Shane fell beside it, streaming life-blood in the same way.

The Well, Ben's old drinking habitat, was quickly becoming his new bad habit. The paramedic sat sipping a tall cold glass of escape, with Forester beside him. It would be a stretch to call them friends, or drinking buddies, but over the last days with Ben off, Erin always on, and Forester circling an epic story but unable to land, they had, like homeless men sharing an alley, forged a trust-free bond of commiseration. They finished their drinks, traded last words, and stepped outside.

Neither Ben nor Forester saw anything. But they heard enough gunfire, shouts, and screams to think they'd stepped into the streets of a banana republic in revolution. They raced to the end of the block, turned the corner, and pulled up to glare at chaos.

A window was gone from a restaurant. The few customers inside were under the tables with their heads in their hands. On the sidewalk, a woman lay in a pool of blood, and what appeared to be black paint; a crying little boy and an overturned stroller and its wailing occupant lay on either side of her. In the lot, a man, also covered in blood, sprawled unmoving beside an unmarked police car. And running across Iowa Street, Ben would have sworn he saw Peter Chandler. Gun in hand, the detective was staring into the decks of a concrete parking garage.

Ben ran for the injured woman and kids with Forester right behind. Ben uprighted the stroller and lifted the girl. The reporter picked up the boy. He had a bloody nose, his sister minor scratches. Both were crying in fear but seemed unhurt. Forester tucked his rolled jacket under Catherine Herrera's head. Ben shouted quick instructions and the reporter took over nursing the family. Ben hurried across the lot to find Detective Shane dead.

Chandler dodged a car on Iowa, counted his lucky stars, and got out of the street. Safe on the curb, he returned to searching the shadows for movement. The thing, whatever it was, had flown into the parking garage on the second level. But all four levels were connected by open ramps within; the creature could be anywhere. Chandler knew he'd have to go in after it. He hurried around the corner, headed for the nearest in-ramp.

A howl reached his ears as Chandler reached the garage entrance. He stopped in his tracks and peered in. Beyond the first few cars, he couldn't see a thing in the dark. But he could hear it, a screech and its echo, the arrhythmic flapping of its wings, distant but chilling. He didn't know if he was being a coward or merely making a sensible choice but joining the monster in the dark suddenly seemed a bad idea. The detective vetoed it for good, opting instead to continue around the structure to the open grass lot on Main Street. From there he backed up toward the Town Clock Center hoping for a better look.

The plaza was empty and deathly quiet.

Then a shriek tore the fabric of the night. The creature exploded from the shadowed third level of the garage swooping thirty feet at Chandler. The detective fired two rounds as he dropped to avoid the grasp. The creature stroked the air and disappeared around the corner. Chandler stood back up with a tear in the knee of his three-hundred-dollar suit and a matching tear in the ligaments of his knee. He groaned and grit his teeth against the pain, and hearing the shatter of glass ahead, limped after the beast.

The Town Clock, one of Duncan's most prominent landmarks, was erected at a cost of $3,000 at the end of the Civil War, atop a downtown department store. Less than eight years later the one-ton gong, half ton bell, four-hundred-pound clock, and belfry toppled, destroying the store and crushing three shoppers. But folks love their symbols, and within a year, the clock was restored. One hundred years later it was relocated to Iowa's first pedestrian mall, aptly named Town Clock Plaza. A new thirteen-ton tower was bolted to a supporting four-column concrete pedestal. The clock's four faces, weighing a combined nine tons, were crowned by a seven-ton cupola and now stood two feet taller than it had in 1864. Add another five feet in height if you counted the creature perched at the top.

Limping, Chandler grabbed a lamp post for balance. The lamp was out, the ground covered in broken glass, and he scanned the empty plaza to see that all of the lamp globes in a row from there to the clock had been shattered. Owing to the dark, and decorative trees, he couldn't see the top of the clock. Nor could he see the creature when it leapt. Again he escaped its grasp and lunged, from post to post to a tree, trying to keep distance between them. He fell through the oval of concrete pylons guarding the site against errant drivers, rolled to his good knee and came up firing. The bullets hit home, but the dark thing wouldn't be denied. Hovering, darting, and retreating, the creature ignored the shots and attacked, wings flapping, arms striking, claws scratching, fangs flashing. But what the hell was it!

Ducking, Chandler pushed himself off from the base of the clock and stumbled nearly to the street before he fell. The creature rose up shrieking, green eyes glowing. Behind Chandler came another sound, an eerie and awful *Tik. Tik. Tik.* The detective ignored it, instead unloading his last three rounds into the green-black chest of the thing above him. Driven backwards, the creature smashed into the south face of the clock and shrieked as glass rained around it.

Spent, badly cut, out of ammunition, Chandler fell. The creature fell too, and lay less than ten feet from the detective at the base of the clock's pedestal. Sirens wailed from every direction. Exhausted but determined to get a look, Chandler dragged himself toward the monster. For his trouble, the creature slapped him with a wing and sent him cartwheeling away. It lifted its head and dragged itself toward the wounded detective. Chandler tried to scream when it grabbed him, but his broken jaw released little more than a groan. The creature unfurled its wings.

Forester shouted through the shot-out window for someone in the Stopwatch to call an ambulance. Shane lay dead. Catherine lay injured. Her son's nose had stopped bleeding but the boy was still crying. (Forester couldn't blame him.) The little girl, back in her stroller, played as if nothing had happened.

Across the street, on the far side of the parking garage, Ben hurried to the plaza. Sirens, cops, and firefighters were just behind him, rolling and running in from every direction. A new, city-sponsored pandemonium erupted. Ben stood on crushed glass and spattered blood, beneath the damaged town clock, searching in a circle for the detective. He searched in vain. Peter Chandler had vanished.

Eleven

Erin's squad was the fourth to arrive, and as the senior, she immediately took over. The patients were removed by ambulance, the children with minor injuries, Catherine Herrera unconscious and unable to tell anyone what had happened. Shane had taken whatever he knew with him. Erin alerted dispatch to send in the scientists, though there were no detectives left in Homicide to investigate. Chandler had vanished.

Her call for witnesses brought her equal shares of delight and anger. Ben had arrived after the shooting started. It had been days since she'd seen him; almost as long since she'd said more than 'Hi' and 'Bye' to him on the phone. Erin was glad he was there. Then, again, he was with that nosy Forester, a constant pain and they'd both been drinking. Come to think, Ben had been drinking a lot lately, and spending time in that dive bar of his, with Forester. She didn't like it a bit. She liked it even less when she got their stories. Neither had seen the perpetrator. They'd arrived after the fact and had seen nothing more than Chandler running across the street. When he was able, Ben trailed the detective to the clock plaza but, by then, whatever had happened to Chandler had happened.

There had been twelve customers in the hamburger joint, but once the bullets started flying, they'd all ducked under tables. No one saw a thing. Strike that, there had been a witness, a non-customer who'd stopped to use the restroom. Rickie Savage, Duncan's eternal child and man about town, left the john after the first round of shots. He'd seen Shane's murderer, and when asked, reported what he saw.

"A bird."

"A bird?"

"Yes."

"You saw a bird?"

"Yes. Big red bird."

That was his story. He had nothing to add but concerns about his bike. It was located for him and Rickie pedaled away.

Two more days elapsed. Two days of collecting glass shards, bullet casings, and blood spatters that added up to nothing. Two days of empty interviews, fruitless searching, and unanswered questions. Two days of grief with no downtime to think about the loss, let alone accept it. There'd been no sleep for Erin since and, outside of interviews, no chance to see Ben.

Now, Erin Vanderjagt had been promoted, against her will, and officially dropped into the heart of the matter. Her protests fell on deaf ears. Taylor was retired. Tankard was beyond reach in the wilds of Moose Jaw, Saskatchewan. With Shane dead and Chandler missing, there was nobody else; she was lead detective. Hell, she was the only detective.

"You're going to have to get comfortable," Chief Musselwhite insisted. "Or be uncomfortable. Incident command has been established. The case files are there. You're in charge and there's work to be done. Chandler wouldn't want it any other way." He pointed at the door to Chandler's office. "Your office, detective."

Erin stepped through like a naughty girl entering church. She approached the incident board, ran her hand over the victims' pictures and the city map. She paused, letting her fingers brush across the Town Clock Plaza where Chandler vanished. She breathed deeply, blinked to hold back the tears, and promised herself a long cry when the situation allowed.

Erin sat, taking in a room she'd seen a hundred times, for the first time from the lead side of the desk. She did not accept Chandler was dead, she refused to believe it. He was missing but she would find him. In the meantime, a murderer or murderers were roaming the city. They were her priority. She reached for the case file on the top of the stack.

Unshaven and unwashed, Ben pulled his rusted Impala to the curb beside Fire Station 2. He lolled his head against the steering wheel and sighed as the engine shuddered and the radio DJ muttered the end of a Public Service Announcement. "...the impending rolling blackouts throughout the city for the next forty-eight hours. The electric company is going to save some energy and, I guess, the city is going to save some money. So be prepared, and careful with those candles, listeners, during those temporary blackouts tonight and tomorrow night." On the verge of a blackout of his own, Ben turned the ignition off and let the Chevy cough itself out.

The last week had been a slice of hell and Ben had spent it all being questioned, by the cops, by nosy Forester, by his bartender. Outside of the nasty business, he'd had no contact with Erin. She hadn't been there for him. He wasn't allowed to be there for her; couldn't even hold her hand in public. She had no time, and if she had, their relationship was the last thing she could deal with now. Ben understood. But Erin didn't. He'd dealt with it the old fashioned way, from a comfy stool at The Well.

Ben climbed out of the car, as rumpled as his shirt and jeans. He leaned on the car, squinting through dark glasses, and deep breathing. He grabbed his duffel and coffee through the window, spilled the coffee, swore, and headed in. Inside the truck floor door, Pontius pounced on him. "What is it, Court, coming in on time doesn't appeal to you anymore?"

"On time?"

"Yes, on time. Or, for that matter, in uniform, shaved, ready to do your job?"

"I'd like to respond with something witty. But I don't have it in me this morning." Ben pulled his turnout gear from its hook and started for the ambulance.

"We're having this conversation too often."

"Then why have it again?"

Pontius lowered his voice. "We're all under a lot of pressure, Ben. Is there something special going on in your life?"

The paramedic paused in stowing his gear. "Nothing I want to talk about."

Pontius nodded solemnly. "All right. If I can help let me know."

Ben watched him go, wondering if Hell had actually frozen over.

Fire station kitchens were simple, table and chairs, stove, coffee pot, and despite the stories, built for quantity, not necessarily quality. The talk of firefighters as great cooks was horse manure. There were those who could whip up a five-alarm chili, requiring a wet towel around the neck to catch the glorious bursts of sweat, no doubt. But in most fire houses the microwave got as much exercise as the oven.

Nestor, Tuck, Arbuckle, Pierce, and the lieutenant had the table surrounded, as usual, reading newspapers, eating breakfast, drinking coffee and spreading lies as Ben pushed in from the truck floor. A chorus of hoots went up in his honor. He ignored them and grabbed a mug, pulled the pot from the machine, and poured himself a cup while the still-brewing coffee ran out onto the burner and across the counter top.

"For God's sake, Ben!" Pontius bitched above the roar. "Do you have to do that every morning?"

"Just like jerking off," Tucker shouted. "Once a day, every day." More laughter followed, this time in appreciation of Pontius' distress, as Ben replaced the pot and half-heartedly ran a rag over the mess. He disappeared the way he'd come, trailing his middle finger at his jeering co-workers.

Ben sipped his coffee, set the cup on the soap rack, and held his head beneath the shower. He closed his eyes, praying for a path through the gin fog, and let the water run over him.

Ben entered the living room, clean and in uniform, but still hung over and looking it. Pontius was there like a gnat in his ear. "The chief just called."

"Who dialed the phone for him?" Ben turned for the paramedics' office.

The lieutenant followed. "Did you hear me, Ben? Castronovo called. I don't know from where. That means he could be on his way here. That means tuck in your shirt."

Ben closed the door in his face.

Nestor turned from the computer, gave his partner and friend the once-over, and smiled. "Much better. You only just look like hell now."

"Thanks," Ben said, thanklessly. "What have I missed?"

"Judging by your delayed motor skills I'd say everything since midnight last night. Meanwhile, I'm working the second half of forty-eight hours in a row and look and feel great." Ben rotated his hand in the air, imploring his partner to get on with it. Nestor pointed at the computer screen. "I was going over the ambulance reports, because of something odd Angelina told me the other night—"

The door opened and Pontius poked in his head. "Pena, the chief called again."

"Is the guy lonely or what?" Ben asked.

"Butt out, Court." The lieutenant returned his attention to Nestor. "There's going to be a temporary shift change. You're being sent to 'A' Shift to cover their ambulance until Cooper's arm heals."

" 'A' Shift?" Nestor moaned. "Who's been working for her?"

"Soetoro. But Captain Ethridge is complaining he can't find his ass with both hands. He wants someone with experience."

"Experience at what?"

"Anything, I guess."

"But Ethridge hates me," Nestor said." He says I'm a screw-up."

"He thinks everyone on 'B' Shift is a screw-up," Pontius grumbled. "He's probably right. But you're a veteran screw up and he wants you, so you're going. Take today and tomorrow off. Report to Station 1 on 'A' Shift day after."

Ben butted in again. "Why can't he work today and report on 'A' Shift after one day off?"

"Whose side are you on?" Nestor demanded.

"Mine. You're my partner. Let Ethridge get someone else."

Pontius growled. "How about this? How about it's not up to you clowns?"

Pierce eased past the lieutenant into the room. "My gear is by the ambulance," she told Nestor. "As soon as you remove yours—"

"We were just discussing that."

"We're not discussing anything," Pontius said. "You're going to 'A' Shift temporarily. Get out of here." He looked at Ben. "You're on the ambulance with Pierce. Shut up."

Ben and Nestor spoke in chorus: "This is bullshit!"

"Count your blessings, Pena." Pontius turned on Ben. "The bull hasn't even started for you. The electric company's rolling blackout is going to effect the downtown area tonight. That means the 9-1-1 Center is going to be without power. That means we're standing by, for three hours, at a phone company junction box in an alley."

"Slavery," Tucker shouted from the living room. "It's slavery, all over again."

Pontius left for the kitchen. Nestor left for the truck floor. Tucker, with Arbuckle in his back pocket, stuck his head in and grinned, his gold tooth gleaming. "Watch your new partner there, Court. She likes to be on top."

"Yeah, yeah," Pierce said, taking it in stride. "I was born on top of you mugs."

The truckies laughed a ton as they headed for the truck floor.

"What was the odd thing," Pierce asked Ben, "that Nestor was saying he found in the reports?"

"I have no idea," Ben said with a sigh. He sipped his coffee, unable to care.

Twelve

It was more than a special Council meeting, and less than a press conference, that took place that night beneath the gold dome (1800 square feet of 23-karat gilded pretension) of the City Hall. It was an attempt by a nervous Mayor Light, and his bulbous city attorney, to save Duncan tourism from rumor, fear, and political fire. The evening started badly before the mayor reached the chambers. Caught in the hall by an impatient Mark Forester, along with Jamie Watts and her WKLD cameraman, Light stumbled. "I don't have any answers. I think it's horrible. But we have to give our police time to stop these murders. Murders are bad. And we don't want them. I don't want murders. Do you? No."

Snappy and impressive it wasn't, and a good many citizens and city employees saw it as they filed in. Light ducked into the chamber like a rabbit into a hole, eager to hand Public Relations off to someone he could blame, his department heads. The room found their seats and settled in, Forester and Watts with the other reporters up front. Light found his throne, and his composure, beneath the Seal of the City. He banged a gavel and called for order. Then he called for the fire chief's report.

Tony Castronovo started to rise, hesitated, then started again, unsure whether to speak from the podium microphone or the councilman's table. The display was nothing new. There were those, Ben Court and the 'B' Shift gang in particular, who considered confusion to be Castronovo's sharpest attribute. "I think you can just stay there," the mayor said.

The chief adjusted his table mic and commenced, reporting in generalities about the Garfield Street explosion and the Fourth Street Elevator fire without revealing anything of importance. Not a word about screams or breaking glass, and absolutely nothing about grenades, gas cans, or flying men in capes. The burned patient from the house was in critical condition and unable to provide any information at this juncture. The Fire Marshall's Office was investigating both incidents. No, his department knew nothing about autopsy reports. Outside of the fires, the Garfield Street, and Fourth Street Elevator incidents were in the hands of law enforcement. The body on the Opera House roof was also a law enforcement case.

"Please, would you hold your questions until later?"

The department had drawn no conclusions regarding recent incidents and, Castronovo stressed, suggestions to the contrary in the newspaper, particularly about arson and murder, were premature and perhaps unfounded. Moving on, he regretted having to report the loss of an ambulance. A temporary replacement had been rented until bids could be taken. Details would hopefully be available at the next Council meeting, but sadly, it was going to be a kick in taxpayers' pockets no matter the numbers.

Forester jumped up with another question. Musselwhite jumped in to save his brother-in-law's bacon, moving the topic away from fire and onto police business, deflecting Forester's question without answering it, and starting his own fact-free department report. Not that it was smooth sailing for him either. There was, after all, the death of one detective to report and the replacement of another. Lead Detective Chandler had taken a leave of absence. No, no further information on either officer was available at present. All investigations were ongoing. Personnel matters were not open for public discussion. Chandler missing? Who suggested any such thing? The idea was ludicrous and wouldn't be dignified with an answer.

"Please, no more questions until we're through."

Erin was introduced as the new lead detective. "Please, no questions for Detective Vanderjagt until she's situated. Everyone can, of course, understand that."

Forester wasn't making any effort to understand. And he wasn't making friends with his repeated interruptions for questions nobody would answer. "Why aren't autopsy reports available on the recent victims? If they exist, where are they? Where is the coroner? The people are entitled to know the cause of these deaths. They're entitled to know if these incidents are related. Is there a connection between the house explosion, the opera house death, the elevator crash, and whatever happened at the Town Clock Plaza? Speaking of which, what happened at the Town Clock Plaza?" Forester was shouting. "I was there and I don't know!"

"All of the incidents you've bagged up together took place under different circumstances," the police chief said. "At this point, we have no reason to assume they are connected."

"Rumor has it the victims have identical wounds. What kind of wounds? Were the victims missing any blood?" Forester ignored the gasps. "One victim was found on a roof. A witness at the elevator blamed a man in a cape. Someone said the perpetrator can fly. Is this some kind of vampire?"

The room went deathly quiet, then erupted in talking, laughter, unintelligible shouts. Mayor Light nearly broke his gavel trying to get everyone quiet and back in their seats.

"I don't think that's funny, Mr. Forester," Musselwhite said. "And it isn't helpful."

"It's nonsensical and childish," the mayor barked. "And it's bad for business."

"Am I supposed to care about that?" the reporter asked.

"Certainly you should care," Light said. "We hope the local newspaper cares about the well-being of the city and conducts itself with some journalistic integrity."

"We just want the facts—"

"We all want to know, Mr. Forester," the mayor shouted, cutting him off. He took a breath, retook his seat, and cleared his throat. "We have no more information at the moment. When we have, it will be made available to the press. In the meantime, for the good of the community, I want to stress the need for calm while the various departments of this city carry out their careful investigations."

"I feel obwiged to add," the fleshy city attorney put in, "that wild concwusions, uninformed guesses, and out-wight fantasies sold as facts will do no one any good. Pwinting or airwing damaging guesses without factual support could do iwweparable harm to the city and its touwism. In such a situation, the city would have no awternative but to defend its intwerests. I will communicate that personalwy to the editors and producers of the media personawities here tonight."

The usual urge to titter at the gummy attorney's speech impediment was stifled by the threat. Instead, those same personalities clouded over en masse, aiming their glares at Forester. Then, as if the city had conspired with the electric company for a dramatic ending, the scheduled rolling blackout struck that section of the downtown district. The lights went out; the council chamber was plunged into darkness. Those assembled filed out, murmuring and trying to ignore a palpable undercurrent of fear.

Engine 2 pulled into the dark alley behind the Masonic Hall, eased down the seedy corridor between dumpsters and stacked cardboard boxes near the rear exit and parked, nose to the street, behind the main branch of the telephone company. There the pumper was shut down. Their watch would last three hours and there was no sense idling the apparatus. Barring World War III, they weren't going anywhere.

Tuck and Pontius climbed from the cab and Arbuckle from his jump seat. They met on the phone company side of the engine. Pontius found the metal door, like a night deposit box, in the brick wall at the back of the building and inserted a key. It took a moment – and a tug from Tucker – before it opened to reveal an old phone, a direct line on uninterrupted power through which the Com Center could send calls of dire emergency. Garden variety emergencies would wait until after the blackout. All part of the joys of living in a quaint town suspended between cave drawings and Enhanced 9-1-1.

"When do we join the twenty-first century?" Arbuckle asked. "Get a real phone system?"

"And lose all our old world charm?" Tuck grinned. Then he spotted the approaching ambulance and bellowed. "Hey, hey! Here come the rock stars. 'Bout time."

Late as usual to department gatherings that did not involve fire or blood, Ben (with Pierce riding doctor) eased 1-Boy-16 past the alley and parked on the street. They looked even more unhappy. Who could blame them? With recent events, it was a horrendous time to plunge sections of the frightened city into darkness. But the power company had refused to alter their schedule. Blackouts it would be. And the phone monitoring (read that 'waiting in a dark alley') began.

An hour later, the watch remained quiet. Nothing was afire and the Station 1 ambulance was just finishing up at the hospital with their only call of the night. The 'B' Shift gang, out of witty banter, had drifted apart and each now stood alone. Ben had stepped from the black alley to the black sidewalk beside the ambulance. He rubbed his shoulders, bothered not by a chill, but by a chilly feeling. In the distance, coming on like the purr of a stalking leopard, the thunder rolled.

"You all right?"

Ben started and glared at the rookie behind him. "Damn. Don't do that."

Pierce smiled. "Sorry. You looked…"

"I looked… what?"

Pierce shrugged. "I don't know. Like something was wrong."

"Something is wrong," Ben said. "Something in this town is very wrong. But I don't know what."

Pierce could only nod. That's all anyone could do. Agree it was bad, whatever *it* was, nod without understanding, and standby. It was a helpless feeling. Despite the press, 9/11 did not make firefighters heroes. And Ferguson did not make cops villains. Both groups were made up of people who were, or were not, whatever they were, or were not, before those incidents. Just people, like everyone else, but schooled in the art of stopping the artless. Braver than most? Maybe and maybe not. Crazier than most? Almost certainly. But not permitted to ask, 'who do we call when we need help'?

They stood a long time, on edge, in silence, when Ben noticed Pierce staring skyward.

"What's the matter?"

"Did you see that?"

He followed her gaze. "What...?"

"I don't know. Something, a shadow, flew over us. And I heard... I don't know. A clicking sound, or a ticking sound, and... Did you ever hear a broken kite flap in the wind? It sounded like that."

Ben turned to look above the roofs, from the bluff on one side to the open expanse of the river on the other, from the roiling gray clouds in the distance to the darkness above. He looked back at the paramedic. He said nothing but the corners of his mouth rose slightly.

"Screw you," Pierce said.

Nearby Tuck and Arbuckle, the Bobbsey Twins of meat, laughed at Pierce's expense. Ben joined in. Truth be told, it wasn't all impish glee. Though they'd deny it, genuine nervousness lurked behind the laughs. The night was dark... and the approaching storm pushed a cold front ahead in its own version of a rolling blackout. Pierce's ticking, flying shadow hadn't warmed them a bit.

Thirteen

The weather in the Mississippi River Valley resembled the little girl in the nursery rhyme: When it was nice it was very nice, but when it was bad it was horrid. You've already seen the fog turn the air thick as cotton. When it rained it poured with lightning like hurled javelins and thunder like war drums. When the wind blew, the river became impassable with cold chop. Even harbored boats were tossed in their moorings like toys. On the bluff and through Eagle Point Park, the ash and maple bowed low to the forces of nature. Those that failed to show respect were snapped like twigs and hurled to the ground. When it was nice it was very nice, but…

A jittery Angelina Pena saw the thunderstorm approaching from the ninth floor service room and knew the weather would soon be horrid indeed. She clocked out, and clutching purse and papers, caught the staff elevator. It had been a long night and, as the doors opened to the hospital's first floor back hallway, Angelina could see it wasn't over yet. The planned blackout had been no problem for the patients. The facility generated its own power with no interruption to care. The same could not be said for the staff. There was no cafeteria, no shift amenities, not even for those on overtime as Angelina had been and now, as her tour finally ended, no lights in the back hall.

Not meant for public eyes, the hall was uninviting at best. In darkness – save for sporadic safety lights – the trip the length of the complex, past the Pathology Annex (*Morgue* to the rest of the world) and

Shipping and Receiving was all she needed. Even the usually ignored Muzak was conspicuous by its absence. The hall was not only dark, but quiet as a tomb. Angelina patted her baby bump to remind herself she wasn't alone. She heard nothing the length of the walk, but the echoes of her own footsteps and, behind that, a strange sing-song that started as she passed the morgue. A mechanical something that, obviously, Maintenance needed to fix.

Tik. Tik. Tik, tik. Tik, tik.

Despite exhaustion, Angelina found herself picking up the pace, her footfalls coming quicker as she hurried from one dim spot of light to the next. Quicker and louder. Quicker and louder.

Tik. Tik. Tik, tik. Tik, tik.

The hall angled to the right past the heavy plastic curtains of the Shipping dock, then back to the left. *Tik. Tik. Tik, tik.* The floor became a ramp to ground level. *Tik. Tik. Tik, tik.* Her heart was racing as she reached the employees entrance and Angelina nearly screamed with relief as she escaped outside.

The relief was short lived. None of the lights were on in the west parking lot. Blackness above with the even blacker silhouette of parked cars below; that was all there was to see. Angelina caught her breath, recovering from the fright she'd already given herself, only to realize a new vulnerability, a new sense of danger, and an overwhelming feeling she was being watched.

Worse, her fear did not change fact. She was in a parking lot which meant she'd forgotten where she parked. She clutched her coat and bag against the wind, a chore made more difficult because, in her hurry to work, she'd grabbed a coat that didn't fit her tummy. She scanned the rows trying to remember, and when it came to her, was off like a shot.

Angelina's Mustang convertible was her beauty, her slave and, at just under forty thousand dollars to purchase, her master as well. Though hers was not a luxury model – it did not have heated seats or an Airscarf –it was still a luxury to her. The power and freedom it afforded reminded her of her new home. Only someone from a cramped Manila could understand the glory of a convertible car and an American road. Besides, Angelina was not fooling herself. When the baby arrived, she knew, her racing days would be over.

Her usual first action when she climbed in was to lower the top. It was, Angelina believed, the American thing to do. Why have a convertible otherwise? But tonight she left the roof in place. Not merely because of the impending storm but for that other thing as well; that sensation, like flames on her nerves that she was being spied upon, perhaps even followed. It made no sense, of course, but feelings often did not. Just the same, what could one do but feel them? Tonight, she would forgo the freedom and surrender to the fear.

She found her car, an ugly maroon in the dark despite its actual red brilliance, and nearly scratched the paint in her hurry to get inside. She relocked it quickly, and breathless, eased back into the seat. She was being crazy and felt embarrassed. But what did that matter? The feeling was inescapable; there was something evil in the air.

She'd feel better when she got home.

Then it dawned on her that Nestor would be home. All that time on 'B' Shift and now a change, temporary he'd said, but a change to which she'd have to adjust. Tonight, though, the thought made her glad and she began to breathe more easily.

Angelina pulled from the lot and turned for home. It was silly, of course, feeling watched on city streets, but there it was. And, in the awful blackout dark, she might have continued to be afraid... but now she'd thought of him her fears were turning to Nestor. Not fears of him; fears *for* him.

Yes, Nestor would be home, but would he be drinking again? Her husband had been drinking a lot lately. Stress, probably. Nerves, maybe, with the baby coming. But he shouldn't be nervous, not more nervous than happy. And he shouldn't be drinking so much. He had never been violent, and she almost regretted having mentioned it to Erin, but he did get quiet and grouchy. He pulled away from her when he was drinking heavily and it made Angelina sad.

Just as quickly, the sadness was replaced by the return of the cloying feeling she was under an all-seeing eye. The feeling she was being followed. It was ten minutes to home and she had herself spooked (was that the word?) by the time she got there. That none of the street lights were working and the neighborhood was black as pitch did not help. Their house did not help either.

Nestor had picked their home; a place that looked like a mansion from an old horror movie. It had gloomy round towers with coned roofs, front and back, and turrets all around. According to Nestor, an architect would have called it Romanesque. The locals called it 'The Castle'. The name fit; it was a castle, falling down and grabbed at a steal – but a castle nonetheless.

Talk around town gave the place forty rooms, when there were merely twenty-four, with two and a half baths; four stories from the basement to attic cupola. It had a tiled swimming pool in the basement, full-sized by 1920 standards when it was built, in which a resident was rumored to have drowned. His ghost, or hers (depending upon the teller), had haunted the castle since. The pool was real. The tale of the drowned ghost did not hold water. But the pool had once held a large collection of potted marijuana plants for a previous owner with a green thumb and no regard for the law. It took the cops a whole day to clear the nursery after her arrest. Nestor denied they'd dropped any seeds. It was his story and he was sticking to it. The Castle was the rumored site of a murder as well. Whether or not that story was true, Angelina did not know or care to know. All she knew was the place had always *spooked* her.

It was a spooky night. The rumbling had arrived and the storm was drawing near. She eased her Mustang beneath the vine-covered trestle and disappeared down the drive through the 'hole in the hedge' that surrounded their home. She pulled up to the old carriage house that in the late 1930's was converted to a three-stall garage. She broke another rule, not bothering to put her precious car away. Angelina had simply had enough. She turned off the lights and was swallowed by the darkness again.

She saw a flicker in the second-floor windows and took a moment to realize it was candlelight. Nestor and candles? It struck her as funny, then odd, then disconcerting. She found herself worrying again about her husband's drinking and pictured her old house on fire. Wouldn't that be all they needed?

Angelina took a deep breath, unsure exactly what she was readying herself for, jumped from the car, and bolted for the door.

Fourteen

Angelina fumbled with her keys again at the door, struggling to hold her purse and papers, holding the door open with a knee. Her nerves, and that ridiculous feeling, made it impossible not to look back at the night. Thunder rolled. A hand grabbed her shoulder and Angelina screamed.

"Hey, hey!" Nestor exclaimed. "Take it easy."

"My God, I can't believe you did that! You scared the life out of me. Oh my God, Nestor. What did you do that for? I didn't even see you. What are you doing out here in the dark?"

"Watching the storm come in." He waved a half empty bottle.

Great, she'd been right, Nestor was drinking. And the door wasn't even locked. She'd been wasting her time and her worries. She turned away, headed in.

"What's the matter?" he called after her.

"I've had a long night. I'm tired. I'm sick of the darkness. And someone followed me home. Other than that everything is fine."

Nestor studied her car in the drive, the wind shaking the hedges, the cloud-filled night sky, and a flash of lightning. His arms turned to goose flesh. He rubbed at the chill, took a hit from the bottle, then started in after his wife, shouting, "Don't see anyone. Who followed you home?"

"I do not want to talk about it on the porch," Angelina called out, feeling a headache coming on. "And I am done shouting."

Nestor entered the kitchen, shivering now, and set the bottle on the table. Seeing it drained below the label, Angelina frowned. "That's what you were doing on the porch, yes?"

"Told you. Enjoying the night air, waiting for you. What did you mean? A car followed you?"

"I don't know what I mean. No, not a car. There was nothing on the road. I just felt it; someone watching me, following me. I do not know what it was."

"You mean 'who it was'."

"Stop it, Nestor. I mean what I said." She started away. "I don't want to talk about it anymore."

"Just trying to help." He followed Angelina into the drafty expanse they used for a living room.

"That is great. But you are not helping. Why are all the candles lit?"

"Why do you think? The blackout."

"I know the blackout. It looks like a funeral home." She dropped purse, papers, and coat. "And you weren't in here. You were outside waiting to scare me to death. You should not be burning candles when you are drinking. You are going to burn our mausoleum down."

Nestor held up his hands in surrender. "Okay. You're tired, hungry, and skittish. Got it."

"I am exhausted. I am not hungry in the least. I do not even know… What is skittish?"

"Nervous. Afraid because you thought someone was watching you."

"I was nervous. Because someone was watching me. And did follow me. But I am not nervous anymore. I am tired and my head aches."

"Would you like a drink?"

Angelina's frown deepened. She laid a hand on her stomach. "You are a medic. You should know that our daughter does not need alcohol."

"Wasn't suggesting we drown you in a vat of wine. Your nerves probably have our son on edge. Was only trying to help."

"I am sorry. It has been a long night. And I am nervous."

"Let me treat you," Nestor said, returning to the kitchen. "Made a nice casserole. Whip you up a lovely non-alcoholic piña colada to go with. Put on some music to remind you of the islands."

Angelina followed him and planted a kiss on Nestor's forehead. "I appreciate it. But I am just going to go to bed."

"What?" Nestor threw up the window, stuck his head out, and over the rumble of thunder, shouted, "Lit candles! Slaved over a beautiful casserole! Picked out romantic music from the Philippines! And my wife is not enchanted!"

"Stop! Our ridiculous neighbor already hates us. He is going to call the police."

"Can't," Nestor said, closing the window. "Except for earthshaking emergencies, there is no 9-1-1 until the end of this stupid blackout. My cooking tastes like dirt, but it isn't earthshaking and I don't count as an emergency." He kissed her. "Sure I can't fix you a little? A small plate?"

"I appreciate it. I am sorry, but I am not feeling well. The shift, and this head, and this storm, and… my silliness. I am going to lie down."

Nestor understood. He didn't like it. He was feeling sorry for himself. But he tried to keep that to himself because he did understand.

Nestor woke to a scream. He wiped the spittle from his chin, struggled up from the couch, and fought to recognize his surroundings. The living room, he'd fallen asleep. His dinner lay picked over and cold on the coffee table, beside a half-burned candle. Again the scream. "Angelina!" He grabbed the candle, cupped the flame, and ran to the hall.

He heard a crash of breaking glass, several heavy thumps, another scream. Angelina's scream from their bedroom down the hall. Nestor was there in an instant, but startled to find the door locked. An old lock on an old door; a lock that had a habit of slipping. The screams continued inside. With them came a series of otherworldly sounds, hissing, a breathy shriek, and the flap of canvas loosed in the wind. "Angelina," Nestor cried in panic. "Angelina!"

He put the candle on the floor, then he put his shoulder into the door. He smashed it again and again until an upright panel gave way with a crack. He held the candle to the opening. He strained to see. His eyes adjusted to the dark and his world fell apart. His wife lay on the floor, on her back, her nightgown torn open, a creature from Hell crouched over her.

It looked to be a huge animal, at first. Then seemed to be a person. It was both and neither. It was hunched over Angelina with its back to Nestor at the door. He could make out few details as the only light was the lightning beyond the shattered bedroom window and, on his side, the sparse glow of his candle through the broken panel. Angelina's attacker had a head of wild hair and, incredibly, wings on its back, folded like a bat's but bigger and hinged like a pterodactyl, or a harpy. Nestor called to his wife. The thing turned, hair flying, to glare with bright green eyes over its left shoulder. It flashed yellowed fangs, hissed, then unfurled a red tongue. It rolled from the creature's mouth like a blowout party favor, a tube over a foot long that ended in a bevel. The creature turned to Angelina and stabbed the tongue into her stomach.

Angelina screamed. Nestor shouted and smashed the door, over and over, a man possessed. The jamb cracked, the lock plate flew, the door sprang into the room with an off-balance Nestor stumbling behind. The creature blinked, hissed furiously and, as the paramedic pushed himself up, sucked its hideously engorged tongue back into its mouth.

Shouting her name, Nestor bulldozed the creature off Angelina. It snapped and bit, claws scratching, wings struggling to open. Its skin was as slimy as a fish, wet from rain, warm with sweat, and gave off the stink of putrid meat. Only his fears for Angelina, and a deep breath, kept Nestor from vomiting in disgust. He pounded on it, driving his fists into hard muscle, coarse hair, and if he wasn't off his rocker, breasts. The thing fought back with the strength of a demon, broke free, flitted to right itself and, using its arms for propulsion, leapt for the window. One of the wings smashed the upper pane. Nestor ducked the flying glass as the monster slipped beneath the sash. Framed by the casement, backlit by lightning and the downpour, the creature hissed again with bared fangs and glistening eyes. Thunder rolled as the thing vaulted out, stroked the air, and vanished into the storm.

Fifteen

Ben turned his phone off. It was a hell of a response in time of emergency, he knew, but he couldn't take the ringing. A hysterical Nestor had called. A shocked Erin had called. An alarmed dispatcher had called. All demanding he come to the hospital; Angelina Pena had been injured at home. Nestor had rushed her to the Emergency Room on his own.

Having abandoned Engine 2 to their communication monitoring, Ben and Kristina Pierce roared 1-Boy-16 into the hospital parking lot like NASCAR veterans crossing the finish line. Ben won the race to the door, but inside, both pulled up. Like everything they'd seen that week, the ER was a madhouse.

Ben heard Nestor before he saw him.

"Trying to tell you what happened. Don't really know myself. It was dark. I just woke up. Angelina was screaming. Had to break down the door. She was being attacked. Don't know what you want me to tell you? I don't understand why we have to do this now?"

Ben turned a corner and saw his partner at the far end of the hall, shouting and crying. Even from that distance, he looked like hell. His shirt was torn and hanging, bruises, scratches, and streaks of blood marred his face. If anything, he sounded more hysterical than he had on the phone and he was giving both barrels to a cop. Ben headed for them, so alarmed himself he was almost on top of them before he realized the officer was Erin.

He could have grabbed, hugged, and kissed her for the relief he suddenly felt. Then he felt the tension and realized she wasn't offering Nestor comfort. Erin had a notebook and pen in her hand and was squared-off on him. Whatever the situation, his girlfriend and his best friend were at odds.

"What *did* you see?"

What Nestor saw was Ben's arrival. He broke from Erin's questioning and shouted, "Angelina was attacked. She's hurt, Ben. The baby... "

"What happened?"

"That," Erin said, interrupting, "is what I'm trying to find out."

Ben glared. He hadn't seen Erin, except to be questioned, for days. She wanted things professional in public and he got that. He was Nestor's pal and she was best friends with Angelina, he got that. But damn... You couldn't have chopped the ice in her voice with a pick. "What the hell's going on?"

"Officer Vanderjagt," Nestor blurted. "Suspects me of hurting my wife."

"That's nuts."

Erin scowled at Ben. "Thank you so much." She turned on Nestor. "That's a gross exaggeration. I'm trying to find out what happened to your wife. For some reason, you are not being helpful."

"Sorry, Erin," Nestor said, sounding like he was. "I'm worried about Angelina and the baby."

"Of course you are."

"Do we have to do this now?"

"You said she was attacked; that the attacker got away. Give us someone to look for."

Nestor stared at Erin, then into space, obviously trying to decide something. Finally, he said, "When I broke the door down, Angelina was on the floor. Her attacker... went out the window as I came in."

"What did he look like?"

"Didn't get a good look," he answered with a shake of his head. "Barely got a look at all. He was going out." He hesitated again. "Just some guy."

"Some guy? Alone?"

"Yeah, I guess so."

"Did you see anyone else?"

"No. Just him. But he was already out the window. Couldn't say for sure."

"What did he look like?"

"Don't know. It was dark. Can't think right now, Erin. Please, can we do this later?" Erin nodded, tucking her notebook away. Nestor headed into Angelina's room.

Erin and Ben watched him go, Erin in annoyance, Ben in confusion. Nestor had always been a rotten liar and Ben knew damned well he was lying now. But why? Erin wondered too. No, she wasn't an idiot and she wasn't fooled. His story stunk to high heaven. Neither Erin nor Ben shared their thoughts with one another.

Erin found herself wondering about Angelina as well. More than once recently, during their many discussions about firefighter lovers and husbands, her best female friend had talked of changes coming over Nestor, nervousness, drinking, too frequent arguments. Pregnancy was difficult enough, without a hubby going through an early mid-life crisis. Angelina had wanted to know if she and Ben had rough patches. Who didn't? Of course, they had moments. But Erin reported fairly smooth sailing.

"Count your blessings," Angelina said. "That you're not pregnant." Erin shuddered at the idea.

Without answers for her friend, she'd tried to be supportive. Every woman on earth knew, in matters of the heart, the strongest men were weak as water. Her suggestion that Nestor was suffering a second childhood had them both in tears, laughing. What firefighter had ever left his first childhood? Maybe, Angelina worried aloud, it was deeper and darker. She told Erin of Nestor's abusive dad. Maybe his past was coming back to haunt him? Maybe, God forbid, the son becomes the father? Or perhaps it was something simple, silly, and natural like Nestor being afraid of becoming a father himself? Erin didn't know. But she'd promised to be there for her friend. Now Erin realized, when Angelina had needed her, she'd been nowhere around.

"There is no way," Ben said, interrupting Erin's thoughts. "No way Nestor physically hurt his wife. He wouldn't have laid a hand on her. The idea is ridiculous."

"She's hurt," Erin said. "And it wasn't my idea. There's a patrol unit at his house right now. I just talked to them. His neighbor says Nestor and Angelina were arguing tonight. He heard shouting. Later, he heard screaming and glass breaking. He thinks Nestor hurt her. I'm just trying..." She was so near to Ben, and feeling so distant, Erin wanted him to take her in his arms. But he wouldn't, she knew, because of her rule, and because Nestor and Angelina now stood between them. "I'm sorry," Erin said. "I'm sorry. I've missed you so much lately. I'm sorry about this, all of it, but I have a job to—"

"I know. I know you do. I'm sorry too." What more could either of them say?

"I've got to go back out," Erin said. "I have to check his neighborhood... for *some guy*."

"You know he lied to you?"

Erin nodded. "Yes. I know."

Ben took hold of her arm. Both shivered at the contact. "I'll try to find out why," he whispered.

Sixteen

The next morning, just relieved, barely home and still in his wrinkled uniform, Ben answered his apartment door to a weary Erin. Her eyes were red, her voice hollow, and her first comment came like a detached police report. "Angelina lost the baby."

"I know. We got a call at the station. What's happening now?"

"I've turned the case over to Ron Musselwhite."

"Musselwhite?"

"The chief of police."

"I know who he is," Ben growled. "I work for the same city you do. That wasn't a 'Musselwhite, who', it was a 'Musselwhite, why'. Why aren't you handling it?"

"How can you ask? Angelina is one of my best friends. It's possible she was assaulted—"

"What do you mean 'It's possible'? She *was* assaulted. Nestor said so."

"You didn't let me finish. It's possible she was assaulted by Nestor."

"That's ridiculous, Erin. Nestor told you what happened."

"And you told me he was lying."

"He's lying about the details. For some ungodly reason that he won't cough up. He isn't lying about the attack on his wife. And he didn't do it."

"We're looking at what he told us and we're going to have to dig deeper. There isn't any choice. I'm not supposed to be telling you, but nothing about what he said is adding up."

"Nestor did not do this!"

"I want to believe that. We all do. But we can't just take his word for it. Or yours."

"Then investigate. But why hand it off to a politician like the chief of police?"

"This isn't Chicago, Ben. Chandler is missing. Shane is dead. Tankard is... God knows where in Canada. I'm the only investigator left and I have a desk full of murders. There's no one else. Besides, I am friends with the assault victim. I'm not going to tear into Nestor's life. I can't."

"But Musselwhite?"

"He's the only one left. And, outside of taking lashes from the mayor, he's a good cop."

"Are you serious?"

"You hate your chief; his brother-in-law. You're projecting. That's not my problem."

Ben paused, gave it thought, and laughed at his own jackassery. "You're right."

"On this," she said, "I know I am. Now can we stop fighting and make up, please?"

They fell into a clinch, without passion but with a oneness both needed. The exhaustion, the pain, the horrors of the week melted as they held each other. "First chance," Erin whispered. "We should get out of here."

"A vacation?"

She pushed her head into his chest. "An escape."

He held her tight. "We need a plan; in case we ever do need to escape. Listen, if one of us has to go, for whatever reason, they go to Chicago. The other follows as soon as they can."

"Why Chicago?"

"Huge city, a couple hundred miles away, what better place to hide and wait? First one there takes a room in a hotel, some place in the Loop so we can find each other, but so seedy, no self-respecting civil servant would be caught dead there."

Erin laughed, still holding on. "What names do we use?"

"Something to honor the hometown. Julian Duncan if I run. Julie Duncan if you go first."

"Can't say I like the names much."

"It's better than Vanderjagt." He took her punch like a man. "We need a group name, too. Some of those places are hinky about giving out guests' names. We say we're with the Court Reunion."

"You never give up, do you?"

"Never," Ben agreed. "Never, ever, ever."

How wonderful it would have been to make love then. But it wasn't in the cards. Neither, just then, was a romantic escape to Chicago. Needing to hurry back to work, Erin broke the hold and escaped to Ben's bathroom. She locked the door, kneeled, and as quietly as she could, threw up.

Later in the day, Ben entered the Intensive Care Unit and asked the clerk for Angelina Pena's room. Not bothering to smile, she politely but firmly replied that the patient was not allowed visitors of any kind. He got the impression it wasn't the first time she'd explained the situation. She added that, outside of the police, nobody was being allowed in. The cops had access only with the doctor present. She pointed to the waiting room.

Ben followed her finger, gazing the length of the hall, to see Nestor in the waiting area in conference with the police. Not just any cops, but Chief Musselwhite himself. A uniformed patrolman, Ben did not know, stood nearby at parade rest, but looking as if he'd rather be elsewhere.

Ben was no expert on body language but he knew Nestor, and by his animated gestures, knew he was more than unhappy. Ben arrived at the room in time to hear the chief say, "Mr. Pena, your story makes no sense."

"The broken window isn't evidence of an intruder?"

"It appears to be. But other evidence makes it questionable."

"So I'm a liar?" Nestor demanded.

"I didn't label you. Many things you told us are true. But the facts of the incident as a whole do not hold together. We need to go over them again. The window was broken from the outside. But there are no footprints, neither wet ones in the room or muddy prints on the ground. There's no evidence anyone crossed the yard or climbed up to enter through that window. I've seen lawns with more grass, I don't need to tell you that. Yours is mostly dirt, mud now with the rain, and that mud is undisturbed. Have you any explanation as to—"

The three turned like clockwork figures to Ben in the doorway.

"This is police business," Musselwhite said.

"Then it should be conducted in a police interview room," Ben replied. "Are you preferring charges against Mr. Pena?"

"Is that any of your business?" Musselwhite didn't wait for an answer. "You're Court, aren't you? The firehouse lawyer? Chief Castronovo talks about you often."

"Yeah." Ben smiled, lifting crossed fingers. "Your brother-in-law and I are just like that."

"That's what he says. But he just uses the one finger. I got nothing against you, Court, but one day, son, you're going to get it bit off." Musselwhite turned to Nestor. "We would appreciate your help in investigating this attack on your wife. Please give this incident serious consideration. Then come see me at the station tomorrow morning."

The cops left without another word.

"They think I did this to Angelina."

"They accused you?"

"Not outright. But you should have heard the questions. What is our relationship like? Do we argue a lot? What about our sex lives? With Angelina pregnant have I been getting it elsewhere? Have I ever hit her? You should have heard them."

"I understand your anger. But that's what they do, Nestor. They start with the spouse and they aren't always wrong. This isn't your first day in long pants."

"I know. I know. But they know me, for Christ's sake. We work for the same city. They treated me like a punk with a rap sheet. My child is gone. My wife is fighting for her life and they practically accused me of—"

"Stop it, Paco. I know you're hurting and I want to help you. But you've got to come clean, bro. You lied to Erin last night, and I goddam well know it. What I don't know is, why? What's it about?"

Ben was cut off by a chime of bells, and an insistent voice over a loudspeaker: "Code blue, I.C.U. Code blue, I.C.U. Code blue, I.C.U." The alarm brought action. All sorts of medicos scrambled into the Intensive Care Unit. Nestor hurried after them with Ben on his heels. Inside, their worst nightmare came to life. The emergency was in Angelina's room.

Lab coats and scrub suits hustled in, around, and over Angelina's bed. Nestor called to his wife, trying to get in, when one of the nurses threw a body block at the door. With a grip usually reserved for hauling hose and swinging an ax, Ben grabbed Nestor from behind and maneuvered his distraught partner back into the waiting room.

Time stretched. Not a word passed between them. Time stood still, but they no longer could. They paced like caged tigers, Ben for Nestor, Nestor for Angelina. When her doctor finally appeared and announced his sincere sorrow, time no longer existed. "We did everything we could. Your wife went into cardiac arrest and we were unable to re-establish…" He talked on, offering heartfelt remorse with the dumbed down explanations of shock from the loss of the baby, stress, infarction, respiratory shutdown, and system collapse. Sometime after, the doctor went away.

"They think I did this to my wife!" Nestor screamed. "They think I killed my family!"

Ben grabbed him, holding him up, holding on.

Seventeen

Ben dreamed that night and, for the first time in a long time, it wasn't a nightmare. It was a dream about the first time he and Erin made love. Officially, the consummation had been wonderful. But that wasn't precisely true and his subconscious knew it. What it really had been was the collision of animal passions in two people too shy, too wrapped up in their professions, and too afraid to display passion. Refusing to commit, unwilling even to admit what was happening, it had been frightening, clumsy, embarrassing, funny, warm, and finally, yes, wonderful. In the middle of a blizzard they'd bumped into each other, two weary civil servants, both out alone, killing matching nights off by attending a local community theater production. She fumbled around. He talked too much. He spilled coffee. She spilled tea. Both beat around the bush endlessly before offering simultaneous invites to each other's apartments for a night cap. He wound up at her place and, somehow, showed enough humor and charm to gain admission to her bed. It had been wonderful.

Once the heavy breathing ended, so did the romance and the evening. In place of afterglow, Erin panicked. Fear of the future? The unknown? Love? A huge mistake? Who knew? Gorgeously naked, she sat up and asked him to leave. Gobsmacked, Ben stared. Erin made it an order. "I need to be alone. You need to go."

It was snowing like hell. He'd taken the bus downtown for the show. And, after coffee, Erin had offered a ride to her house. The tourist town had a lovely bus service but not with routes that far off the main drag. And they didn't run at three in the morning. The only cab company had two drivers with the flu and two cabs on the fritz. "I'm really sorry, but you have to go."

He went. She was of age and welcome to her emotional somersaults like everybody. He was a big boy. Besides, it wasn't so bad. How often does a man get a blizzard entirely to himself? In a whiteout, Ben trudged three miles down and around the bluff (no elevator at night or in winter), across the frozen downtown, to his place in the lonely Port District. All in all, it had been a memorable first date. Ben's dream brought it back in all its hot and cold glory.

He was just dragging his ice-covered rear into his dream apartment when reality intruded. The phone's insistent ring yanked Ben back to this world. He groaned his displeasure as, again, the old saw 'Life is so much easier to handle unconscious' proved itself true. He lifted the receiver and got another slice of bad news from Erin; this one definitely not a dream.

Ben arrived at Nestor's to find the street barricaded and The Castle surrounded by squad cars and cops. Engine 1 and an ambulance were there as well. The sun was barely up. The shocks were coming too quickly and Ben swore in helpless response. He parked, was allowed through to the hot zone, and met a tired and pale Erin. "Are you all right?"

"I'm fine," she snapped, obviously not fine.

"I'm sorry. You look sick."

"I've never felt better!"

"Fine!" Ben pointed at The Castle. "What the hell is going on?"

"Nestor's inside. He's supposedly suicidal and he's threatening others."

"That's ridiculous. Nestor is making threats?"

"He hasn't spoken to us at all. But his neighbor says—"

"His neighbor? The same asshole who said Nestor and Angelina were fighting the night of the blackout? When in the hell are you guys going to get it? His neighbor has a bone to pick. The guy hates foreigners, even when they're not. He thinks our New Mexican is a Mexican, the racist rat bastard, and he throws Nestor a cold hard one every chance he can."

"I'm not arguing with you, Ben. I just said, Nestor won't talk to us. We received a complaint. Now we're here we can't just go because you say so. He's barricaded inside. He's forcing this standoff. And there's no way around the fact he's still looking at a possible manslaughter charge."

"Oh, give me a break," Ben said. "Is Musselwhite still on that?"

"He's not the only one, Ben."

"You think Nestor hurt Angelina? You really think that?"

"Somebody killed Angelina and the baby. Nestor has a long way to go before he clears up some very cloudy facts."

"He's *our* friend. He's *my* friend. Even if he wasn't, how could you come away from an interview with him without knowing he's innocent and that he and Angelina were okay? Musselwhite's thick as mud, but I'd have never guessed it of you."

"I don't appreciate that. I didn't call you to give me a hard time. I thought you'd help."

"I most certainly will." Fuming and feeling betrayed, Ben turned and started around the squad.

"Ben! Ben, you can't go in there!"

"Fuck that!" Ben ran for the porch. Weapons went up all around and several officers started his way. Ben didn't care and didn't slow down. He ignored their shouts. Erin shouted louder, at her people now, calling them back. What was the point of turning Ben into a target? Besides, in his place, she'd probably have done the same. For all Erin knew, though she didn't ponder the question, this may have been the reason she'd called him to the scene. Ben leapt to the porch, found the supposedly barricaded door unlocked, and went in. He pushed the door shut, leaned on it, and breathed deeply. His goal had been to get inside and he'd done that. Great. *Now what,* he thought, fresh out of plan.

The hall was empty. Should he stride in, he wondered, like he'd done a thousand times over the last ten years? Or should he stay put and call out like a hostage negotiator? Hell. He started in, feeling an alien fear, and goddam his best friend for that.

Nestor's disembodied voice stopped him. "I almost shot you."

"Yeah?" Ben called back. "With what? Do you even own a gun?"

Nothing but silence.

"I'm coming back." Ben took a step.

"Don't!"

"Oh, bullshit," Ben hollered. He pushed off, surprised how angry he was, and started down the hall. "I don't care if you treat the cops like punks. Some are card-carrying jack wagons. But Erin doesn't deserve it. And what? You're going to treat me like a punk? I don't think so. Where are you?"

"In here."

The door to the living room was ajar. "I'm right?" Ben asked, his hand on the door. "You don't have a gun? And, even if you do, it won't be pointed at me?" He stepped through.

Nestor stood, unarmed of course, peeking out one of the windows across the room. He turned to Ben, sagged against the wall, and slid to the floor. He covered his face with his hands and shook while he cried. Ben dropped beside Nestor, hugged him tightly, and held him for a long time.

Later, neither was sure how long, the phone rang. Both stared without moving.

"It's the cops," Nestor said. Crying again, he added, "There's no one else it could be anymore."

"Screw 'em," Ben said.

A loudspeaker blasted. It was the police chief himself. "Pena. Nestor Pena," Musselwhite said. "We need to know that Ben Court is all right. Let him show himself, so we know he's all right."

"Christ," Ben said, rising. With his head to the side, he slid the window open and shouted, "This is Court. Don't be stupid. I'm not a hostage, for Christ's sake. I'm all right. Everything is all right."

"We need you both to come out."

"We're talking. Give us a few minutes."

"We don't have a few minutes, Court. There's a lot of people waiting out here."

"Go the hell home. He didn't ask you here and neither did I."

"We aren't going to do that."

"No. Didn't figure you would."

"Tell Pena he needs to come out now."

"What do you think I'm doing, you moron. We'll be out in a few minutes." He slammed the window and scowled at Nestor. "Jesus, have you stepped on your cock! Yours and mine both."

"I've screwed up, Ben, as a husband and as a human being, but I never laid a hand on my wife."

"Don't you think I know? I know. But you are making yourself look guilty as hell. Not to mention this crap about killing yourself." Ben jabbed a thumb at the window. "They think you have a gun."

"I can thank my neighbor for that."

"No. You can thank yourself. Your neighbor's always been an ass. This new wrinkle is yours. I know you're hurting, man, but you've got to cut this crap out, Paco. You've got to answer the cops' questions and help them catch the guy that destroyed your family."

"There was no guy. I can't answer their questions because there's nobody to catch."

"What are you saying? Are you telling me you—"

"No. I didn't do it. But neither did anyone else. Nobody human."

"What are you talking about? What happened with Angelina? What happened here?"

"You're not going to believe me. Nobody will believe me. There isn't one chance in a million."

"I don't know what you're saying, but it's obvious you're serious. I've got that, brother. So why can't you tell me? Why would I doubt you?"

Nestor studied Ben. "My Angelina," he said in a whisper. "My baby... were killed by a monster."

"But who? Who did you see?"

"No, Ben, you don't hear me. You don't get it because you're not listening. I need you to listen. I'm not talking about a man. I'm choosing my words carefully and I mean what I say. My wife was attacked and killed by a monster. A creature. A demon right out of Hell."

Nestor told it all, there on the floor in Ben's embrace. He relived the night, the storm, the rolling blackout and, in detail, led Ben to live it with him; Angelina insisting she'd been followed home, their friendly skirmish over the candles, the nightcap, the casserole he'd slaved a whole fifteen minutes over, his yelling out the window, her going to bed with a headache, his waking to breaking glass, splintering wood, and his wife's screams. They relived his breaking in the bedroom door. Then he described the hideous thing on top of Angelina. "It hissed and growled. Its obscene tongue was buried in her belly. It was sucking like it was a straw. It killed our baby. It killed my wife."

Ben wiped the sweat from his lips and forehead. "Why didn't you tell the police any of this? Why in God's name did you make up a story about some guy—?"

"Would they have believed a word of this? Do you believe it?"

Ben studied the inside of his head, wondering whether or not he did. He couldn't answer.

"You see? It's the absolute truth but who would believe it?" Nestor caught his breath, calmed himself. "Ben, do you remember Aswan?"

"Isn't it a dam or something?"

"Not the dam."

"The ruins, you mean? That old city in Cambodia?"

"Not Angkor. Jesus, what are you talking about?"

"Easy, Paco," Ben said, "you ain't the only fireman under stress here. You asked a weird question and I'm trying to answer it. I think I've heard the word, but I can't think of where, so I guess the answer is no. What's Aswan?"

"It's one of the words our patient was shouting, our burn patient from the Garfield Street explosion. It's one of the words he kept yelling in the ambulance. Aswan, remember? When I was holding her in the car, on the way to the hospital, Angelina said it too. I swear. Aswan. Aswan. Over and over, just like the burn patient. Then she said, "Demon." She could barely get it out, but she said, "Demon. That's what attacked Angelina." Nestor stared at Ben with swollen red eyes. "A demon."

Eighteen

They were still on Nestor's living room floor but Ben's mind had taken flight. He'd returned to the rear compartment of their ambulance, reliving that trip to the hospital. Cooper was there, holding her injured arm, but he was busy pouring water on the patient, Soomnalung, holding his mask while he screamed, 'Aswan', 'Mennon', 'Gal', and 'Tick, tick, tick', like a coked-up clock.

Aswan. Aswan? Had Nestor heard Angelina right? He was upset. He'd been drinking. She was hurt. Going back, had he heard Soomnalung right? He was out of his mind with pain. Maybe he hadn't said any such thing? Aswan? A demon?

Nestor broke Ben's concentration. "Do you believe me?"

"I don't know a thing about monsters or demons," Ben said. "I know you. I believe you are telling me what you believe is true."

"I know," Nestor said. "It's a long way around to get to my side."

"I am on your side." They gripped hands.

"Ben, I can't live without Angelina and the baby. I don't want to."

"You don't have a choice. You're a stupid heathen like me, but you were raised to be a good Catholic boy. Your wife was devout. You have to take what life gives you and do something with it. Angelina wouldn't accept anything else. That rules out rash self-destruction. You are also barred from killing your neighbor, no matter how much the prick deserves it." They shared a pained laugh. "So what are you going to do? What kind of life are you going to make to honor your family?"

"Firefighter Pena! Firefighter Court!" It was the police loudspeaker again. This time with a different voice, the worst voice in the world. "This is the Fire Chief!"

"Goddammit," Ben groaned, throwing his head back. He peered out and saw Tony Castronovo, bullhorn in hand, leaning against the police chief's squad. His brother-in-law was beside him. "Ladies and gentleman," Ben muttered. "Badge *and* bugle are in the house. Looks like they came together." He sat back down by Nestor. "On the bright side, Erin isn't in charge anymore and she shouldn't catch any flack for whatever dumb shit we do next."

"I order you to come out!" Castronovo growled, with reverb. "I'm not kidding. Or waiting."

Ben looked to Nestor. "Well, Paco, the sand has run out. There's no more time. Either we both go out now or we both kill ourselves. What's it going to be?"

They laughed. Then Nestor dropped his head to Ben's chest and cried. Ben held him, crying too. A moment later, his brown cheeks flushed and marred with tears, Nestor said, "They're going to send me to the booby hatch."

"Yes, brother," Ben said, nodding. "That's the drill. For observation at least. But is that so bad?"

"To be hauled off to a psych unit?"

"To walk out of here like a man who, though he's been to Hell and back, understands he's got issues that need sorting. To check yourself in voluntarily. To get some rest. To talk with people that, though they're just as full of shit as you are, if not more, might hear you. Where's the downside?"

"I'm going to lose my job. It's all I know."

"Why would you lose your job? Outside of your neighbor's wet dreams you haven't threatened or harmed anyone. You've suffered two devastating losses and you've reacted like a devastated man. Now you need to pull it together; even if you're not sure how. But you've got to decide, brother, before Castronovo and Musselwhite piss themselves."

Nestor nodded wearily. "I'll get my head candled on one condition. You've got dig into this mess. You've got to promise to investigate; find out what happened to my family."

"How am I supposed to do that?"

"I don't know. I've got my own troubles. But you've got to promise."

"Okay. I promise. I'll detect. As soon as I figure out where to start."

"That's easy. Start where this started. Go back to the Garfield burn victim. He said it; he must know what 'Aswan' is. He's the only survivor from these incidents that can talk. Question him."

"The guy doesn't speak English," Ben said. "He's been in isolation since the fire. One paper said he's in a coma. The police haven't even been able to question him."

"I don't know about the cops but the coma stuff is bull, a rumor, or a story cooked up to keep the reporters away. Angelina worked there. So does a cousin of hers from the old country, Bennie Bagtas. He works in the kitchen. Coma patients do not eat three squares a day. They're being sent to his room on the Burn Unit."

"Assuming you're right. Assuming I could get in to see him, and he wanted to talk, and he was well enough to talk," Ben said. "He's Filipino – I couldn't understand a word."

"Pena! Court! Are you coming out?" Castronovo sounded ready to pop a vein.

It wasn't funny, but Ben and Nestor laughed. "We've got to go, Nestor."

Nestor grabbed Ben's arm. "Take an interpreter. Angelina's cousin, Bennie, he's right there at the hospital. He's a native Filipino, speaks the two most common languages in the country. Call him. Tell him I need his help. Tell him we're going to revenge Angelina. You've got to see Soomnalung. Talk to him; see what happened. Find out what he knows."

"Bennie will help us?"

"If you pay him enough." Ben stared incredulously. Nestor laughed. "What? It's America, who does anything for free?"

The paramedics had yet to clear the porch when a band of city employees in blue descended to give the New Mexican a set of steel bracelets. Ben told Erin they weren't necessary. She agreed, but said, "No choice. It's the rules."

"Can you take him in?" Ben asked in a whisper.

"Of course," Erin said. "There aren't any charges right now. We're going straight to the hospital."

Soon after Erin drove off with Nestor, the police chief grabbed Ben. He wasted no time and few words chewing the paramedic out for interfering. But, with no reason to fit him for municipal jewelry, Musselwhite let it go at that. Then Ben's own red-faced department chief stepped up like incoming mortar fire. "What the hell's the matter with you?" Castronovo demanded.

"Nothing, sir," Ben said. "Thanks for asking."

"Don't even bother being a smart ass. You intentionally disobeyed the police chief's order."

"I was already inside by the time you and the police chief arrived. Nobody gave me an order. Had they, I'd have told them to kiss my ass. I'm not on the Police Department. As for your brother-in-law, we both had the same objective and I achieved it without violence on anyone's part. As Nestor is one of your men, you ought to appreciate it. Musselwhite made his feelings known without pressing any charges against me. So it's all fixed."

"Nothing's fixed." Castronovo sneered. "In my book, the ends don't justify the means."

"Your book?"

"I know; you didn't know I could read. You're hilarious, Court. My sides hurt every time I'm near you. You are also suspended for the next three days without pay. And I don't need the permission of the Civil Service Commission. Laugh that off, funny man."

Ben sat on The Castle steps until long after the last engine, ambulance, and squad disappeared. It took ten years, but Castronovo had finally been right about something. Ben didn't feel like laughing.

Nineteen

The last request Nestor made of Ben in public, as Erin told him to watch his head and helped him into the back of her cruiser, was that Ben not give up on him. They were best friends, Ben replied, how could he? The last request Nestor made of Ben in private, before they'd come out to face the music, was that he get to the Garfield burn patient and learn what started this horror show.

As good as his word, despite knowing it was crazy, Ben arrived at the hospital prepared to do just that. Then fate tried to derail him. Whether by accident, coincidence, or – an even creepier thought – stalking, Mark Forester was somehow there to accost him in the hospital parking lot and, as reporters always do, to turn 'Hello' into a question.

Instead of answering, Ben asked, "Why aren't you downtown?"

"At the press conference? I was. If that's what you want to call it. Roses and hearts from the mayor but no answers. Autopsy reports, finally, but heavily redacted. No access to the coroner. Nothing new from the lead detective." Ben bit his tongue; Forester missed it. "If the administration has any news, they're keeping it to themselves. It's ridiculous, I know, a member of the press expecting something from a press conference."

"You have my sympathy. But you're not going to get any news following me around."

"Come on, Ben. I thought we understood each other." Forester jammed a thumb at him. "Protect the public." He turned the thumb on himself. "Inform the public."

"It'd make a great comic book," Ben said, starting away.

"I'm telling you," Forester shouted. "We'd make a good team."

"Wonderful," Ben shouted back. "But there's no game. We'd just be standing admiring our matching uniforms." He disappeared around the corner into the hospital's west lot.

Forester stood alone, still with no story.

At Nestor's urging, Ben had phoned Bennie Bagtas, Angelina's cousin, a hospital employee and a Philippine native who spoke both English and Tagalog, the most common languages in the islands. Not surprisingly, he even spoke Angelina's Taglish. Ben arranged to rent Bennie's services as a translator, and his silence, and laid out their caper. Having passed through the Burn Unit many times during work, Bennie suggested the post med, meal time break as the best opportunity to sneak an interview. Most of the nurses would be in the cafeteria, two floors below. Those still on the unit would be off their feet doing as little as possible. With luck, Bennie had said, they'd get in and out unnoticed. Ben kept the status of his recent luck to himself.

Bennie, early twenties, copper skinned, dressed in a hospital scrub suit, was at the hospital's west entrance, holding two more sets of scrubs in sealed plastic, and had been for ten minutes. He was ready to quit when Ben arrived on the run. "Man," Bennie complained. "You said you'd be here."

"I'm here."

"You didn't say you'd be late. I look like a pervert standing here. I'll be lucky if someone didn't report me to security."

"I was unavoidably detained."

"This is going to cost you a hundred bucks."

"What? I don't want to adopt the guy. I just want to talk to him. We agreed on fifty."

"I'm unavoidably raising it. You made it harder on both of us. I got a bigger chance of losing my job now and you got to pay." Ben shook his head. "I nosed around," Bennie said, sweetening the pot. "This Soomnalung, he's not allowed visitors. Even family, if he has any, which he prob-ly does not, are restricted. The cops pass through regular, keeping an eye 'cause he is hot. No pun intended. You don't have a chance of seeing him without me. And, if you get in, then what?"

"I don't have a hundred. I've got what we agreed on, fifty dollars."

Bennie raised his hands in mock apology.

"I'll get the other fifty," Ben said in disgust. "But you have to take this for now and do the job. Or Nestor and I will whip your ass."

"Okay," Bennie said. "I'll trust a fireman. All you got to do is swear on the virgin."

"I don't know any." Bennie eyed him with suspicion. "Oh," Ben said, getting it. "Fine." Ben handed Bennie the cash. "There's the fifty we agreed on. And I swear – on the virgin – you'll get the extortion money when we're done, even if I don't eat this week."

"Think of the information you will have to digest with an interpreter."

Ben followed Bennie into the depths of the hospital. They passed the shipping dock, the pathology annex, and the house kitchen where the patient meals were prepared, doing all they could to avoid the security cameras. They took a back elevator to the eighth floor Burn Unit, then marked time in the service room, peeking occasionally until the north hall was free of traffic. With the coast clear, Bennie led them like panicked mice to a mop closet across the hall from Soomnalung's room. It surprised Ben, at first, to find no police guard. But considering the condition of the patient, and that of the town, using the manpower elsewhere made sense. Soomnalung wasn't going anywhere. They donned the sterile scrubs, turned out the light, cracked the closet door, and waited their chance.

The hall stayed quiet but the target room had a brief and unpleasant flurry. Nurses came and went, and by their equipment and the sounds of agony coming from the room, the paramedic realized they'd arrived in the middle of a debriding session.

Flame and human skin do not mix. Second and third-degree burns, over eighty percent of his body, meant most of Soomnalung's skin was damaged and much of it gone. The nerves were burned or exposed. The oozing wounds were a breeding ground for infection. Such burns required debridement. The dead skin tissue had to be removed with enzymes and scalpels, and antiseptic patches applied to replace missing skin, making the patient look like a screaming quilt. The process, not unlike skinning the patient alive, had to be repeated frequently.

Soomnalung screamed. Bennie moaned in a whisper. "This isn't for me, man. I'm sorry. I don't think I can do this."

"Think again," Ben whispered back. "You agreed and took every nickel I had."

"Not for this. I transport food; I'm not a nurse. I don't like sick people."

"You work in a hospital, you fool."

"*Whoa.* Is that any way to treat a friend?"

"You're Nestor's friend. Not mine."

"I'm Nestor's cousin, by marriage, I'm not—"

"I don't care," Ben said, cutting him off. "You're my employee. You're going to do the job or I'm going to beat you with one of these mops."

Bennie considered the options and, deciding to be happy in his work, nodded his surrender.

Across the hall, the screaming stopped. Ben peeked and saw two nurses vacate the room with relief on their faces. The procedure had been no fun for them either. Ben gave Bennie the high sign and they sneaked across and into Soomnalung's room.

Seeing the man again, lying there swathed in bandages, brought the horror of their first meeting flooding back. Ben stifled the memory, leaned over the bed, and whispered, "Soomnalung, my name is

Ben Court. I'm the medic that brought you to the hospital. Can you hear me?"

The patient's eyes opened to slits. He groaned and closed them again.

Ben looked to Bennie. "Tell him, in his language. Say I need to ask a few questions."

"I don't know what his language is. I can try Tagalog." He did. The groaning patient looked at Bennie, then Ben, then Bennie again. He mumbled something. The interpreter furled his brow and renewed his efforts. Again Soomnalung mumbled a reply. It was gibberish to Ben, and he was about to discover, mostly gibberish to Bennie. "This guy may or may not be Soomnalung," he said. "I don't know. But if he's from the Philippines, I'll eat his bed sheet."

"What? He's not Filipino?"

Bennie shook his head. "Prob-ly been to the islands, I don't know. Every once in a while, he says a word in Tagalog. Maybe he's seen an Eddie Romero movie. But he isn't from the Philippines."

"That doesn't make sense."

"I'm just telling you."

"Try again," Ben said, desperately. "Ask him what Aswan is?"

"What? Aswan? What's that?"

"That's what I'm trying to find out. Ask him?"

"You don't mean *aswang*, do you?"

The patient groaned loudly. Both Ben and Bennie turned to look. His eyes were open, bloodshot, filled with tears, and suddenly, with terror.

"I don't know," Ben said, answering Bennie but staring at the patient who was staring back at him. "Do I? I might have misheard the word. I could have been mispronouncing it all along. What's aswang?"

"Aswang!" the patient cried.

"It's goofy, that's what it is," Bennie said. "This guy is not Filipino." He pointed at Ben. "You're not from the Philippines. But you're telling me the word we're all going to get together on is aswang? That's just goofy."

"Why? What is it?"

"It's nothing. It's superstition. Old ladies use it to scare their kids into being good."

"It's a ghost?"

"No. Filipinos don't believe in ghosts. It's more like a—"

"A monster?" Ben asked. "Is aswang a demon?"

Bennie studied Ben. The firefighter returned it. The staring match was interrupted when the man on the bed, in pained but perfect English, said, "You know aswang? You know about the demon?"

Ben and Bennie both turned. The patient licked his lips through a slit in his bandages and repeated the question. "You know about the demon?"

"I've heard of it," Ben said. "My best friend's wife is dead. He says she was killed by a demon. I don't know anything. What it is? Where to find it? How to stop it? Can you help me, Soomnalung?"

The patient shook his head, winced, then nodded in the same slight fashion. "I'm not Soomnalung. My name is Dylan Ruzicki. I'm an American." He began to shake. His groans turned to sobs. His wet eyes began to soak the surrounding bandages. "You're telling me it's still alive? Please, God, no. The aswang is destroyed. Isn't it? Isn't it? I destroyed it! Didn't I?"

Twenty

"I sent the monster back to Hell," Ruzicki insisted, raising his voice.

Ben shushed him. "Take it easy. We're on the same team. But we're not going to be able to help each other if they throw us out of here." Ruzicki nodded. Ben dabbed at the man's eyes with a tissue.

"Are you sure?" the patient asked. "It's still alive?"

"I'm not sure of a thing, brother," Ben said. "I don't know. I don't know if I can even believe in this… aswang. But something in this town wasn't here a week ago. People are dying because of it."

"It's my fault," Ruzicki said. "My fault it's here. My fault it wasn't destroyed."

"Don't get upset again. We don't have time to keep drying you off. The minute they find us here, they're either going to throw us out or arrest us. If this thing exists, if it's out there, I need to know what it is, where it came from, and what I can do to stop it."

"Promise me," Ruzicki said. "Swear you won't stop until the creature is destroyed."

Ben frowned. He thought of the promise Nestor had insisted on. And the promise Bennie had insisted on. Then he looked at the wrapped mummy on the bed. These guys, Ben thought, and their oaths of honor. What was he getting into? "Fine," Ben said. "What's one more? I promise. I won't stop until the thing is destroyed. Now tell me about aswang."

Ruzicki nodded slightly. "It's a long story," he said in agony. He pointed to a water glass beside the bed. Ben held the straw while he sipped. "I'll try… to get through it."

"We were mercenaries. Soldiers for hire, handling mostly black operations for whoever paid the bill. Hired to do the dirty things a country's own military couldn't or wouldn't do. We moved a lot, got in and out, fighting Communist insurgents in one country, garden variety revolutionaries in another, Islamic extremists in yet another."

"Over a year ago, I was sent to the Philippines, one of the islands south of Manila, commanding a small group of men posing as military construction workers. We were working covertly for their Army. My men took orders from me. I took *suggestions* from the local commander with their mission in mind. The Philippine authority needed plausible deniability, a way to disavow our group and activities in the event the operation blew up. We were stationed in a mountain jungle," Ruzicki said, licking his lips. "I don't mean a rainforest; I mean a fucking jungle. In daylight, we hacked our way from a base camp to the mountain top, to build a communications tower. That was a cover. By night we ran guns, shipping them in and out from an abandoned port on the other side of the mountain; the west side of the island. Those details aren't important now." He stared into Ben's eyes. "They have nothing to do with your promise."

Ben nodded, renewing the agreement.

"Let's say I had no moral quibble with our actions. The world is full of bad guys that need to be swatted like flies. We sold fly swatters. We sent shipments to China, Vietnam, Korea, and the African coast, Somalia, Ethiopia, the Sudan. Lots of dead rat bastards because of us."

He paused to gasp. Ben held a box of tissues and Ruzicki dabbed at his blinding tears. He got hold of the pain and continued. "We had the equipment needed to make the cover real, generators, backhoe, a trencher, tools, concrete mix and lumber, spools of electric wire, pallets of metal tubing. When we weren't in the port or sleeping, we worked the cover, steadily erecting a communications tower that was never going to communicate with anybody. Everything was aces until, one night, some equipment disappeared. Not the munitions, the weapons and ammunition, they were secure. I mean the equipment for the cover, for building the tower. A whole shitload of it vanished overnight in a robbery so smooth it had to be an inside job. The night guards had to have had a hand in it. The Philippine commander, a major, was incensed and turned their camp upside down. He discovered the responsible individuals and had them brought to the scene.

"There were five of them, four privates and a sergeant. He accused them of the theft and got their confessions. Then it got crazy. Right there in front of us, the major ordered all five to strip. We were speechless; we didn't get what was happening. The five were scared shitless but they did as they were told, stripped to their skivvies and put their uniforms in a pile. Then the major pulled his service pistol and, without so much as a kiss my ass, shot all five dead. No charges, no trial, no last words. It was the goddamnedest thing I ever saw. As each one took it, the others stood terrified and shaking, waiting for theirs. It happened so fast, the killing, my men and I stood there with our mouths open. When I found my tongue, I protested, but it fell on deaf ears. The major said discipline had to be maintained and that was that. Not that it mattered. They were dead as dirt; what good was I doing them? Worse, we were made accomplices. The major reminded me that, at great expense, we had been detailed to him and *suggested* I order my men to dispose of the bodies.

"We carried them into the jungle for burial. There was no service. As far as the major was concerned they were trash to be gotten rid of. We were to hurry up, dig one hole, pack the corpses in like sardines, and be done. I put my men to work digging the grave. That's when the trouble started."

Ruzicki gritted his teeth against the pain. "My guys attacked the job. We wanted to be done and out of there. They hadn't been at it long when Janeke hit something with his spade. I had no idea what it was but there was my best man, shouting like a frightened school girl. I cleared the hole, jumped in, and brushed the dirt away. He'd hit a chunk of bone. I teaspooned around until I figured out it was a skull. It was the goddamnedest thing you ever saw. Sort of round, but misshapen, tortured, with nasty yellow fangs in a long jaw. I thought it was an animal, but I'm not a biologist or an archeologist. I dug it out for a look. The more I looked the less I believed it. It was too big for a jungle animal; had to be human. But there was something wrong. We were soldiers; we'd seen every horror of war, but this thing—

"Beneath the jaw, something stuck out of the ground. I didn't know what it was; a root, a hunk of metal. Janeke saw it too. He jumped into the grave beside me and yanked it out. When he wiped it off, we saw it was a tarnished green metal rod, pointed on one end like a tent stake. He thought he'd spotted treasure. Turned out it was a murder weapon.

"When you make war for a living, you're not easily frightened. But I'm telling you, something about this was wrong. I wanted nothing to do with the thing. I jumped from the hole and ordered Janeke up. I told my men to come away, that we'd dig elsewhere. We left the grave and the creepy feelings. The men thought I was crazy; said one hole was good as any, asked what difference another body made? I told them to knock it off. I couldn't help it. Touching that skull got to me. Several hundred yards on, I had them start a new grave and told them to be quick. I couldn't tell them, couldn't understand, how terrified I was. We'd exposed more than a skeleton. I felt it to my core; we'd unearthed a dormant evil.

"With my men sweating blood, with five corpses growing ripe in the jungle heat, all I could think of were the stories I'd heard from Soomnalung."

"Soomnalung?" Ben asked. "There is a Soomnalung?"

"There *was*," Ruzicki replied. He took another sip of water, suffered another wave of pain, dabbed at his eyes, and when he mastered his agony, continued. "He was a priest from the nearby village. The island was his parish and he volunteered as chaplain for the Army unit." Ruzicki laughed. "With us heathens it was mostly an honorary position. Still, he was one of us."

Ben nodded. "I saw the dog tags."

"Yeah, the tags," Ruzicki said, taking in air with a hiss. "I'm getting to those. Soomnalung was an old man but with a mind as strong, a spirit as fierce, as on the day he'd arrived in the mountains from Manila five decades before. We got to be friends of a sort. What he told me... In the late sixties, the world was in revolution. But he found his new parish, there on that island, in an uproar of its own having nothing to do with the world. Nothing to do with this world at all. He found the island tortured by a hellish plague. The people, particularly the children and pregnant women, were dying in the night. The superstitious villagers blamed their evil gods. The priest resisted that notion."

Ruzicki coughed and shuddered. "Soomnalung never explained, the memories were too painful. And I've talked too long. I've about had it," the mercenary said. "Skip ahead. Soomnalung came to believe, then to know, that evil – honest to God evil – was responsible for the killings and the terror. A creature, a demon from Philippine mythology was attacking the women and killing their children in the womb. Soomnalung believed the creature ate the souls of the unborn children."

Despite his pain, Ruzicki nodded. "I see your look. I know. I thought the same when Soomnalung told me. I won't try to convince you... Ben, isn't it? I won't try to convince you, Ben. You've promised and I'm going to hold you to it, so I'll just tell you... Fifty years ago this creature—"

"But fifty years...?" Ben interrupted.

"Listen!" Ruzicki cried. "Listen, I'm out of air. It wasn't a plague on that island, it was a creature. It attacked the women, killed their unborn children. It killed any who tried to defend them. I don't know what it was; I don't know that the priest knew. He called it a worldly manifestation of evil. He said it walked in human form and called itself *Vong*. But when it attacked, it changed form and became aswang."

Ben fought every urge to walk out as the poor fool, clearly out of his mind with pain, droned on.

"The young Soomnalung led a few courageous men from the village to Vong's lair. They trapped it and destroyed it. Understand, Ben, they did not kill it. Aswang isn't human; it's a demon. They destroyed it and buried the detestable thing in unhallowed ground in the jungle. It lay in that unmarked grave for fifty years, locked between death and its hideous life." Ruzicki was crying again. "Last year, burying the corpses of five executed men, we dug it up again.

"I'm not superstitious," Ruzicki insisted. "If you'd told me this story two years ago, I'd have laughed louder than anyone. Now I know different. We unearthed an aswang called Vong. I don't know what limbo it occupied while buried. But I'm proof, the last surviving proof, the creature did not appreciate its resurrection. Vong turned the island into a charnel house, attacking every night; our camp, the base, the village. It satisfied its lusts on the women, its needs on the children, and its hatred on the men.

"It killed dozens. It toppled the unfinished tower. It burned the Army camp, destroyed most of our munitions. It burned the church and exacted its revenge upon the priest." Ruzicki suffered a coughing jag. He sipped water but his voice and strength were fading. He fought for breath, winced, and hissed at the pain. "I found Soomnalung dying in the ashes of his church. With his last breath he begged me to take up where he had failed; to destroy aswang and return it to limbo. I did. I promised because my friend was dying in my arms. He pushed his dog tags into my hands to seal the promise. Then he died. But I'd lied to him. I had no intention of staying to fight that thing. I didn't tell you… I married a village girl named Corazone. She was in danger because of me; she was pregnant. I had to get her out of there, off the island, away from the horror we'd unleashed.

"I couldn't fight it in its world, I told myself. I took what weapons I could, and my wife, and I got out. I had no way of knowing the extent of its hatred. Vong chased us, from the islands to South America, to Mexico, then into the modern world. It followed us, across the border into the United States, up the Mississippi. Over and over it attacked. It became clear there was no escape, no rest while the creature lived.

I had to fulfill my promise. I had to make a stand. But the creature struck before I was prepared. It attacked our home, here. I couldn't get to Corazone, couldn't save her or our child. I had no choice but to... I blew up the house, I killed my wife, destroyed myself, to save our child's soul. I thought I destroyed it. But you tell me I failed; that the creature still lives." Ruzicki grabbed the front of Ben's scrubs, pleading, "You must take it over. You must destroy this creature. I must atone for what I did, but Vong must be destroyed and that is beyond me now. You must find the creature's hiding place and send it back to Hell."

Ben stared incredulously. Behind him, Bennie watched helplessly. Behind Bennie, unannounced, the door came open. An angry growl escaped a livid nurse. "Who are you? What are you doing here?"

"We're... we're the paramedics that brought Soomnalung in," Ben said, easing Ruzicki's hands back to his sides on the bed. He forced a smile. "We were just seeing how he was."

The nurse darted her eyes from the patient to Ben, to Bennie. Her gaze lingered on the kitchen transporter as if in recognition. "You're going to have to leave now. The danger of infection..." She opened the door and pointed to the hall. "He isn't allowed visitors."

Twenty - One

Erin stared into the box of grenades, just stared. She was a trained marksman, could handle any gun you gave her, could turn a Danish into a donut with one shot at forty paces. But she couldn't make heads or tails of a hand grenade and didn't want to. What she'd wanted was to see all of the evidence Peter Chandler had collected. The grenades, though not on any inventory list, and not to be spoken of, were part of the evidence. But what were they doing in the Garfield basement? She closed the box again, turned, and took in Chandler's office. She sighed, backed up and tried the thought again: her office.

She stared at the city map, the crime scene photos, the stacked files, considering for the umpteenth time where to begin. She needed a crack through which to sneak a peek at the answer. She needed a clutch to get her murder investigations into gear. Hell, she needed a decent metaphor.

She stared at the Garfield Street photographs (selected by Chandler from hundreds taken during the Fire Inspector's investigation). She thought of the victims.

The press knew the corpse was female and the fire of undetermined origin. They did not know it was a homicide. They didn't know about the stomach wound, originally thought to be a gunshot but known now to be a stab wound from an unknown weapon. They did not know the victim was pregnant. The investigation, they'd been told, was ongoing.

The surviving burn victim, known only as Soomnalung, had yet to be interviewed. His dog tags suggested he was Philippine; that guess had yet to be confirmed. Outside of gibberish at admission, the subject hadn't uttered a word. Arrangements for an interpreter had been made, then postponed, when the hospital refused the interview. Normally cooperative with law enforcement, the hospital claimed this case was different, the threat of infection too great. No one saw Soomnalung but his doctors and nurses. And, according to the nursing supervisor even their attempts at communication had netted only screams of pain. Soomnalung's knowledge of the incident on Garfield Street remained his own.

Who were those two, Erin wondered? Were they man and wife? Companions? Enemies? What caused her death and his torture? Was he a murderer? Or had he failed in a rescue attempt? Was a perpetrator still out there? An interview, perhaps, held the answers. But that would have to wait.

She studied the pictures of the other victims each in their turn.

Linnea Keddy, attacked in an alley, left dead on the locked and inaccessible opera house roof. What was thought to be a gunshot wound in her stomach was, like the basement Jane Doe, found during autopsy to be a puncture. The same weapon? Probably. No weapon was found.

A question entered Erin's thoughts and she dug through the files for Keddy's folder. She examined Stanley Pickles' autopsy report; this time for a specific fact. She'd read it before but hadn't considered it in connection with the others. There it was; Linnea Keddy was pregnant. She dug further, found the autopsy report for Crystal Evers, the victim in the Fourth Street Elevator crash. A glance showed a similar puncture on the stomach. And, yes, Evers was pregnant too.

Catherine Herrera was obviously pregnant, eight months along, the night she was attacked. The night Shane was killed and Chandler disappeared. The children had been turned over to child services, and Erin understood, taken home by their maternal grandmother. But Herrera had no matching wound. Why? Had Chandler halted the attack? Herrera was hospitalized, out of danger, resting, and awaiting a second interview. But the first talk with her had offered little. She'd guided her children from the restaurant to the sidewalk like ducklings. There she was hit on the head. She woke in a hospital with no memory of the incident whatsoever. A rap on the door startled Erin.

"Sorry," Traer said, waving a pair of notes. "The mayor called to remind you a press conference has been scheduled for—"

"There is nothing new to report," Erin barked. She took a breath. "I'm sorry, Traer. I shouldn't kill the messenger. Thank you, Mayor Light's summons has been duly noted. What's the other one?"

"From your snitch, Mickey."

Erin grinned. The snitch was an invaluable weapon in the arsenal of the street cop. But to afford Mickey Cooke that title was a stretch even the athletic Detective Vanderjagt doubted she could make. He was an incorrigible gambler and small-time criminal, a bottom-feeder who occasionally swam close enough to the surface to do her a favor in return for a little folding money. She'd had no luck tracking down the elusive Garfield Street landlord, and with nothing to lose, had put Mickey on the trail. The note, his call back, read: '*Landlord – Horace March. Garfield house rented Corazone Quezon. No prev. address. No ? Asked. 3 months paid in full.*'

That was it. Missing the mayor's call had been okay but Mickey's note inspired a dozen questions to which Erin wanted the answers. They had a name now, Corazone Quezon. But was it the name they wanted? Was it Filipino? Was she, if it was a she, the burned Jane Doe from the basement? What, if anything, were Corazone and Soomnalung to each other? More, if Corazone and Soomnalung were the victims, there was still a perp out there and that perp stayed somewhere. Erin thought of another shot in the dark Mickey might take. She needed a check of all the realtors in town, this time for apartments and houses recently rented or sold to foreigners or furtive individuals. It wouldn't be much to go on, and she'd need to define furtive for Mickey, but they were grasping at straws. She tried his number and got what she expected. No doubt he was off to the casino, his usual haunt.

She'd barely hung up when Traer appeared in the doorway again. This time, he carried nothing but a curious expression. Erin returned the look. "One of the Fire Department paramedics is here," he said. "Wants to have a word with you."

Erin's heart jumped into her mouth. "Oh?" was all she managed. It had to be Ben. But, if it was Ben, what was he doing? Both agreed the relationship would be kept quiet. That meant he was either breaking their agreement or the visit was official. But if it was business, what business? She hadn't seen him since she'd left The Castle with Nestor. She wasn't sure how he felt about her hauling his best friend off. She wasn't sure how she felt about what he'd done. She was proud he'd taken action and mad at the action he'd taken at the same time. It made no sense but that's how she felt. She loved Ben Court, but just now, she didn't like him very much. "I'll see him."

Traer disappeared and, a moment later, returned with the paramedic. Yes, it was Ben, wearing his yellow turnout coat and smelling of smoke. Erin excused herself and walked Traer back to the squad room. It wasn't that he needed an escort, or that she had anything of import to tell him, she simply wanted Traer as far away from her office as possible. And to give herself another moment before she faced Ben. She wouldn't be kissing him at work, she knew. But she couldn't guarantee she wasn't going to bite his head off.

She returned to her office to find Ben studying the corkboard of crime evidence. He was holding several file folders she didn't recognize, that he'd apparently brought with him, and wearing a sheepish expression. Erin moved to her chair, putting the desk between them, and sat. Her heart, briefly in her mouth, had returned to her chest where it was madly racing in place.

"Hi," Ben said. "I wanted to… You got Nestor to the hospital?"

"Safe and sound."

"I wanted to thank you—"

"It was my job."

"And I wanted to apologize to you. If I made your job harder."

Erin nodded. That was all. Ben cleared his throat and waved the folders. "I was snooping through our recent paramedic reports. I saw a few similarities came up with a few questions, and thought I might run them by you."

"Such as?"

"Such as a recurring round wound over the stomach. I don't have access to your autopsy reports. You are probably aware, but I wanted to make sure. The wound was noted on the opera roof victim, the elevator victim, and on Angelina. Several of the women were pregnant too. I thought you might want to double check the rest." He set the files down. "If you ask me, there've got to be connections."

"Why do you say that?"

Fact was, he said it because of his interview with Dylan Ruzicki. He'd stopped at the station afterwards, and grabbed the files for an excuse to see Erin and feel her out, and to decide how much to tell her of what Ruzicki had said. But he hadn't been all that happy with his reception. He was less happy with Erin's attitude toward him personally. And he wasn't sure now he was going to tell her a thing.

"You're a cop. Don't you think the evidence suggests the same killer?"

"Yes, Ben, I do. But 'suggests' is a long way from 'got to be'. The world is full of coincidence."

"Maybe. But little Duncan, Iowa is not. We've had three homicides, Erin. And an attempt on a fourth. Whoever he is that's doing this—"

"There have been five homicides. Shane's doesn't feature a stomach wound. In fact, his wounds are entirely different from any we've seen. And, to the best of my knowledge, he was not pregnant. You didn't come to apologize or share information. You came looking for information. Right?"

"You don't want to give any out?"

"I'm not paid to give out information. But, for free, I'll agree with you. If these crimes are connected and we do have one killer, it's most likely a filthy man."

Ben smiled pleasantly and waved it away "I don't know what killed them."

"Don't you mean – who?"

Ben didn't answer and an uneasy moment of silence passed between them. Then he said, "I want you to quit working nights." And a much longer, much more uneasy moment passed.

"People in Hell want ice water."

"I'm serious."

"That's what's so sad, you probably are. But I'm not taking you seriously."

"Can't they move you to days?"

"What's the matter with you? I'm the lead investigator now. There are no day or night shifts. I'm on them until they're closed. Or until Peter strolls back in and takes them over again. If there were such a thing as a day shift, I wouldn't take it. I have a sworn duty."

"I'm worried about you."

"In another setting, I would probably appreciate that. But you're breaking our agreement by trying to have this conversation here."

"You're right and I'm sorry. I came to tell you something else."

"What?"

"Nothing. It isn't important. Let's just leave it at a lame, I was worried about you."

"If I get into trouble," Erin said, "I'll call the Fire Department and you can rescue me."

Now the silence was on Ben's side. Finally, with no way around it, he said, "Not for the next three days. Castronovo has suspended me for butting in on your standoff with Nestor."

"That isn't fair. You resolved the situation. That's why I called you. Do you want me to—"

"No." Ben raised a hand. "Thank you. One of the things we have in common is the need to fight our own battles." Erin nodded. Ben leaned on the corner of her desk. "Did Nestor say anything to you on the way to the hospital?"

"No. It was a quiet trip. Why?"

"Thinking of battles," Ben said. "I was reminded of what Nestor told me we are up against."

"What did he say? You did report what he said?"

"I didn't report anything. And I'm not reporting now. I'm talking to you, Erin, about what our friend said. I don't have a thing to report to Detective Vanderjagt."

Erin shook her head. "I can't—"

"Then I have nothing. Nestor was talking to me, not a city firefighter. I'll tell it to you, not a city cop. Or I'll let you get back to work."

Erin leaned on her desk and laid her chin on her hands. "What did Nestor say?"

"He said Angelina was assaulted by a monster."

"Of course he's a monster."

"No, Erin. I don't mean a bad guy. I mean..." Ben made claws with his hands. "*Raaahhh.* A monster. He said the thing that attacked Angelina was not human. He admitted what he told your chief was crap and that he lied because he knew he would not be believed. His wife was assaulted by a demon."

"I'll have to take that to Light's press conference. It will calm the citizens. Nestor said that?"

"Because his nosy neighbor blew the situation out of proportion. Not because there's anything wrong with Nestor's mind."

"I'm not going to argue about it. As far as Nestor goes, I agree. I don't think there's anything wrong with his mind either. I think he's pretending there is so he doesn't have to face what he did to Angelina."

"He didn't do anything to Angelina."

"Then the facts will prove that, Ben. And we can concentrate on bringing whoever did to trial. Along with whoever killed these other women."

"I know it sounds crazy. But if Nestor is right there won't be a trial. Not if you're after—"

"A demon? If you expect me to buy that, Nestor should have gotten a room with two beds." Erin moved the folders around on her desk, the better not to look at Ben. "Thanks for sharing this with me. I've got a press conference I have to get ready for."

Ben pursed his lips and nodded. He'd served in the military and knew when he'd been dismissed. He pulled a photo of Nestor and Angelina from his files, pinned it to Erin's board with the other victims, and left without looking back.

Twenty - Two

Big surprise, the press conference was a waste of time. The department heads reported generalities, Mayor Light offered his patented smile and repeated reassurances all was well in Tourist Town, the reporters (Forester in particular) pressed for answers to unanswerable questions, and Erin repeated the reply, "We have nothing to add at this time; the investigation is ongoing," so many times she felt dizzy. She wasted more time listening to Mickey Cooke's phone ring and decided to get out and get air. She wanted time to think with movement around her. She wanted to make something happen. And she wanted her snitch bothering realtors. That meant finding Mickey, which meant going to The Mystery Casino, out on the island and pushing him off his stool at the roulette table.

The Mystery, formerly the Duncan Greyhound Park, was a combination dog track and casino. The tourists thought of it as Vegas on the Mississippi – the cops thought of it as 'The Racino' –income for the city and a headache for law enforcement. Located on Chaplain Stevens Island, The Mystery boasted 30,000 square feet of gaming space with a thousand gaming machines, sixteen card and Roulette tables, and three restaurants: The Bur Oak Grill, Buffalo Bill's Steakhouse, and The Jackpot. Between all they fed, and occasionally fleeced, over a million visitors a year.

That night, members of the management were not the only ones with an eye on taking customers. That night Vong walked the casino floor.

Vong was a gorgeous copper-skinned beauty, an inch under five feet tall, slender but firmly curved. Like most women of the Philippines, she had long straight black hair and a wide nose and mouth with full red lips. But she had thick brown eyebrows and her almond-shaped eyes were hidden behind sunglasses. The glasses looked pretentious indoors, but revealing her eyes in public might have caused a stir. Vong's eyes had an interesting effect on people. One other difference separated her exotic features from those around her, though one had to look closely to notice it. She was missing the philtrum, that vertical groove running from the nose to the middle of the upper lip. Vong didn't have one. Vong wasn't a mammal, nor was she a human being.

Vong circled the bright, boisterous gaming room, taking her own gamble, she'd admit. Desperate as she was for sustenance, she had no choice. She sniffed the air, searching. She ignored the stares of those passing, thinking, *let them look and wonder.* She had half a mind to doff the sunglasses and really give them something to stare at. Americans disgusted Vong. American men were cowards, more women than men, and the women were revolting bitches, all helpless to protect themselves or those they claimed to love. So selfish, they couldn't generate enough interest to propagate their own species. Fat, lazy Americans didn't have children anymore; didn't even bother to replace themselves. The men remained children, playing with toys, while the women pretended to be mothers, dressing little dogs in human clothes and pushing them in baby carriages. It was useless – the scent Vong wanted was absent.

Outside, Vong scanned those coming and going. More of the same was all she smelled as the sun began to set. She was about to give up when she caught the scent. She inhaled deeply relishing the *liquor amnii* and the promise that came with it. She followed the scent and spotted the target opening a car door. The woman barely showed; less than twelve weeks along to be sure. But the fetal heartbeat was there, meaning the soul was there, and Vong was hungry. She stepped up noiselessly and grabbed the woman by the hair. The woman screamed. Vong grabbed her throat, pinching off the sound.

But she'd been heard. Two men, well-lubricated and laughing, stepped from the casino at the precise moment Vong attacked the pregnant woman. They focused on what looked to be a strong-arm robbery, by a small female robber no less, in the parking lot. They shouted in unison and ran in Vong's direction.

Vong shoved the woman into the silver Ford and pushed into the driver's seat after her. She squealed the tires pulling out and left the rescuers in her wake. The woman, screaming again in the passenger's seat, had suddenly become her kidnap victim. *That,* Vong thought as she slapped the bitch into silence, *was unfortunate.* She'd only meant to kill her.

Vong sideswiped two cars escaping The Mystery lot and turned onto Greyhound Park Road without looking back. She followed the curve left, beneath the underpass and then, with a shriek of rubber, made a hard right onto Sixteenth and raced like a bullet toward the bridge heading off the island.

Coming from the opposite direction, toward the Mississippi and the Sixteenth Street bridge, unaware a carjacking had taken place, Erin passed through the Port District, driving around a parade of Easter celebrants congregated at the corner of Maple and Fifteenth. The annual walk of 'The Stations of the Cross' was underway and the parish priest stimulated those gathered with the first of many selections of Holy Scripture.

" 'My soul is sorrowful even to death. Remain here and keep watch with me.' He advanced a little and fell prostrate in prayer, saying, 'My Father, if it is possible, let this cup pass from me; yet, not as I will, but as you will.' When he returned to his disciples he found them asleep. He said to Peter, 'So you could not keep watch with me for one hour?

Watch and pray that you may not undergo the test. The spirit is willing, but the flesh is weak.' "

"Isn't it just?" Erin muttered as she eased past them and on toward the bridge.

There were only two ways onto the island; the Wisconsin Bridge, the second largest arch bridge on the Mississippi, and the virtually unused Sixteenth Street bridge. Feeling lonely herself, Erin took Sixteenth Street. The marina lay to her right. She followed the curving road to the left, toward the casino. It was then she spotted a car, with extensive front end damage, coming toward her like a bat out of Hell.

Two women occupied the front, a dark driver in darker sunglasses, and a blonde passenger swinging roundhouses at her. It didn't take a cop to see something was amiss. The car, a Ford Focus, was coming so fast, Erin had no time to react. It blazed by, swiping her cruiser and forcing her to spin out in the Greyhound Road intersection. The baseball fields beyond the Chaplain Stevens loop spun past her windows as if she were riding a carnival Scrambler, and the nausea that had plagued Erin for a week returned. It was all she could do not to barf. She got the squad under control, breathed deep to shake the sick stomach, pulled a U-turn, and mashed the gas pedal, taking up the chase. The Ford had a lead on her, speeding off the island, over the bridge and back into town down Sixteenth Street.

Vong shot across the four-lane Kemper Blvd without slowing. From all sides came squealing brakes, smoking tires, and the frantic honking of horns. Seconds later, Erin's squad carved its way through the same intersection, just missing a Camry pointing in the wrong direction.

The pursuit continued down Duncan's 'tree' streets, Sycamore to Maple then left onto Pine. At Pine and Fourteenth Street, Vong skidded to a stop. She'd have laughed herself silly were in not for the woman beside her, screaming and slapping, and the police bitch behind her, siren blaring. Before her an immense crowd of Passion walkers paraded, crying and gyrating as they celebrated Easter; a hundred undulating bodies holding up traffic as they moved down the street. Those in front – at the elbows of the priest and the stand-in messiah toting an impressive wooden cross – carried candles or cringe-inducing whips, while the worshipers trailed behind singing the traditional Stabat Mater. From behind, at odds with the enthusiastic singers, came the shrill siren of the police car. Caught between The Rock and a hard place, Vong jumped out, abandoning the vehicle, leaving behind what may have been the luckiest woman in Duncan, and disappeared into the parade.

Erin found the stolen Ford at Pine and Fourteenth with the victim inside, terrified but unhurt. She noted the woman was pregnant, and with a racing heartbeat, reasoned she might have stumbled upon more than a carjacking. The killer she'd been chasing might well be at hand. Erin told the victim to wait in her car and she would send help, but first, she needed to get after the driver. She ran into the crowd, searching.

Vong shoved her way to the front of the crowd as the snaking parade reached the Second Station of the Cross. The cross bearer arrived on the heels of the priest and turned with his burden to face the throng. The candle bearers moved to either side, their light necessary as the sun was nearly set. The priest raised his hands and told his long line of followers, "Here Jesus, betrayed by Judas, was arrested." He lifted his voice to the heavens. "We adore you, O Christ, and we bless you."

Around Vong, the crowd replied, "Because by your holy cross you have redeemed the world."

The priest opened his Bible and began to read, "Then, while he was still speaking, Judas, one of the Twelve, arrived, accompanied by a crowd with swords and clubs, who had come from the chief priests, the scribes, and the elders. His betrayer had arranged a signal with them, saying, 'the man I shall kiss is the one; arrest him and lead him away securely.' He came and immediately went over to him and said, 'Rabbi.' And he kissed him. At this, they laid hands on him and arrested him."

Vong looked back and spotted the lady cop closing the gap, moving forward through the crowd of believers. She gave no indication she'd seen Vong.

"Lord, grant us the courage of our convictions," the priest prayed. "That our lives may faithfully reflect the good news you bring. Lord Jesus, help us walk in your steps."

The last ribbons of light were going; darkness descended on the parade. The marchers produced candles of their own, and as they sang, set them to light. The priest pointed up Fourteenth toward Washington Street and signaled the advance. Like a well-trained army, the parade began to move.

The cop was getting too close. Vong butted into the pantomime behind the priest. She grabbed the new cross-bearer, who had only just taken the burden, and yanked him from beneath the cross. Then Vong threw the Christian symbol of torture and divine sacrifice onto her own shoulder.

"Hey," shouted the worshiper, sounding betrayed himself. "It's my turn!" His complaint was lost amid the joyful noise of a hundred choral singers. The parade moved on with the priest leading, Vong carrying the Cross of Christ, the candle bearers walking beside her, two men behind pretending to whip her, and a disgruntled, displaced cross-bearer *wanting* to whip her. And finally the parade of faux Judeans in concert.

Erin hung behind at the Second Station, watching the Passion snake disappear. Whoever the carjacker was – an insane joyrider, an interrupted kidnapper, or their murderer – Erin had lost her.

The parade neared the corner of Washington. Vong let the cross drop, out of danger. One of the pair flailing behind her tripped over it and fell on his face, amusing Vong with his involuntary genuflection.

Those nearby scrambled to help; all but the disappointed cross-bearer, whose place Vong had stolen. Seeing his opportunity, and ignoring the whip man's plight, he dropped the candle he'd been given as a poor replacement and raced to the fallen cross. He struggled to lift it onto his shoulder and reclaim the role of martyr.

Some further back in the parade were in a panic. Though none had a good view, it looked as if the Son of God had taken a header. Several moved toward Vong, to discover she was all right. But, finding her upright, their attitude changed. Several surged forward, demanding to know why she'd dared to—

Vong yanked off her sunglasses, giving those nearest her a view of green, blood-shot eyes. The abused cross bearer, and the candle-bearers beside him, saw themselves, the cross, and their flickering candles in a bizarre and inverted reflection in her gaze. Vong shrieked in a voice no more human than its owner.

From behind and above Vong's head came a loud and grating noise. *Tik. Tik. Tik, tik, tik.* A brilliant flash of light followed and a huge, hellish red bird of prey appeared, flapping its wings frantically. Screams and shouts of alarm went up through the crowd, paraders shoving at each other to escape. Vong ducked away, laughing, and disappeared in a riot of running people. In the chaos, without anyone seeing how or to where it went – the bird vanished.

The priest shouted, trying to get the attention of his flock. It took some doing, but he finally managed to still their panic, to restore quiet, to revive reverence, and to get the parade back on track headed for the next station. What all the to-do was about, was beyond the man of God. He'd seen the bearer as she accidentally dropped the cross, but had witnessed nothing of import before or after. His attention had been on the service, the cross, and the deep and bothersome unanswered question – why was a woman playing Jesus? With the crowd calm again, and a man bearing the cross, the priest redirected the group's energies to a rousing verse of the Parce Domine. The passion walk, and its players moved on. The Third Station of the Cross, Jesus' condemnation by the Sanhedrin, awaited. The Easter Service was in full swing and there was no time to stop.

Dylan Ruzicki leaned back against the shadowy corner, gasping for breath. Half his brain urged him to scream and run. Half told him to lay down and die. He couldn't obey either, yet.

It had been quite a day. First the physical hell of repeated skin debridements. Then the even worse, more frightening and painful, return of the hell of his past. He'd been partly responsible for unleashing aswang in the Philippines. The deaths of those innocent villagers were on his head. Then he'd run. To save his wife assuredly, but to save himself as well. He'd run like a bitch. When he finally faced the creature, when he finally grew a pair and fought it, it was because he'd been forced into the battle. And when he'd attempted to end the monster's existence, he'd murdered his wife and child instead. He'd failed them all. With Ben Court's revelation that Vong still lived came the understanding he'd failed everyone. And in so doing, had again unleashed a literal Hell-spawn on the world.

Following the ejection of Ben and his partner, following his last debridement, the nurse stood as usual and wiped his tears until he could govern them himself. She'd cooed reassuring pleasantries at him with the best of intentions and, finally, she left him to his pain… and his plan.

Biting a folded washcloth to stifle his screams, Ruzicki climbed from his bed. Slowly, in mind-numbing pain, he examined the hall and found it empty. He left his room and, as quickly as he could manage, the east wing of the hospital's eighth floor Burn Unit. The lights were lowered for the evening and Ruzicki used the shadows and his military skills to advance; one doorway, one corner, one alcove at a time, waiting with endless patience between each move. Throughout, he commanded a control over his mind and his pain that surprised even him. Every nerve ending which had survived the blast, and the numbing shock that followed, now screamed with indescribable pain. Ruzicki held on and continued down the hallway. He was almost to his goal. He could see the door; the red-striped metal panic bar, the bright yellow *Warning* sign, the wiring running from the door to a nearby electronic panel and the alarm above.

It had all gone wrong. His efforts to save his men and the inhabitants of the village. His efforts to save his wife and their unborn child. His effort to destroy the demon aswang. In the end, it had all come to disaster. He'd had no choice but to kill his wife, to save her soul and that of their child. But there was hope for this town, and perhaps, the world. Ben Court had come, had promised to take up the mantle. Now, a forgiving God permitting, he could join his family.

Ruzicki pushed himself from the shadows, every fiber shrieking with pain, and hit the red panic bar. The alarm box above blared as the door opened. Cool night air bathed the sweat on his forehead and face, stung the burns on his body like ice. He stepped, nearly falling, onto the fire escape balcony of the west wing of the eighth floor. He ignored the shouts from the hall behind. He ignored the screams from his burnt nerves. He looked out over the lights that blanketed the city, spread out so wide – so different from the little village where the horror started – so far below. He saw the moon on the river and thought of his wife. "Forgive me, Corazone," he whispered. "For releasing this thing, for failing you. Forgive me for not dying with you."

A nurse running from the far end of the hall cried out, "Soomnalung!" Nobody here had ever called him anything else, nobody until Ben Court. Next time he'd steal an easier identity … next time. The nurse screamed again, sounding louder, nearer, more frightened. Ruzicki ignored her and the mind-numbing pain, as he climbed the balcony rail. *If suicide really was unforgivable,* Ruzicki wondered, *wasn't eternal damnation a fair price for his wrongs? His mistakes?* He heard their shouts. He felt someone at the door behind him. He saw what might have been Corazone, beckoning to him from empty space. Dylan Ruzicki let himself fall.

Twenty - Three

Forester was a rare creature ; an investigative reporter who looked for news, checked his facts, ignored politics and his own agenda, and reported. One hell of a reporter, and to those in charge, a huge pain. It wasn't his goal to annoy, but Forester was on the biggest story of his life and determined to get it no matter who it bothered. At that moment, he was waiting to bother Erin Vanderjagt.

He wasn't expecting much. Facts in the case of the mysterious Duncan murders were as rare as hen's teeth. But hope sprang eternal, hope for a crumb of a portion of a detail, and to stay on the safe side, he wasn't holding his breath. He was merely waiting, lying in wait really, for Erin outside her office. And he'd been there for hours. The detective was more than a little late coming in.

When Erin finally appeared, Forester didn't ask if she'd overslept. She didn't look to have slept at all. And he got that. With the murders, the dead cop, the missing detective (leave of absence, his ass) and the damage to tourism, he'd been going without sleep himself. Forester learned later, much later, that on top of everything else, Erin had been feeling ill for days and was late that morning because she'd been to her doctor. He hadn't given her health or personal cares a thought. All he knew then was she had plenty on her mind and he wanted some of it for his readers.

To list the questions Forester asked would be pointless. You've heard most of them, so had Erin, and she still had no answers. If she did, she was still reserving them. In truth, none of his questions pierced her thoughts, until the last, when he asked for details about the hospital suicide. That drew a pause, and a perplexed look and, Forester thought, was about to draw a response when Traer slid between them to shoo the reporter away. The uniformed officer spread his arms and moved the news hound down the hall to the exit, like a janitor with a squeegee pushing out filthy water.

Rid of Forester, Traer returned. "Where were you this morning?"

"Oh, I… I had an appointment."

"Erin, is everything all right?"

"Yeah. I'm okay." She spilled her coffee and snapped at him when Traer tried to help clean it up.

"Am I interrupting you?"

"I'm having a moment," Erin said. "And taking it out on you. Did you need something?"

"I did. I don't mean to crowd you, but I thought you should see this." For the first time, Erin noted the file tucked under Traer's arm. "When you have a few minutes."

She took the folder, saw the name 'Soomnalung', and sagged against her desk.

"When you've had a chance to read it, I'll be glad to fill in any gaps."

She nodded and took a breath. "Go ahead."

Traer made an attempt but Erin couldn't seem to concentrate. "Are you all right?"

"I am. Traer, if you could give me a few minutes?"

"Of course. I've got to run up to the fire chief's office." He indicated the report. "That's incomplete. I understand a couple of firefighters visited the patient, not long before he jumped. I'll try and find out what that's all about." He disappeared without further question.

Left alone, Erin broke down, crying.

One three-by-five-foot section of Fire Chief Anthony Castronovo's office – a framed cork board on an interior wall – was all business. It featured a large city map, department memos, City Attorney-issued documents, Mayoral proclamations, and a number of Chiefy-do lists, wish lists, and schedules. The outside edges were pregnant with pamphlets. The rest of the room was nothing but firefighting fun; antique photos of antique firemen (from a time when the ladders were made of wood and the men made of iron), photos from his own firefighting past (including a few with the young face of a then-blameless rookie, Ben Court, peering from the crowds), photos of fire apparatus through the ages, a toy ambulance, a model quint, a Gamewell box, and an old Klaxon horn; in fact, a run-of-the-mill fire chief's office. With three file cabinets and a desk under all. And, behind the desk, Mount Etna was erupting.

"According to the charge nurse at the hospital, there were two men claiming to be firefighters on their Burn Unit. They were caught in the room of..." Castronovo paused, studied a scrawled note, then decided against giving the name a try. "The room of the burned patient from the Garfield Street fire. They claimed to be the medics who brought the patient into the ER. Bennehoff and Cooper don't know a thing about it. Pena is still in the bug house. That leaves you... and someone else I don't know. I want to know. Who were you with? And what you were doing?"

Despite the rumors – many spread by Ben – this time, Castronovo wasn't yelling at himself. He was yelling at Ben, with Parker Traer (Erin's pet police trainee) looking on from the corner of the room. Ben glanced from the chief to Traer, and back again, and for a nano-second, considered admitting his visit to the hospital. After all, what harm had been done? Then again, why should he? He couldn't repeat a word of his discussion with Ruzicki. They'd never believe it. Hell, *he* didn't believe it. He was already deep enough in a mess he couldn't understand. With Erin in charge of the murder investigations and Traer snooping into this, every angle had grief for him written all over it. The cops had no clue. They were still calling Ruzicki by the name 'Soomnalung'.

Without Erin here to gauge the situation, Ben felt no inclination to inform them differently.

"You want to know?" Ben asked. "Or the police department wants to know?"

"Don't be a clown. I'm not clowning."

"Neither am I. If this is a Fire Department matter," Ben chucked a thumb at Traer. "Then this strapping section of the Big Blue Wall shouldn't be wasting his valuable time here. If it's a police matter, I would think I have some civil rights to consider that don't involve you… sir."

"Yeah, yeah. Don't try to think either, Court, it hurts everybody. Tell us what's been going on."

"A lot has been going on. So much that I don't have any clear memory of last night. I doubt I was at the hospital. If I was, I doubt I visited a patient. If I did, I doubt I was with anyone else. If I was, it was on my day off and none of your damned business."

Castronovo started to sputter but Traer stepped forward. "Excuse me, chief." He turned his emotionless stare to Ben. "This is not for the public yet. I would appreciate your discretion. Immediately after his visitors left, the burn patient, Soomnalung, committed suicide. He did a half gainer with a twist off the eighth floor fire escape balcony."

Ben felt as if he'd been kicked in the stomach. He tried not to show it, but failed miserably.

"Anything that anyone could tell us would prove helpful," Traer added.

The firefighter gritted his teeth, inhaled slowly through his nose and exhaled through the slit of his thin lips, trying to corral his thoughts. "If…" Ben said. He swallowed his spit. "If I'm able to think of anything, I'll let you know."

Traer was unhappy, to say the least. But he had nothing to go on but guesses and the agitated finger-pointing of the fire chief. He thanked Ben and Castronovo and left. Ben was on his heels when the chief called him back. "I didn't dismiss you."

"I didn't realize I needed to be dismissed. There was something else?"

"There's plenty else. You'd better take a look at who you're talking to." Castronovo flicked his starched collar. "Apparently you've forgotten these bugles make me the boss around here?"

Ben grinned. "Did you hire me? Can you fire me? You don't sound like much of a boss to me."

Castronovo's face reddened. "We'll just see what the Civil Service Commission says about that."

"That's the point I'm trying to make," Ben told him. "You'll have to."

"Now you get my point," Castronovo said acidly. "Mind your own business. Stop digging into shit that doesn't concern you. Stay away from this fire investigation. Stay out of the investigations of these deaths. And, unless it's related specifically to your job, stay away from the hospital."

Without answering, without waiting to be dismissed, Ben started for the door.

"And," Castronovo yelled, "stay the hell away from Nestor Pena."

Twenty - Four

Of course, obeying Castronovo was out of the question. A gulf had opened between Ben and Erin. Their idyllic relationship suddenly felt a dozen strains. Without his girlfriend's companionship, Ben needed his best friend more than ever. Especially as, now Ruzicki was dead, that friend was the only one with insight (however crazy) concerning recent events. Ben made a beeline for Nestor, a temporary resident in the same place you'd find any so-called 'attempted suicide' – the Duncan Memorial Psychiatric Unit, known by local medicos as 'Four East'.

"Did you see him? Did you see Soomnalung?" Nestor demanded when Ben arrived.

"Yes and no." Ben explained the burn patient's alias, a fact to which only he, Nestor and Bennie Bagtas were privy.

"No kidding? The cops don't even know? And?"

"And only his burns prevented Ruzicki from being your roommate. He was crazier than you."

"He agrees there's a monster?"

"He did. He insisted there's a monster."

"Yes!" Nestor threw his fists into the air. Several staff members near the unit clerk's desk looked their way. Nestor mouthed 'Sorry' and moved Ben further down the hall. "Why do you refer to… what's his name? Ruzicki? Why refer to him in the past tense?"

"Because he's passed on. Right after I talked to him, he killed himself."

"Damn!" Nestor whistled low. "But he did know about the creature?" Ben nodded. "Okay," Nestor said. "What's next?" Ben stared a hole through him. "What?"

"What do you mean, What's next?" Ben shook his head in disbelief. "Nothing's next. I did as you asked and told you what Ruzicki told me. That's it."

"That's not it. We know what killed my family. Now we have to do something about it."

"We don't know anything of the kind. We – meaning I – heard the delusional fantasy of a badly-burned guy, doped up on morphine, who's had the same traumatic experience with his family that you had. What the hell are we supposed to do about it?"

"Not we. *You.* Look around, Ben. The doors and windows are locked. If I sneer, they sedate me. They stole the cinch string from my pajamas, for Christ's sake. I can't help. You have to do it."

"Do what?" Ben demanded.

"Find it! Find this thing, this creature."

"Geez, you sound like Ruzicki. How am I going to find it? I don't know anything about it."

"You didn't ask him?"

"There wasn't time. We heard a fairy tale about a demon's resurrection, then a nurse chased us out."

Nestor hesitated, thinking, always a dangerous situation in Ben's opinion. Finally, he nodded. "If we need to know more about this thing, you go and ask someone who knows."

"Great," Ben said, looking for a seat. There wasn't any furniture. Could patients hurt themselves with furniture? He shook off the thought. "Who, in Duncan, can I ask about a living Philippine demon?"

Nestor smiled. "I got that. I've been talking to one of the housekeepers here, a Philippine girl with an unpronounceable name who goes by Chesa. She has an aunt, also with an unpronounceable name, who goes by Poni. Poni runs a shop in the Philippine section of town."

"There's a Philippine section of town?"

"Certainly. Where do you think Angelina lived when I met her?"

"How do I know? This is America, she could have lived anywhere."

Nestor made a noise. "It's not on a map. But there *is* a Philippine section of town. Poni's shop is there and Poni, according to Chesa, knows everything about the old country and the old superstitions."

"Okay," Ben said, in a tone that suggested it wasn't. "What do I do?"

"You loan me money."

"I loan you money?"

"So I can pay Chesa to meet you and introduce you to her aunt."

"I paid your cousin to talk to Ruzicki. Why am I paying your housekeeper to talk to Poni?"

Nestor frowned and pulled his pant pockets out to hang empty. "Kiss the bunny's nose," he said. "They took my shoelaces. If they think you'll hang yourself with shoelaces, they know you'll cut your own head off with a dollar bill."

Ben sighed, reaching for his own pocket. "What's a housekeeper cost nowadays?"

Nestor was right, there was a Philippine section of town. It was only four square blocks, and other than a few signs, no different from the surrounding streets, but Ben was surprised all the same. Ten years a firefighter and he'd never known. He found the curio shop, *Whatnot*, with Chesa waiting. She led them in to the tinkle of a bell atop the door.

The shop was small with a massive counter, fronting a row of shelves which took up three-quarters of the length of the right wall. The shelves made the shop look smaller, and were overstuffed with... *stuff*. Paintings, statuary, clothing, books, furniture, bric-a-brac, postcards, tools, timepieces, garden stone and garden plants, mounted animals, dolls, and enough Catholic imagery, rosaries and crucifixes, to send the Pope into a fit of envy. Not a nook was empty, not a cranny sat idle. The word *menagerie* came to mind or, then again, *Whatnot*. Chesa called for her aunt.

A beaded curtain behind the counter parted and an old woman appeared from a back room. In Ben's limited experience, many Asian women, stunningly beautiful in their youth, did not necessarily remain so. This one hadn't. She was under five feet, under a hundred pounds, and looked to have come from under a bridge. She saw her niece and chirped like a magpie; she saw Ben and squawked. Screaming what must have been abuse, she darted for the shelves behind the antique cash register. She pulled the lid off a jar, grabbed out a handful of what looked like dust, and held it above her head. Ben froze, giving the troll his full attention. Trembling, chanting, ready to throw whatever she had fisted in her hand, the woman held that pose.

Reddening, Chesa barked something at her aunt. The pair began a high-pitched squabble in Bennie Bagtas' Tagalog. It ended when the aunt, still shouting, dust-filled hand still aloft, disappeared through the beads into the depths of the shop.

"What was that all about?"

"You scared her!" Chesa snapped. "I'm sorry. It's my fault. With your eyes covered, you frightened her. Please, take off your sunglasses."

Dumbfounded, Ben did as he was told.

Chesa called into the back and the verbal tennis match started again. Ben stood by for the next several minutes, understanding squat, except the words 'Ben' and 'Court'. The old lady reappeared but did not venture beyond the beads. Chesa sighed. "Ben Court, this is my mother's sister, Poni. Aunt Poni, this is a friend of Angelina's husband. He has questions about the old country. You agreed to answer. The sunglasses were my fault. I should have told him."

"Hello," Ben said cautiously.

Poni disappeared again. Ben and Chesa sighed, both at a loss, before Poni suddenly reappeared again. Still clutching her dust, she carried a magnifying glass in the other hand, demanding… something.

"She wants to see your eyes and will not speak to you or answer questions until she does."

"My eyes?"

"The evil creatures of our land will not look at you. Their eyes are blood-shot from nights spent peering into funeral houses for bodies to steal. She is afraid you might be one. In the demon's eyes, your reflection appears inverted, upside down. Show her, please, your eyes are normal."

Making a mental note to kick Nestor square in the ass at the next opportunity, Ben pocketed his sunglasses, put his hands behind his back, and smiling, leaned forward. Chesa said something soothing to the old lady. She nodded, approached warily, and raising the glass, stared into Ben's eyes. She stepped back a moment later, satisfied Ben was human, and chirped something at her niece.

Chesa waved Ben forward. "She will speak with you now."

"She speaks English?"

"Yes," Chesa said. "Now she has chosen to speak with you."

Ben scowled. "Sorry I frightened you."

The old woman scowled back. "What do you wish to know?"

"I want to know about your superstitions. I mean, the superstitions of the Philippines."

"Our people are superstitious. There are as many tales as there are tellers."

"Okay. I want to ask about a creature I understand comes from your country."

"There are as many creatures as there are tales. The western world is ignorant of the spirits around us, the creatures that walk among us, of the demons in our midst."

What, Ben wondered, *had he gotten himself into?* What had he let Nestor talk him into? Maybe he was dreaming? Maybe he'd fallen asleep waiting to see Nestor? Maybe their last meeting had yet to take place and he was still leaning against the wall by the psych unit's nurses' station? That must be it. The old biddy was a patient who'd wandered from her room to entertain him until Nestor came.

Poni cleared her throat loudly and asked her niece, "Is he asleep?"

Ben surfaced to find Poni and Chesa staring holes through him. "No," he assured them. "I was thinking. Can you tell me about the Philippine monsters?"

The old lady shrugged and wandered behind the counter. She returned the dust to its jar, wiped her hands on her apron, and leaned on her elbows on the countertop. "The west regions of our islands, Visayan, the Iloilo, the Antique provinces are rich with supernatural activity. There are some *multo*, ghost stories, but not like here. Americans believe in ghosts, Filipinos do not. Ghosts are not our evil. There are provinces known for goblins, ghouls, and for the *tikbalang*, a giant horse-man. The Capiz province, on Panay Island, is rife with covens of witches, what we call *mangkukulam*. All over the Philippines, on every island and in every province, live the terrible *manananggals*."

"Menon? Gals?" Ben exclaimed. "You mean that's one word?"

Poni nodded. "*Manananggal* is the name of the most feared creature in the Philippine islands."

"I've heard it. I didn't understand it to be one word. But that's it – Manananggal. There's another word I wanted to ask about. Aswang? Do you know—"

"Aswang, of course," she said. "These are the same creature. The manananggal. The aswang."

"But what is it?"

"Even the native peoples cannot agree on this, on who or what is this creature. They cannot agree, but all fear it. To some it is a viscera sucker. To some, it is a drinker of blood like the vampire. To others, aswang is a demon that can possess a human being and inflict great harm on its host and those it hates. To some, especially the young, aswang is, how would you say..." Poni threw her head back, searching for the words she wanted. "A bogeyman. They have no respect for good and evil. They frighten their children with these stories to keep them off the streets and home at night. But to others, to many, the superstitions are real."

"But the creature," Ben said. "Aswang? Manananggal? Whatever you call it. What is it?"

"It is a being of enormous power. It can transform itself into any shape, even inanimate objects, to get near to its victim. Like many creatures, it will kill to defend itself. But it preys upon children. And women who are pregnant. And the sick and the weak. Sometimes aswang will play tricks. Once it has overpowered a victim, it will take a bundle of sticks, some talahib grass, and rice or banana stalks, and make with these a replica of its victim. It breathes unholy life into this replica and sends it back home while taking the real victim to kill and eat."

Ben laughed. "The folks back home don't notice the difference?"

"You joke because you are ignorant. No one goes near because the replica looks sick. It quickly dies. By then the real victim is gone with manananggal."

Ben quit laughing. Ridiculous or not, Poni believed the tale she was telling and was afraid.

"Some say aswang eats children, favoring their livers and hearts. Others say the creature eats the child's soul. They are said to love the souls of the unborn. Pregnancy is a time of great fear for Philippine women because Aswang causes miscarriage and sickness. They rob graves, kidnap children, and fill the night with strange noises."

"And it can look like anyone?"

"Or anything," Poni said. "Aswang can leave its human form, transform into the likeness of a dog, a snake, or a bat."

"Like a vampire?"

"It is not a vampire. Manananggal is not undead. During daylight hours, it's a living being. Male or female, but usually female. It may appear quite young, ageless, even when the creature is very old. It does not speak without great need. It is quiet when acting human, when not in another form and not detached from its body—"

"Wait. What? Detached from its body?"

"Manananggal means 'to separate'. Aswang, it is said, can separate at the waist, leave its legs behind, and growing wings, can take to the air to stalk its victims. After it feeds, it rejoins its legs, and returns to human form. They are not vampires; they are demons."

"Assuming this thing was real," Ben asked. "How could you beat it? Destroy it?"

"It is best to not meet aswang. If you look for them, they will know and they will come for you. If aswang wants you, run away. Run and take your loved ones with you."

"What if I couldn't?" Ben asked. "What if I had no choice but to meet this creature?"

"It can be fought. But not by a non-believer." The old woman studied him. "It can be beaten. But you must be properly equipped." She turned, searching the shelves behind her, and pulled a shining stake from a box. "Copper," she said. "A copper stake is best. Real copper. Guaranteed."

"Guaranteed to work?" Ben asked.

"No," she said pointedly. "Guaranteed to be ninety-nine point nine percent pure copper." She held it up. "Point 625-inch diameter by twelve-inch copper round rod. With excellent electrical conductivity for pinning aswang's life force to eternity. Twenty-nine dollars thirty each."

Ben laughed. "If I had twenty-nine dollars thirty for one of these stakes, what would I do with it?"

"You would stab the creature, of course." She scowled, sounding suspicious that Ben was wasting her time, and put the stake back on the shelf.

"Stab the creature in the heart, Aunt Poni?" Chesa asked hurriedly.

"No, no, no." Poni waved her niece's response away, turned, and pulled her gray hair aside. She pointed a withered finger at the nape of her own pale neck. "In the back of the neck. It is better done by a priest, or man of God but, if there's none, it can be done by a true believer in the goodness of God." She eyed Ben dismally. "Perhaps you can find one."

Ben smacked his lips.

Poni went on. "The believer stabs the creature through the neck with the stake of copper, and in doing so, pins the monster to its afterlife."

"Aswang holds still for that?" Ben asked in disbelief.

Poni frowned and looked to Chesa. Chesa frowned at Ben. Poni said something in Tagalog, or maybe Angelina's Taglish. Chesa clearly agreed but didn't translate.

Ben got the message. "I'm sorry," he said. "I don't mean to be ignorant. I appreciate your aunt's help. I appreciate both of you. Could you please ask..." He stopped, remembering the old girl spoke English, and turned to Poni. "How do you get close enough to the monster to pin it with copper?"

"You cannot wait for aswang to come upon you. To do so is to die."

"Right. That's what I'm saying. What do you recommend?"

"I recommend you forget this. If you will not, if you are determined, you must find the creature's lair and trap it." Poni lifted a crystal bottle from a collection on the shelf and held it up. "In a glass container, a vial or bottle you can see through, like this, you must carry with you blessed oil, coconut oil prayed over by a priest, the prayer stirred in with the stem of a banana leaf."

Ben pointed at the bottle. "Is that blessed coconut oil there?"

"Just so," Poni pointed at the bottle. "When aswang is near the oil begins to boil. It will boil until the demon has departed. Twelve dollars ninety-nine for the bottle."

Ben bit his tongue.

"Like your vampire, you can keep aswang away with garlic. They abhor the smell." Poni grabbed a necklace of garlic bulbs from the counter, shook it, then hung it around her own neck. "This is mine; not for sale. I don't sell enough to keep them fresh. Get it at any grocery store." A light went on behind her old gray eyes and she was off again, to the jar of dust she'd visited before. "Sacred ash," she said. Instead of grabbing out a handful, she merely tipped the jar so Ben could see the contents. "You hold the monster at bay with ash, blessed by a priest."

"How much?" Ben barked.

"Eighteen ninety-nine a box, already blessed. Crucifixes, pocket to altar size. Six ninety-nine to ninety-nine ninety-nine." She didn't wait to see if she'd made a sale. "You can drive the creature back using the tail of the manta as a whip."

"The manta?" Ben asked.

"A Devil Fish," Poni said. "The creature called the manta ray. You cut the tail off and use it as a weapon, a whip, against aswang."

"Do you have one?"

She lifted her eyebrows. "Where would I keep it?"

"Blessed by a priest, I imagine?"

"Yes."

Ben shook his head. He'd heard a lot of nonsense in his life. He'd also wasted a lot of time over the years. Never had he heard so much bullshit *and* wasted so much time all at once.

"Why do you ask this?" Poni demanded. "How do you know this creature?"

Ready to walk, Ben paused to indulge the old lady. "There've been a number of deaths in the city. Unexplained deaths of pregnant women." Poni crossed herself. "But not everyone has died in the same way. One, a man, had completely different wounds. I doubt aswang was the culprit."

"Do not be so quick. Perhaps there is more than one creature."

"More than one aswang? They travel in groups?"

"There are many kinds of aswang. Look for peculiar people, odd habits, these give aswang away. There is the sigbin, the little aswang, said to look like the chupacabra or Tasmanian devil, with spotted fur, a wide mouth, and fangs. There is the witch aswang, a common creature who appears as a hag with unkempt hair, uncut nails, and a long, black tongue."

Ben sighed, and without meaning to, rolled his eyes. He would have laughed, but it wasn't funny anymore. He was tired of the whole thing and fighting the urge to say so.

"You do not believe?" Poni asked sharply.

"It's a little unbelievable."

"You ask about aswang, I tell you. But, if there is a second monster, it may not be aswang."

"Good grief, a second monster? You mean there are two creatures? Two different creatures?"

"There could be. It could be aswang and its familiar. Like the witch's black cat, or the shark's remora, aswang has a familiar. It is another demon spirit, summoned to do its bidding. The herald of aswang, it sings a warning at the creature's approach. The tik-tik is named for its song."

"The tik-tik?"

"A huge bird-like creature that prowls the night with aswang. It is cursed to warn of aswang's attack, to sing at its approach. But the tik-tik is a damned creature and a liar. It confuses those it warns. It sings loudly when aswang is far away, quietly when aswang is near and ready to strike. You know aswang comes, but it lies as to when. Aswang, with the long tongue, is the stealer of unborn souls. Tik-tik, with the talons, is the drinker of blood, feeding on that which aswang leaves."

The old biddy was really putting on a show, and in spite of himself, Ben was suddenly breathless. Still it was ridiculous and he couldn't help but shake his head. "Two monsters."

"Yes. They kill alone and together. That is what is so frightening." Poni drew near and stared up into Ben's eyes. "There is a saying, repeated all over the islands: Pray to the virgin when the tik-tik sings."

Twenty - Five

"Did you go?" Nestor shouted. "Did you hook up with Chesa? Did you see her aunt?"

"Yes," Ben said, holding his phone at a distance to save his hearing. "I did what you asked. I talked to everyone you asked me to talk to. It was a complete bust."

"Didn't she help?"

"Yes. She helped me to see this is all nonsense. That old woman's crazy. The meeting was a scam to sell me worthless junk."

"Forget what she tried to sell you. What did she tell you?"

"Stop screaming at me." Ben sank onto his couch. "I was fed Philippine lore until I couldn't swallow another bite. It was entertaining, but there's less horseshit in a racing stable. To be honest, Paco, I feel like such a fool I don't want to talk about the details."

"You knew it was going to be strange."

"Strange I could have handled. This was bug house." Ben paused, reconsidered to whom he was speaking and where Nestor currently resided. "Sorry. I didn't mean it—"

"What did she say?" Nestor demanded, ignoring the comment and the apology.

"She agreed with you. Our problem is a monster, aswang or manananggal, the words Ruzicki used, and its familiar, the tik-tik, which is another word he used, not a sound I thought he was making. We can only fight it with… wait." Ben dug into his pocket. "I made a list when I got back to the car. I didn't want to spill a drop." He studied his own scrawl. "Let's see… We need coconut oil to warn of the creature's presence. A copper stake for, get this, driving through the monster's neck to pin it to the afterlife. Ashes, blessed by a priest, to sanctify its lair. And, lucky us, she sells each of those items, not cheaply. It was a joke."

"What else did she say?"

"What else?" He consulted the list again. "Oh, it doesn't like garlic. But Poni doesn't carry garlic; can't keep it fresh. You might know the one item I could afford, she doesn't carry."

"Ben, I don't have a lot of time. The phone is a privilege they shut off at night and whenever they feel like it. It could go dead at any minute. Will you please tell me what she said?"

"I'm telling you. It jumped between a sales pitch and outright craziness. Here, you'll love this. We can fight the creature, hold it at bay, by whipping it with the tail of a manta ray. Have you got one of those in your back pocket?"

"You're forgetting where I am. I don't have a back pocket, or shoelaces, or a belt. Why is that crazy? It's a creature from the Philippine Islands. Rays are plentiful. If you believe there's a monster, it makes sense. Hey, there are rays in town!"

"Nestor, what are you talking about?"

"There is a manta ray and a stingray, right here in Duncan."

"Hold on a second; I can barely hear you. The street's full of sirens." Ben waited for the wails of engines, ambulances, and squads to pass. "Man, they're burning the town down. Okay. Anyway, you were saying? There's a manta ray? In northeast Iowa? Swimming around and breathing?"

"Yes, I'm telling you. There's one at—"

"And you want me to maim it?" Ben demanded, interrupting. "Probably kill it? By cutting off its tail? Because an old crone in a Philippine carnie shop wants to sell copper scraps and banana oil?"

"You said coconut oil before. Which is it?"

"It was coconut. And who gives a damn? This is all insanity."

"Stop saying that! You weren't at The Castle. My wife and baby were killed by a monster from a Philippine nightmare. That nightmare is alive and feeding on… What, by the way? Did she tell you? Chesa's aunt? Did she tell you what this thing wants?"

"Well, that depends on which creature it is and which lust it has. Seems the island people spend all their free time dreaming up new monsters."

"Quit fucking around!" Nestor screamed. "You sound like a whistle prick in paramedic school. Signs and symptoms, brother, what are the signs and symptoms? Take the evidence of your eyes and ears and combine them with the knowledge the old woman gave you."

"That's what I'm telling you, Nestor. The old woman didn't give me anything. She's a shyster. She was trying to sell me some sort of demon hunter's kit."

"That's what we wanted! Look, forget your disbelief. You knew going in we were dealing with the unbelievable. Her beliefs aren't yours, I get it. But assume what Poni gave you was fact. She wasn't an old biddy in a voodoo shop, she was a textbook. Take the signs and symptoms this case exhibits and hold them up to the light. Make a diagnosis."

Why not, Ben thought. After the day he'd had, what was more wasted time? "The victims have been female," he said, starting his list. "Most pregnant. Most with an abdominal puncture wound. The male victim had different wounds entirely. You saw a monster. Ruzicki claims he fought a monster. Several of the words Ruzicki shouted are the names of—" Ben hesitated, closed his eyes, comparing the real evidence to the old lady's goofy legends. "Pregnant women. Babies' souls. Aswang. Manananggal," Ben whispered into the phone. "Pray to the virgin when the tik-tik sings."

A heavy moment of silence hung between them.

"You've got to fill that list," Nestor said. "The oil, the ashes, a copper stake. You need to get a manta tail. For Angelina and the baby. For the promise you made Ruzicki. This evil has killed dozens, maybe hundreds, and will keep killing. We've got to stop it. We've got to find aswang and destroy it."

It was lunacy, bat-shit crazy. Ben listened, politely, intending to fully ignore Nestor's rant. But the rant ended abruptly. On the other end of the line, someone barged in on Nestor. It took a moment to realize it was his nurse. In passing, she'd heard Nestor's agitation and now she politely but firmly told him the phone was being shut off. Then her voice was in Ben's ear, as firm but without the politeness, informing him he'd upset the patient and the call was done. The line went dead.

Ben stepped from the shower arguing with himself. What was he supposed to do with the mess he'd been handed? He'd promised Nestor he'd kill the monster. He promised Ruzicki he'd kill the monster. He didn't even believe in the goddamned monster. He couldn't wrap his mind around all the craziness, the bizarre deaths, the horrors visited upon Nestor and his family, the wrecking ball of stress hanging over his relationship with Erin, the fairy tale spun by Ruzicki, the wacky old lady at the Whatnot shop, let alone a Philippine demon. How could he sort the mess? How was he supposed to fulfill his ridiculous promises? What else could go wrong? Before he had time to regret the questions, his doorbell rang.

He pulled his pants on, and still drying his hair, opened the door to find Forester on the other side. "Oh," the reporter exclaimed. "You are here. I'm surprised."

"Why? I live here."

"I know but I thought you'd be at the fire."

"My day off. They can put out a few without me."

"That's what you think. They're burning another one to the ground as we speak."

"Yeah?" Ben asked, pulling on a shirt. "What now?"

"A store over in Little Manila."

"Little Manila?"

"The Philippine part of town."

Ben stared. "Does everybody know about that but me?"

With no idea what Ben was talking about, Forester shrugged.

"Never mind," Ben continued. "What did you say was burning?"

"Burned. Already a basement. A junk shop mostly, tourist trap selling Philippine trinkets. Doubt if anyone but the insurance company would even care if it weren't for the fatalities."

Ben lowered the towel from his hair, stared at Forester. "Fatalities?"

"Yeah. Two women, one young, one old. They just hauled them out. No other details yet and won't be for a while. I had to dig like a terrier for that."

"Two women?" Ben felt as if the floor had dropped away beneath him. "The store, was it the *Whatnot*?"

Forester nodded. "You don't know about Little Manila but you know the name of the shop? You psychic or something?" Stunned, Ben wandered back into the apartment. Forester followed. The reporter pointed to the liquor cabinet. "May I? It's been a night."

Ben waved absently. Forester helped himself to the whiskey, and between gulps and gasps, studied the firefighter. "How did you know which store?" Miles away, Ben offered no reply. "Doesn't matter," Forester conceded. "I doubt this fire will help my career. My editor probably won't print the story. He isn't printing half of what I write. Other than angry shouts, he isn't even talking to me. He doesn't mind the blood and guts I've been turning in, and he loves the explosions, but the mystery crap is putting him off his lunch. Like it would harm him to stay off his lunch. He says I'm hurting tourism. That means the Business District, or the mayor, or both, have accused him of hurting tourism. Screw it. I'm not willing to ignore facts in favor of agenda. Yo, Ben. Should I save the rest of my sad story for whenever it is you're coming back? Because you ain't here, brother."

"I'm not interested in your sad story. I'm trying to digest this fire."

"Why?" Forester asked. "Something special about it? Is it connected? Is that what you're saying?"

"I'm not saying anything. I'm not doing an interview!"

"Do you see a notebook? I'm not asking for one. I'm asking a friend what's happening in our town. I'm asking what can I do to help?"

What could Forester do? Hell, what could Ben do? What options did he have? Poni and Chesa were dead. But were they murdered, their shop burned to the ground, because they'd tried to help him? For giving him information? It made no sense. They'd told him fairy tales. So what? Even if they were true, how could the creature have found them out? What had the old lady said? 'It is best to not meet aswang. If you look for them, they will know and will come for you. If aswang wants you, run away and take your loved ones with you.' Was the killer Ruzicki's Vong? Was Vong Poni's aswang? Did any of this matter? As far as Poni and Chesa were concerned, nothing mattered now.

Ben wondered if he should empty the bag for the reporter. He wandered the room, considering the question and wound up pouring himself a drink and staring out the apartment window. He looked into the port, saw the brightly-lit casino and its partially filled parking lot. Besides it, he saw the empty lot of the darkened water park. Further down, the river museum and the solid black mass of the William T. Greene, the dredger permanently moored on the museum side of the harbor.

Ben stopped. There it was again, as he'd seen it days before, when Nestor and Angelina had dropped in – someone walking the deck of the old steamboat. The security guard, Ben thought, out for a smoke? A trick of shadow? It was gone as quickly as it had appeared. *Where to,* Ben wondered, *below deck or back into the realm of fractured light from which his tired mind had conjured it?*

Lost in thought, Ben didn't hear the bell. Forester did and opened the door. "Detective Vanderjagt. Don't just stand there looking surprised. C'mon in."

"Is Ben… Is Ben Court here?"

"Certainly," the reporter said, closing the door. "He's daydreaming, so I came to your rescue."

Erin's face showed little appreciation. She had no clue what was going on here, but knew she didn't like it. News gatherers, while not necessarily enemies, required careful watching. On the rare occasions they were useful, still they were not often helpful. Ben had spent a lot of time with Forester lately; more than he'd spent with her. Much of that was her fault, the requirements of her job. Still they'd been together a lot, bellied up to the bar in The Well. Now, on another rotten day, with another fire and two more deaths added to the epidemic roaring through Duncan, with the maddening discovery she'd just made in her own office, she found Forester at Ben's apartment. And Forester had found her at Ben's apartment. She didn't like it.

Ben was still in the living room, still staring out the window. "What are you looking at?" Erin asked.

"Hey," Ben exclaimed. "Hello."

"Hello. What were you looking at?"

"Oh. That eh, that shadow on the dredger. I mentioned it before. I saw it again, someone on the deck. The one I… Well, you know."

Erin stole a look out the window and saw what she expected, darkness falling over the Port District, lights blinking on in an attempt to fight back, and nothing else. "There are lots of shadows in the port at night. What's so compelling about this one?"

"I don't know. Just catches my attention once in a while." He tried to laugh it off. "Probably the security guard out for a smoke."

"I've known Walter Dunn for years," Erin said, humorlessly. "He doesn't smoke."

"Okay. I'm paranoid." Ben attempted a smile, but failed. Erin had come in with claws extended and he didn't like it. Besides, he was being pushed to believe real darkness moved in the shadows. Despite his shaky convictions, Ben was starting to feel it and more. The shadows, he feared, whatever they were, were watching back.

"Ben!"

Hell, he'd been daydreaming again. He found Erin and Forester both staring at him as he came out of it. The reporter looked confused. Erin looked mad. "Can I speak to you?" she demanded.

They disappeared into the kitchen leaving Forester to wonder what was going on.

"What's going on?" Erin asked. Her tone made it a demand.

Ben didn't feel like meeting any demands. "Are you on duty?"

"As you may have noticed, I'm always on duty nowadays."

"I've noticed. I wasn't sure whether or not that was by choice."

Both were feeling it, a clash of emotions, love and anger, magnetism and repulsion, a desire to unload and a sudden alien distrust. It was crushing. But neither could push the weight away.

"I don't feel like I have choices," Erin said.

"So you didn't choose to come here?"

"I need to talk to you. And I don't want to do it with a reporter on hand. Just seeing me here, he's learned plenty."

Forester didn't take it well, being asked to leave. But he couldn't tell Ben and Erin to go to Hell when he was standing in Ben's apartment. He'd thought Ben was on the verge of a revelation when the lady cop arrived. He hadn't complained. He'd even been nice and not asked any embarrassing questions. For his trouble, he was being shown the door. To Hell with it. To Hell with them both.

"He wasn't happy," Erin said as Ben returned from seeing the reporter out.

"Did you expect he would be? What's up, Erin?"

"That's my question for you. Where have you been keeping yourself?"

"You know where. I've been looking into these… odd events. Nestor believes some creature from Philippine mythology, something the world does not understand, is responsible for these killings, including those of his family, and I agreed to look into it for him."

"So," she said, bristling. "You listened to a campfire story, then you and the reporter spent a week pouring alcohol on it, and now you're ready to present your findings? A Philippine monster?"

"Erin," Ben said. "I know it sounds crazy—"

She put up a hand. "I wouldn't have a problem with crazy, Ben. You're a firefighter. Crazy is your strongest attribute. What I can't take is stupid, childish, and drunk. Those wear thin quickly. I have a question for you. When I came, I was merely going to ask as a matter of routine. Now I not only don't want to ask but I'm afraid of the answer. More than anything, I really hope you won't lie to me."

"I can guarantee that, Erin. I'll never lie to you."

She nodded. Then she braced herself. "There's evidence from the Garfield Street arson fire missing from my office. One of the hand grenades was taken from its box. Did you take it?"

"After not seeing you as a friend or lover for a week, you stopped by to fill out a theft report?"

"There won't be a theft report because the mayor refuses to allow us to admit the munitions exist. But they do exist, and they are deadly, and one has been stolen from my office. You did something the other day that you have never done before; you came to my office. Damn it, Ben, did you take it?"

"Before you get angry at me all over again for refusing to answer, please note, I kept my promise that I would never lie to you."

"I have two new bodies to start reports on," she said, making a beeline for the door. "I need to get to work." A half-dozen pithy exit lines flashed through her mind. Erin ignored them as each, regardless of how much of Ben's blood they drew, would have cut her too. She had no clue if he was trying to prove some bizarre point, or was drunk, or was crazy. She didn't know why the man she loved was trying to hurt her. But she wasn't going to reward him with tears. Erin left, without bothering to close the door. For a long while, Ben stared after her, feeling as empty as the dark hallway.

Twenty - Six

Two hours laying in silence, thinking about what he intended to do, had been undiluted hell. Ben had run the emotional gamut – doubt, guilt, anger, pity, resolve, determination, right back to doubt in a circular argument. But events left him committed. He was also stifled, stiff, and his left hand had gone to sleep. He couldn't take another second. Groaning despite fear of discovery, he squeezed out from under the seats, sat up, gulped a badly needed breath, and peered around the darkened theater.

Two hours earlier, he'd walked into the National Mississippi River Museum & Aquarium looking, he hoped, like any tourist. A volunteer took his ten dollars and returned a ticket stub and an apology. He'd arrived too late to see the whole museum; they would be closing soon. Ben said he'd do his best, threw a studious-looking backpack over his shoulder, and moved through the exhibits without seeing them. He wasn't a tourist; he was a man on a mission.

Ben skirted around Catfish Planet with its one hundred species including, Electric Catfish, Glass Catfish, Walking Catfish, and a Catfish that ate wood. He denied himself a walk through a twenty-two-foot long catfish with interactive innards. He passed up Native American artifacts. He passed the National Rivers Hall of Fame, where the stories of Mark Twain and early explorers could be heard while you practiced your captain's skills in the Towboat Pilot Simulator. He passed glass doors looking out on a boardwalk, where visitors could 'explore the river's natural habitat at living history outposts' and see an authentic Native American wikiup in a recreated wetland, a fur trader's cabin, and stations for demonstrations of fishing, clamming, refuge management, and pioneer boat building. In sunlight, one might see turtles sunning on logs, or a great blue heron, or a bald eagle perched aloft. But night was here and Ben moved on without a glance at the blue moonlight.

He rounded a corner and entered the main display room. There, on the far side of the expansive floor, beneath the wide stairs, surrounded by awe-struck children, stood a massive round feeding tank; a 200,000-gallon aquarium that could have held a whale. A banner circling the top of the tank read: AT THE MOUTH OF THE MISSISSIPPI. Scattered posters proclaimed the glories of the Gulf of Mexico on the river's southernmost border. In the massive tank, an incredible variety of sea life swam, flipped, and fanned out, over sand and rock, through and around undulating flora and fauna. Apparently all well fed, for there were as many small fish as there were big, each going about its business with no sign of distress. Ben searched the busy water. A big turtle paddled by and there – he swallowed hard – cruised a four-foot shark. *They're well fed,* Ben told himself again, and started through the crowd.

"Manta. Manta," he muttered, his head bobbing, his eyes bouncing from creature to creature in the tank. He finally spotted it, a black swimming kite with a disappointingly short tail. Ben's expectations collapsed. While certainly odd, Ben was forced to admit the manta wasn't that impressive.

"That's not the manta," a small voice said, jolting him.

Ben looked down at an angelic blonde boy with deadly blue eyes, watching him watch the fish.

"Excuse me?"

"If you're looking for the manta," the child said. "You're looking at the wrong fish. The manta is bigger and, unlike other mobulids, its mouth is in the terminal location, not the inferior."

"You don't say?"

The kid scanned the depths and pointed. "That's the manta ray."

The stingray they'd been watching swooped to the bottom as a huge shadow covered it in gloom. Ben followed the kid's finger to the source, a giant underwater bat, an alien flying saucer, an undulating monster from a fifties' B movie. It was twelve feet wide, if it was an inch, with dark blotches marring the vast white underside of its disc body. Then, with a graceful flap of its pectoral fins, the creature dived, showing a top so blue it looked black. For a second time, Ben swallowed hard.

His eyes fell from the monster to a placard bearing its picture. It featured a list of names from the obvious; manta ray, Atlantic manta, Pacific manta, to the odd; Prince Alfred's ray, eagle ray, blanket fish, skeete, to the intimidating; giant devil ray, devil fish, giant manta, and sea devil. It reported the creature had eighteen rows of teeth on the center of the lower jaw, with twelve rows on either side; a fact that hit home as he reached the Latin at the bottom: Cephalopterus vampyrus.

"That's the manta," the brat said again.

"Great." Ben sighed heavily. "Just great."

Indigenous to the waters of the western Atlantic Ocean, the sign read, with a migratory range from San Diego to the Bay of Bengal and the South China Sea (around the Philippines) to the temperate waters of the Gulf south of Louisiana and the Mississippi River. The average manta was twenty-two feet wide and weighed several thousand pounds. At twelve feet, this one was just a kid. Then he found the target, the manta's spineless tail, easily as long as its body; a formidable whip indeed.

His plan, little more than a plot element from a cheap thriller, was to hide until all had left. Alone in the closed museum, he'd have hours to accomplish his goal. He'd need them. Watching the glorious creature swim past, Ben knew, he'd need to convince himself all over again of the necessity.

He took the stairs to the second floor, entered the small theater on the balcony, and slipped into a seat in the back row. The featured attraction, attended by a scant few, was an adventure film called *Mississippi Journey,* an educational boat trip down the famed river. With his backpack beside him, Ben settled in to watch. The picture played out and the room cleared, except for Ben. New theatergoers filtered in, and on the half-hour, the film started again for a final showing. As it ended, Ben slipped to the floor with his backpack, and tucked in under the seats against the back wall. There he lay until the theater emptied, the lights went out, and the museum went quiet.

Now, stiff and cold, Ben got to his feet.

He sneaked from the theater to the museum's first floor and to the feeding tank. This time, he went out of his way to avoid seeing the shark or face the monstrous manta ray. He stripped to the trunks he already wore beneath his clothes, pulled a mask, snorkel, and Bowie knife from his backpack, and gulped a breath. Hating himself, but convinced he had no option, Ben climbed atop the tank and crawled to the feeder's hatchway. The lady who fed the fish did so in full scuba gear. Partly, Ben imagined, because it took so long and partly because it looked good for the tourists. Ben could use a tank and regulator, of course, but getting them into the museum would have been a trial. He didn't plan to be in the water that long.

He dunked his lens, donned his mask, and lowered himself through the hatch. Like the engine on his old Impala, Ben gasped out his snorkel exhaust. Tropical or not, the water was freezing. To continue the jalopy metaphor, his headlights came on and his stick shift shrank as the creatures of the Gulf darted in excitement. The manta swam slow vertical loops around him. Ben saw none of it. He'd closed his eyes to hold off seeing the abhorrent work ahead. Something brushed him in passing. And again. And again. It suddenly occurred what a disappointment he must be. Used to a human presence that signaled food, the fish must have been wondering where the grub was. He felt an impressive nudge and opened his eyes to find the shark circling. Ben panicked, dropped his knife and surfaced. The poor shark, probably thinking he was nuts, juked and went by showing no more interest.

The foot of air at the top of the tank was stale and warm, but it was air. Ben refilled his lungs, found his courage, and dove to reclaim his knife from the bottom. Weapon in hand, his mind back on his mission,

Ben scanned the depths for the monster ray. He felt a sharp pinch at his hip and turned to see the turtle making off with a piece of his trunks. It occurred to him, if he wanted to escape alive, he'd better finish and go. He found the manta, and battling a new wave of guilt, swam after it. There was no choice but to maim this beautiful sea creature. Countless human lives depended on it. But, goddammit, how could he? The devil fish swam by, trailing nearly twelve feet of tail. Ben tightened his grip on the knife and stretched his free hand.

Across the museum floor, Walter Dunn watched in terror.

The old guard had entered the hall, as he had a thousand times before, on his rounds. But this time, *Jumping Jupiter*, was anything but routine. There was a diver in the feeding tank. A man with a knife going after the fish! With trembling hands Walter pulled his flashlight... and his gun.

In the tank, knife in one hand, manta's tail in the other, Ben was suddenly and inexplicably blinded by light. He heard a shout, unintelligible through the water and beneath the hum of the aerators, but a shout all the same. He let go of the manta, and again, dropped the knife into the waving flora below. Through his mask, through the Plexiglas wall of the tank, the startled paramedic glared out into the museum at the museum's security guard, staring back at him. The old man dropped his flashlight and Ben saw terror in his eyes. He saw his shaking gun. Then Ben saw a brilliant flash as the old man fired.

Twenty - Seven

With the muzzle flash, everything went into slow motion. The snorkel popped from Ben's mouth as he screamed. A torrent of bubbles rose to the surface. He sucked water, his eyes growing to the size of fried eggs behind his fogging mask. The bullet hit the rounded glass wall of the aquarium in front of him.

He expected an explosive *thwack*. He expected shattering glass and a thunderous deluge with an encyclopedia of exotic fish, and his silly dead ass, pouring out of the tank and onto the polished tile floor of the museum in a waterfall of horror and gore. But his nightmare failed to materialize.

The shot puckered the glass, with an oddly impotent *tick*, and the fish scattered. That was it. There was no shatter, not even a slow and sinister spidering crack in the glass, and he wasn't dead. Amazingly the tank held. The pucker, mostly heat and moisture, began to fade. The waters calmed and the fish returned to cruising. But Ben Court had damn near had a heart attack. And, through the water and glass, in the gloom across the museum, on the other end of the gun, to his horror, the paramedic saw the old guard grab his chest. He saw him grimace, and though it was muffled, heard him cry out in pain and fear. Walter Dunn *was* having a heart attack.

Ben scrambled up and out of the tank. He dropped the mask and snorkel in a puddle of salt water at his feet. Some adventurer he's turned out to be. He'd brought a knife to a gun fight, and dropped it at the bottom of the tank. He'd failed spectacularly in his hunt for a manta tail.

He examined the obviously bulletproof tank that had proved itself more impressive than him. It looked as solid as ever. He looked across the museum and forgot his worries that the old boy might take a second shot. Walter, collapsed on the floor, could not have looked less solid. Ben hurried over, slipping twice on the tile, and found the guard conscious but in respiratory distress. He lifted him to a sitting position and propped him against the nearest wall. Overwhelmed with guilt, Ben only felt worse when the breathless old man began pleading that he not hurt him.

"It's all right," Ben assured him. "I'm the last guy in the world who's going to hurt you."

He unbuttoned Walter's shirt and loosened his collar. He tried to assess his condition, but the guard was too frightened to answer questions. Ben saw he had no choice. He lifted Walter's portable from the floor. "Your radio," he asked. "Who's on the other end?"

"My... dispatcher," Walter replied breathlessly. "Just... my dispatcher."

Ben wiped the river of sweat from Walter's eyes, then the river of sea water from his own. He keyed the transmit switch. "Dispatch?"

"Walter?" the radio squawked. "Walter is that you? The P.D. is on the way."

"We need an ambulance as well," Ben said.

"Who is this?"

"Did you get that? We need an ambulance at the river museum. Tell them it's a possible M.I."

Several minutes of silence followed before the dispatcher returned to say an ambulance was coming. He called for Walter again, then hurled threats at the voice that wasn't Walter's. Ben turned the radio off. Walter, crying now, renewed his pleas that Ben not hurt him.

Ben knew plenty of cops, knew how and what they were thinking. Someone in the Port District would have heard the shot and phoned it in. And Walter's dispatcher was in hysterics. The police would question what there was to steal at a river museum, and they would seriously question the presence of militant criminals, but they would still be responding to a '2-11 in progress with shots fired' and they would arrive ready to rumble. There was no sense trying to hide anything. There was no time to dress and Ben was trailing water everywhere. He wasn't going to cover his tracks. The only two things to do now would be to ensure Walter did not buy the farm, and to show no threat when the cops arrived. God, he just hoped Erin was busy elsewhere.

He borrowed Walter's keys, unlocked, and blocked a front door open. Sirens were fast approaching. He returned Walter's keys, told him help would soon be there, then sat down to wait on the wide stairs. From there he could watch Walter, lit by a tank in the wall above his head, and the shadowed hall to the front doors, and wonder about his uncertain future. The sirens arrived and died as red and blue flashes stole into the museum hall. He looked to the tank, couldn't see the knife and hoped the cops wouldn't. The fish, including the manta, swam on, uninterested in the drama. Ben didn't care anymore either.

The cops, paramedics, and firefighters entered en masse, flashlights and badges, wheeled cot, stacked medical equipment, and turnout gear. With the exception of Traer's partner, Ben knew every last one of them by name. God, it was embarrassing. Still maybe the universe didn't absolutely despise him; Erin was not among them. Walter was their immediate focus of attention and Ben was grateful.

Eventually, of course, Traer made his way over and asked, "What were you doing in the tank?"

"What tank?" Ben replied.

"Okay," the cop said with a shrug.

Ben wasn't doing himself a favor being an ass, he knew. But any charges, other than trespassing, would be based on Walter's statement. Ben didn't know what he'd said or seen. He could still hope they knew nothing of the manta, or the knife, and there was little sense confessing to crimes about which they were ignorant. All things considered, he didn't have a thing to say just then.

Then the universe spat in Ben's eye. Erin arrived, looking a thousand questions, and followed Traer's pointing finger. She recognized Ben at the same instant he recognized her. Two worlds crashed at once.

Ben watched as the paramedics loaded the security guard up, and with lights and sirens, started away. Then he went for a walk himself, in handcuffs, past the remaining engine crew. His colleagues stared back, some in confusion, more in amusement, as Erin wordlessly frog-marched him to the parking lot. She pushed on the top of his head, not gently, 'helping' him into the back seat of her cruiser. She got behind the wheel, with a wire screen separating them, and rolled into the night.

Ben felt like a caged monkey. The silence was deafening. His mind raced as he struggled for words, any word. "I suppose you're wondering why I've called you here tonight?"

"Don't."

"Erin, I–"

"Don't say another word." She didn't turn, just glared daggers in her rear view mirror while, Ben could see, fighting back tears. Another horrible minute of silence passed. "Do you know how many cops and firefighters have hit on me?" she asked. "More than I can count."

"I never hit on you."

"I know," Erin shouted. "That's one reason I wanted you. Lucky me. I had to fall in love with a lunatic!"

"It's not that bad, you know."

"It's worse," she barked, so mad she was spitting the words. "It's way worse." Erin's reflected glare was full of fire. "Haven't you noticed I've been sick, every morning? Even Nestor knew I was sick and he doesn't know anything at all."

"I haven't seen you. You've been sick?"

"Morning sickness. I'm pregnant, you idiot. Your condom, like my life, apparently came apart. I didn't just fall in love with a lunatic, I made a baby with one." She turned from the mirror, pleading to the heavens. "My God, I'm the idiot. I let you make me pregnant, then you're off to chase monsters. And I don't even know what to say about the grenade other than, if you took it, and we both know you did, give it back before someone finds out. Now this! Now this! Walter Dunn may die. You scared the poor old man… probably to death. And why? What the hell were you doing in that aquarium?"

"Erin, I can explain."

"Shut up! I don't want to hear it." The dam broke. "God! Oh, God, I'm scared to death to hear your explanation for this."

Ben watched in guilty silence. Erin strangled the steering wheel with white knuckles, breathing deep, fighting a tremor trying to take control of her body. In through the nose, out through the mouth, without meaning to, putting on an exhibition of strength as she reclaimed a grip, on her emotions and the situation. She pulled the squad off of Iowa Street into the municipal drive. At the bottom of the ramp, she dried her eyes as she waited for the always slow overhead door. Then she pulled the squad through and underneath the Law Enforcement Center. She parked and turned the cruiser's engine off.

"I…" Ben started uncomfortably. "I don't suppose… you could bail me out?"

"I'll call my brother in Galena," she said, checking her face in the mirror. "See if he can come over." Her reflection glared. "I don't think anyone here knows him." Ben mouthed an 'Ouch' but said nothing, not even when she added, "Then I'm going to think up a legal way to kill you."

Ben wasn't sure where they'd come from, but the cops from the museum, Traer and his partner, were suddenly beside Erin's squad. A third, a booking officer, wandered out to meet them wearing a shit-eating grin. Erin spoke to the trio then opened the back door of the squad.

"Come on, Captain Ahab," she said, too loudly. "All ashore that's going ashore." She grabbed his arm and 'helped' him again, the cuffs biting his wrists like a mad dog.

They formed a parade, Ben in bracelets and damp trunks, the rest in dark blue. They were buzzed through the garage door, a few steps further on buzzed through a second door and, down a short hall, buzzed through a third door into the booking room where, Ben imagined, the fun would continue into the night. All kidding aside, the tiny part of his psyche that occasionally touched base with cold hard truth realized things were about to start tasting like hell.

The three blue goons stared holes through him. Erin went out of her way to avoid looking. "Traer," she said, starting to shake again. "Can you... write this collar?" She hurried out.

Traer nudged Ben toward a wooden bench. "Have a seat." It wasn't a request.

The occasional red light and siren did not a big city make. Neither did the sporadic bar or pizza joint staying open late. Despite the best efforts of Mayor Light, the City Council, and the Duncan Outreach (read that 'Marketing') Committee, the fact was, Duncan remained a mid-west farming community that rolled up its sidewalks at midnight. By one a.m., every hard-working, law-abiding human was in bed.

Vong, on the other hand, hungered with nagging lusts. And the Duncan Memorial Obstetrics Ward seemed a lovely place to fulfill them.

Known to the civilian world as Labor and Delivery, the ward was hidden away behind the second-floor surgery suites (and a sign reading: *Hospital Staff Only*), for two obvious reasons. One; logic and the law required staff and patients be free of unwanted traffic for security, sterility, privacy, and peace. Two; because, though advanced medicine had made childbirth as easy as breathing, it was still no cakewalk, and they needed surgery near in case things went pear-shaped during the blessed event. That meant, with the exception of nervous fathers (or whatever stand-in the expectant mother's lifestyle decreed), the public was not allowed. Family, friends and well-wishers could gush and snap pictures upstairs, through the viewing window of the fifth floor Nursery. Steps were taken to make that so.

Gaining entrance to the supposedly secure ward was child's play to Vong. She moved stealthily up an interior stairwell, without anyone being aware of her presence. She glanced through a door window, then sure she was alone, stepped through into the Obstetrics hall. With the late hour and the low hospital census, save for emergency lights, the wing lay in darkness. There came an echo of laughter from the nurses' station down the hall, a spot of light in the gloom. Otherwise, the floor was empty and quiet.

The elevator in front of the nurses' station *pinged* its arrival. Vong slipped back into a shadow to watch as the doors slid open and an Emergency Room clerk rolled a wheelchair, with a voluminously pregnant patient aboard, onto the floor. A nurse in blue scrubs, chewing the last of a bite, stepped from the station to meet them. The clerk introduced Theresa Meyers, the patient, adding the husband was in Admitting and would soon be up. The nurse took charge of the patient. The clerk recalled the elevator and vanished.

Vong moved to another shadowed doorway, nearer the station, and watched the new patient being rolled into Delivery Room Four. She watched the arrival of the disheveled husband, a bundle of jangled nerves at the prospect of daddy-hood. Vong leered, knowing she'd take care of that. He introduced himself as Scott Meyers and Vong watched as the nurse showed him to his wife's room. "You can have a few minutes," the nurse told him. "Then we'll chase you out while we get her ready."

Vong slipped into a dark and empty Delivery Room Three, immediately across the hall, leaving the door ajar. A few minutes, that was fine with her. Vong loosened the straps and let her dress fall to the floor. She could wait a few minutes.

Twenty – Eight

City protectors were a lot like family. Firefighters were brothers and sisters to all firefighters. Cops were brothers and sisters to all cops. Firefighters and police officers, while not brothers, were distant cousins and usually friends. At the very least, they tended to be on the same side. Most of the time, they had each other's backs. It was a benefit Ben enjoyed at that moment. Embarrassed and defeated, he'd been photographed and fingerprinted (there'd been no way around it), but afterwards, owing to the unspoken familial relationship, he'd been left relatively comfortable in the booking room with no immediate plans to toss him in the clink. It wasn't the Hilton, but it wasn't a cell either.

There he sat with hundreds of plaques, trophies, patches, badges and photographs glaring down at him from the sterile white walls, the history of law and order in Duncan, Iowa. Every new toy, every department innovation from the turn of the century on: the jump from horses to motors in 1922 with a motorcycle, two cars, and a paddy wagon. Eighteen Gamewell Telegraph call boxes, with lights and bells, to replace the original seven. The first machine guns to fight the Prohibition gangs of the 1930's. The rank designated uniforms, with threatening patrol officers wearing guns on their hips while the sergeants, captains, and chief wore long coats to hide them. The photographs changed from black and white to color in the 1970's. All of them, like history, like the exhausted firefighter returning their stare, fading rapidly. The department's first chief seemed to glare with disapproving eyes. Ben didn't blame the old boy. Who in 1901, when the city hired its first police matron, could have conceived of the day when a female police detective would haul her nutty boyfriend, a city firefighter no less, in on charges. Ben smiled sadly. *You've come a long way, baby.*

The door to the booking room came open and Ben did a double take as Art Blackmore walked in. To say he was surprised by the Union president's appearance was to put it lightly. He hadn't seen him since he'd called Art a prick with ears at the Garfield explosion, and hadn't missed the company. He had no clue what Blackmore wanted but knew he'd find out in short order; a friendly chat wasn't likely.

Blackmore sneered. It took Ben a full second to tire of that. "Art," he said. "You're the last person on earth I expected to see."

"I'm not here by choice." He didn't spit, but it was close. "If it were up to me, you could rot."

"That's plain enough. Why are you here?"

"As long as you're a Union member, you're entitled to legal representation. As long as I'm the Local president, it's my responsibility to make sure every member gets their entitlements."

"Well, aren't I the lucky one?"

"I don't know what you are; I never knew. Tonight hasn't cleared up a thing."

"I appreciate your coming down."

"Keep your appreciation. I told you, I'm not here by choice. If you need an attorney, I can put you in touch with one. The initial consultation, at least, will be paid by the Union. What happens after depends on a number of things we don't know yet."

Ben smiled. It was a pleasure watching Blackmore do his duty.

"Tomorrow morning," the president continued. "I intend to do all I can to have you suspended and, as soon as possible, fired."

"You consider that your responsibility as well?"

"I certainly do. I owe it to the Union I run and the city I serve. Once you're out on your ass, your legal problems are your own."

"I really don't know what to say," Ben said. "Other than fuck you and the horse you rode in on."

"That's clever. Well worth getting out of bed in the middle of the night to hear. While you're thinking up your next clever bit, maybe it will occur to you to do the decent thing and refuse our help. What the hell, Court, you don't need it. It's a criminal case and they'll appoint you an attorney if you can't afford one. If you had any decency, or a set of balls, you might even go a step further, quit the department and save your Union brothers the embarrassment of being associated with you."

"Thanks, Art. I'll give your offer and commentary all the consideration they deserve."

At the door, Blackmore paused for a parting shot. "As you never come to meetings," he said. "You may not be aware Sandy Cooper is our secretary. Let her know if you want our legal assistance. For myself, I've said all I have to say to you." Blackmore disappeared.

Ben tried to think, but nothing came to mind but expletives. Outside of fire suppression, he knew little about physics but, really, how black could a cloud over your head get? What Art Blackmore said, did, or thought didn't matter, he was merely another straw for the camel's back. But Ben's life was quickly unraveling, in regards to those he cared for, and that mattered a lot. Erin was pregnant. God, Erin was pregnant with his child. And she wanted to kill him. She had every right. And, if anything Ruzicki, or Poni, or Nestor said was true, Erin was in more danger now because of him. Could it be true? The whole damned monster thing, could it be true? If he didn't think so, why was he here, under arrest for… what he'd done? But they didn't know what he'd done. They weren't going to find out. Not from him. Because he was done talking about demons. Yet, he knew he wasn't done with monsters. He had no choice now but to find and kill aswang by himself. If he ever got out of jail.

The hours ticked by. Ben counted the floor tiles, counted the squares in the panels of the ceiling, counted sheep. He was counting the framed photographs again, to make sure his first count had been accurate, when the door opened and he was once more on display. This time, the oglers were Ron Musselwhite, the police chief, and an elderly fellow with spectacles hogging his face. The old man groaned, nodded to the chief, and left. Musselwhite entered the booking room and closed the door. He plopped down on the bench, heaved a sigh, and said, "Court, you are without doubt, the luckiest son of a bitch I have ever met."

"Is that a fact?" Ben asked.

"It is. And if, just if, you can get through this little meeting with me without cracking wise, by which I mean, saying something incredibly stupid, your luck may hold and you may again breathe fresh air. It's a big *if*, so mind your mouth."

Ben nodded without a word.

"That gentleman," Musselwhite said, pointing at the door. "Was Llewellyn Crossbinder, the curator of the river museum. He wanted to get a look at you and, after the night you gave him, I thought we both owed him that." Ben said nothing. Musselwhite went on. "I don't know where to begin, so I'll just lay out the examples of your luck in no particular order. The feeding tank at the museum where, God knows why, you decided to go for a swim, is undamaged. The Plexiglas was developed for sharks and is bulletproof and able to withstand incredible water pressures. Lucky you.

"Walter Dunn, the museum security guard, has been released. He didn't have a heart attack. His medical emergency was one-part angina and two-parts anxiety. It's clear your clown act brought it on. But it's also reasonable to assume, if his life was in jeopardy, your response also saved him. Neither the curator nor Mr. Dunn wants to press charges. So instead of a second-degree murder charge, you get a pat on the back. Like I said, you're luckier than shit.

"I've spoken with Detective Vanderjagt, and with the mayor, and your chief or, as you delight in calling him for some reason, my brother-in-law. With all that is going wrong in this city, nobody wants a headline about an arrested firefighter. Particularly if the screwy details were to come out, which they would if we pressed for them. The bottom line is; you're being released without charges."

Ben nodded. "Thank you."

"Don't thank me," Musselwhite said. "I've asked no questions about the museum because we found the knife and, frankly, I don't want to know. I think you're a fool, and I'm not certain you're sane, and I don't give a damn about either. But I'll tell you this, Court, if you ever upset Erin again – like you upset her tonight – your next prank is going to end with a Fire Department funeral." Musselwhite stood. "Get the hell out of my police station."

The air off the Mississippi River was cool and crisp. It tasted sweet as Ben stepped from the Law Enforcement Center where, it seemed, he'd been for years. Dawn threatened an arrival. He started across the lot, stretching his legs for home, when a stranger climbed from a compact car and blocked his path. He was young, thin but muscled, with sandy hair but a dark expression. He said, "Excuse me," but nothing in his tone sounded polite.

"Can I help you?"

"You're Ben Court?" the man asked. When Ben admitted it, he went on. "My name is Tony Vanderjagt. I'm Erin's brother."

A second look showed the resemblance; the same thin nose, the same eyes, and a heat behind them identical to the anger he'd seen in Erin's earlier that night. Ben smiled and extended a hand. Tony ignored it and Ben pulled it back.

"My sister called me, pleaded with me to drive over here to bail you out."

"I appreciate–"

"Don't bother. I came for her. Because she asked it of me, despite my advice to leave you in the can. Turns out I wasn't needed; bail wasn't needed. I don't know the details and, unless Erin chooses to fill me in sometime in the future, I never will. But for whatever reason they've dropped whatever charges they had against you. Great. Congratulations."

"I'm sorry you wasted your trip."

"It wasn't a waste. I got to see my sister. That happens too infrequently. And I get to warn you… I don't want Erin hurt."

"Of course you don't."

"No." He turned, squaring off and balling his fists. He seemed to grow right in front of Ben. "Hear what I'm saying. I don't want my sister hurt."

Ben nodded. "I hear you."

Twenty – Nine

Scott Meyers got the bum's rush. On tip-toes, moving backwards, straining for a last glimpse of his wife, Theresa, over the nurse's shoulder, Meyers was ushered from Delivery Room Four. "We'll let you back in a few minutes," Virginia Silas, the nurse, the sergeant at arms in scrubs said as she maneuvered the nervous father-to-be. "We need to get her ready for the doctor. We'll get you a cup of coffee at the nurses' station." Silas didn't argue with patients or their significant others. She did her job, friendly but firmly, leaving the door to the delivery room ajar. She'd be back in a flash. Their steps echoed as they disappeared down the hall.

Delivery Room Three, across the hall, was dark and unused but not unoccupied. The door inched silently open and the occupant listened as the echoes died and the hall fell silent. The door jerked wide and the dark thing pulled itself into the hall. The naked abomination of a human female torso shown sickly green-black in the dim fluorescent light. Leathery wings on its back folded down and in, wrapping the body, as long arms stretched clawed hands to pull it quickly across the tiled floor. Undulating like a paraplegic thrown from her chair, long black hair in riot on its head, the aswang reached the door to Room Four, nudged it open, and vanished inside. Then came an ear-splitting scream.

Silas stepped from the nurses' station, glaring down the hall, trying to localize what she'd heard. The scream could only have come from one room, that of the new patient, Meyers. But it wasn't a shout of pain, it was a scream of terror. Silas took off for Room Four. Behind her, the husband, holding a Styrofoam cup while a unit clerk poured, watched after the nurse with his mouth open. His wife screamed again. Meyers dropped the cup and ran after the nurse.

Nurse Silas shoved the delivery room door open. She gawped inside. Then she screamed, too.

The patient was on the bed as Silas had left her. But there the normality ended. Atop the patient lay some kind of animal or alien creature, the nurse had never seen the like. It had huge wings, wild hair, the upper body of a woman and, from what Silas could see, no lower body at all. The blanket and sheet were pulled down, Theresa's hospital gown shoved up, the mound of her belly exposed. The thing grabbed the patient by the throat, cutting off her screams and pinning her to the bed while, with the other clawed hand, it reached down and massaged her ripe belly. The wings fluttered in excitement beneath the ceiling light, throwing a strobe of shadows about the room.

With its green eyes glued on Theresa's belly, the creature opened its mouth and extended a glistening red tongue past rows of yellow fangs. It was round, thin, and incredibly long – unlike any tongue Silas had ever seen. It ended in a keen point like the tip of an IV catheter, perfect for injecting or drawing off body fluids. With a hiss, the dark thing drove the tongue into the patient's stomach.

Silas gasped. Scott Meyers arrived demanding, "What's the matter? What's happened?" The nurse couldn't answer, couldn't catch her breath. He looked past her into the room, heard a ghastly sucking noise, and saw the animal on the bed defiling his wife. The creature lolled its head to the side with only the bloodshot whites of its eyes showing, the irises rolled up and back. The thing fed in ecstasy.

Meyers added his screams to the chorus. The creature's eyes rolled down, shining green in its filthy head. It saw the husband and nurse gawking and, continuing to feast, hissed around its tongue like an agitated snake. The nurse shrieked again. Meyers pushed past her into the room.

At the nurses' station, the unit clerk was in a panic. She had no idea what was going on but knew, whatever it was, it had never happened before. She dialed security, screaming for help, as a groggy OB doctor joined her from his on-call sleeping room. Both turned at a new shriek.

Scott Meyers stumbled backwards out of the delivery room like a wrestler tossed from the ring. His arms windmilled on either side of him. He vomited an arc of red through the air in his wake. To the unit clerk, it looked like he'd spit a mouthful of cherry Kool-Aid. The doctor guessed red liqueur. Meyers hit the wall on the far side of the hall and collapsed. Only then did clerk and doctor see the bright deluge down the front of his shirt and realize his throat had been slit.

Hysterical, the unit clerk started dialing again. Where were those security guards? The doctor ran to the fallen man and, with one look, saw there was nothing to be done. He turned for the delivery room, took a step, then screamed as something scuttled out toward him.

The doctor saw what you've seen, coming at him at incredible speed, crawling low on the floor, wings folded, torso squirming as it *clicked* grotesque nails on the tiles, hair flying, gore coated tongue flicking over stained fangs. It hissed, howled, and bit viciously at him. The defenseless doctor's screams lasted mere seconds and he went wherever Meyers had gone. Dripping blood and shrieking, aswang scuttled back into the dark of Room Three.

Terrified but needing to know, the clerk tip-toed down the hall. The patient's husband, no longer an expectant father, was propped against the far wall. The doctor lay at his feet a few steps away. Their hearts had stopped, but both continued to leak blood onto the polished tiles. Hugging the wall as far from Room Three as she could, the clerk peeked into Room Four. Nurse Silas lay butchered on the floor. Theresa Meyers lay lifeless on the bed, her sheets painted with blood. Gulping air so as not to puke, the clerk hurried back to her desk and grabbed up the phone again.

The door to Room Three opened and Vong stepped out. The clerk didn't know her. She knew only that a darkly exotic woman, wearing a sun dress and sporting the freakiest green eyes she'd ever seen, had stepped out into the middle of that bloody carnage, stared straight at her, and smiled. Then, despite it being night and their being indoors, she slipped on a pair of sunglasses, turned, and walked away like a tourist strolling down the beach. She stepped over the doctor's corpse and the body of the murdered husband as if they were puddles on a wet sidewalk.

Vong passed two security guards coming the other way. The unit clerk pointed, screaming, "Her! It's her! It's her!"

The rent-a-cops spun in their tracks. "Hey! Hey, you! Stop!"

Though it happened before her eyes, the next few minutes became a mystery the stunned unit clerk would be unable to help the police unravel. She wouldn't remember a thing.

The larger of the two guards laid his hand on Vong's shoulder. She grabbed it and tossed him from one wall to the other, and back again, like a billiard ball off the table cushions. He collapsed in a heap. She jerked the smaller one over the top of his unconscious partner, carried him to the end of the hall, and threw him against the window. Overlooking downtown Duncan, it was made of Lexan, not glass. Vong smashed the guard into it three times before it shattered to create a wide enough opening through which she could throw him. The drop was only twenty-four feet. But, if the crunch was any indication, the angle of the fall and the quick stop combined to cleanly snap his neck. Vong followed him through the hole, enjoyed the view for a moment crouched on the window ledge, then leapt out.

Everyone within the clerk's sight was dead. She finally gathered her wits enough to get an outside line and dial 9-1-1. But somebody was ahead of her. Outside the broken window the night was already alive with red and blue flickering light, police sirens, squealing tires, and slamming doors. In minutes, gunshots and screams were added to the list.

From the radio traffic, it was a good guess all hell had broken loose at the hospital. From the sound of gunfire as Erin approached, the guess was confirmed. She squealed her tires turning onto Williams Park, the street bordering Duncan Memorial to the south, and was fast approaching the first entrance when something indefinable shot across the street, four feet off the ground, in front of her vehicle. Her brain registered something flying, before her eyes had a chance to see what. She hit the brakes, fishtailed, and slid the car into the hospital lot. She grabbed the rearview mirror, trying to find whatever it was she'd nearly hit. Then something huge smashed the front of her car. The windshield popped; the glass spidered. Her airbag exploded in her face.

Somehow the vehicle came to a stop. Stunned, Erin fell out of the driver's door, pulling her Glock as she staggered to her feet. She turned back to an ear-piercing shriek, and fired at a brilliant explosion of red and black in the air above her squad. She turned, following and firing, emptying the clip at the moving target. Between the god-awful squawks and the barking of her handgun, she caught part of the eerie song she'd heard before.

Tik, tik, tik. Tik, tik, tik.

Knocked stupid by the airbag, blinded by the muzzle flashes, her nose full of burnt powder, Erin struggled to see past the parking lot lights to the night sky. The dark thing, whatever it was, had gone. The red thing, whatever the hell it was, had gone too. Both – just gone. But, finally, she had proof the damned things had been there. An oozing black substance which, other than the color, might have been blood, spattered the broken windshield. And brilliant red feathers, a handful of them, were lodged in the windshield frame.

Wobbling, in a private fog, Erin took in the scene. Four patrol officers, one a supervisor with chevrons on his sleeves, stood in a pool of amber near a light pole at the edge of the drive. Two held smoking guns, looking into the darkness to the east. The other two, also with smoking guns, stared into the darkness to the north. Heading forward, toward the hospital, Erin found three patrol units between parking spaces and a fourth bridging a curb. A hospital guard lay dead on the sidewalk. Four bodies in blue were sprawled at various spots in the lot. Two moved slightly. Two, she discovered, would never move again. One of the dead officers was Parker Traer. Erin collapsed beside him.

The Obstetrics' unit clerk, the only person left alive on the ward, stood staring out the busted window above, watching Erin cry.

Thirty

The tally at Duncan Memorial Hospital was monstrous. Nine dead, including another of Erin's closest friends. Three officers had been hospitalized in critical, stable, and satisfactory conditions. The critical officer, a married father of three, was beyond answering questions. Of the others, both bachelors, stable had no memory of the incident, and satisfactory, who'd been climbing from his squad when the attack came, hadn't seen a thing.

The havoc in the streets became rage in the corridors of police headquarters and panic beneath the glistening dome of City Hall. In the lead investigator's office, the chief divided his gaze between the board of evidence and the detective as Erin tried to update him on the OB incident and the investigation as a whole. Her report somehow carried more weight as she delivered it with a frightening goose egg on her forehead. There were plenty of witnesses now, including herself, but the descriptions of what were believed to be three perpetrators were as ludicrous as the plot of an old Bela Lugosi movie. The ringleader was an exotic and beautiful dark-haired woman, Asian or Polynesian maybe, with two animal accomplices.

"Animals?" the chief asked.

"Right. Both fast as lightning, as they appeared out of nowhere, and both able to fly. One was dark with leathery wings—"

"You mean like a bat?"

"If so, it was a damned big bat. But the wings were somehow different. And a second creature, bright red, with a black head, and a murderous beak and talons."

"You mean like a bird?"

"At the risk of repeating myself," Erin said. "If so, it was a damned big bird."

"Can we get sketches distributed to patrol units?"

Erin tilted her head, looking for a way to field the question. "We can try, if you think it would help. Pictures of a giant bird of prey, a hundred-pound bat with human arms and tits, and their fashion model Asian organ grinder? I don't know what…" Erin let it trail off.

The chief hesitated, nodded his understanding. "Skip it. We'll come back."

"Right." She picked up the instant Ice Pack she'd swiped from the First Aid kit and held it to her head. She returned to her list. "I've alerted DMV, car dealerships, and realtors to try to get a handle on the exotic woman."

"Could the FBI help with the ID?"

"Certainly, but you and the mayor wanted to keep the grenades, the gasoline, and Chandler's disappearance out of the hands of the feds. Are you ready to let go?"

The chief rose, swore under his breath and took a lap around the room. It came to an abrupt end when he met Mayor Light entering the office unannounced.

"Did I hear my title? And is that any way for a police chief to be carrying on?"

"When you barge in," Musselwhite said, returning to his chair. "You get what you get."

"Yes, well… We're all stressed," the mayor said. "We'll let it go. I stopped to say that, following this evening's events, we've arranged a press conference for…" He consulted his watch. "One hour from now. I'll expect you both to be there."

Erin exploded. "I don't have time for another press conference."

Light looked as if he'd been slapped. "You're going to have to make time, Detective Vanderjagt. It's part of your job."

"I'm doing my job. I'm trying to stop a killer. I have no new information to share with the media."

"You can tell them that," Light said. "In the most uplifting and informative manner possible."

Erin looked from the weary police chief seated near her desk, to the sneering mayor, doing his best to loom over them. She leaned back in her chair, folded her arms, and asked, "What's the point of holding repeated press conferences when the events being covered are so unbelievable they can't be told? When nearly all of the facts and evidence have to be withheld?"

"We have an image of honesty with the public that must be upheld."

"Even if we have to lie to everyone to do it?"

"I did not ask you to lie, detective," Light said. "I simply want you to meet the press and couch your comments in terms that comfort an alarmed citizenry."

"We have an absolutely inexplicable eyewitness account of the most recent events at the hospital, mine included. We're searching, so far in vain, for an undetermined number of suspects who, after causing the deaths of an expectant mother and her child, a husband, a nurse, an OB doctor, and two security guards, was shot repeatedly by over a half dozen police officers. Two of those officers have since died. The suspects escaped the scene so fast witnesses said they flew. The bullets didn't even slow them down. My squad was destroyed. And the organic evidence left on my vehicle decomposed before the forensic team could collect it. Nothing was left but the busted cruiser. And unless all of our officers are liars, Mr. Mayor, when the suspects bled, they didn't bleed blood." Erin stared through hard, red-rimmed eyes. "Feel free to go couch that," she said. "I've got work to do."

She turned to her chief as if the mayor no longer existed. "I know you're appointed, Ron. You have to walk on eggshells. But I would genuinely appreciate it if you would either tell *His Honor* to stay the hell away from me or accept my resignation."

Light blustered. "This is the sort of discipline shown by your lead detective?"

The police chief smiled. "Jerry, even you have to admit the circumstances are extraordinary. I've got the press conference covered. You, Tony, and I will go make a solid show of it. Meanwhile, Detective Vanderjagt has work to get to, and I think we'd better let her do it."

The police chief rose, pointing to the door. The tight-lipped mayor, savvy enough to know when to retreat, took the hint. The chief winked at Erin and followed him out.

Unaware the mayor had already tussled with Erin, Mark Forester set upon the politician the moment he took his seat in the Council chambers. The police chief had veered off to make last minute copies leaving Light alone and ripe for the picking. "Mayor, can you clear this up? Wasn't one of your firefighters taken into custody at the river museum last night?"

A blast of air escaped Light's lips. "Oh, I'd be surprised if that were true."

"Is that a denial?"

"Please, don't put words in my mouth. Be nice."

"I'm not trying to make up a quote. I'm asking, was a firefighter arrested last night? If so who? And why? And where is the arrest report? If not, what happened last night at the river museum? And who was involved? Beyond that, what in God's name happened at the hospital?"

Forester was unaware that Jamie Watts, with her microphone, big ears, and bigger mouth had entered the room. His casual one-on-one with the mayor was doomed. In seconds Watts crowded in, going over ground every TV station in the mid-west had been over for a week. Forester could have kicked her in the slats. Had she not interrupted, he knew, the mayor would have spilled something printable. Instead, Light expelled more bad air and rotated in his chair like a kid waiting for the *Tilt-a-Whirl* to start. He laughed, getting a joke nobody told, then beamed. "The City of Duncan is proud of its firefighters and police officers."

The non-sequitur ended the interview and cued the arrival of the fire and police chiefs. On their heels came the remainder of the department heads, reporters, a small riot of interested citizens, and a bored janitor. With the opportunity for news gathering past, the press conference began. Updates were presented without revealing anything of value. The mayor led marvelously, driving the gathering to a rapid conclusion. Then Forester stuck his nose in again.

He arrived, he claimed, at Duncan Memorial after the blood bath but in time to hear some incredible rumors and wanted to know what was true. "There were eyewitnesses at the hospital. Are sketches of the perpetrators being developed? Will we have images to print?"

The mayor offered a humorless smile. "There were eyewitnesses. We're withholding their identities for obvious reasons. The investigations are ongoing. When more information is available... we'll avail you of it. Now, can we get on?"

"Certainly," Forester said. "Answer this: You blew raspberries when I asked about a vampire. The rumors persist. Is some kind of monster responsible for these killings?"

"Is that what you're going to print in your paper, Mr. Forester? A monster? You think it's all right to terrify the public with nonsense like that?"

Musselwhite rose and cleared his throat. "All personnel within the Police Department, Sheriff's Department, and Iowa Highway Patrol are working sixteen hours a day. We are taking this situation seriously. We would appreciate it if the media did the same."

Thirty – One

The Civil Service Commission governed Fire and Police Department entrance exams, appointed firefighters and police officers, and conducted promotional exams. Its three Commissioners, the appeals board in all matters of discipline, were appointed by the mayor with Council approval. A Human Rights Director sat as an Ex-Officio Member. The four were about to judge Ben Court.

Ben arrived early at the City Hall. He found a handful of reporters, including Forester, being advised that, as the fire chief's complaint fell under the umbrella of a 'personnel matter', the Commissioners would meet behind closed doors. The news hounds groaned; Ben sighed in relief. Witnesses would be called to support Castronovo's contention that he, Ben, was insubordinate, but they'd do so in private. Ben's attorney, not paid by the Union, was asked in by herself. Ben was left outside the chamber. He repeated, "No comment" all the way to an uncomfortable seat on a hard bench, then stewed in shame, embarrassment, anger, resentment, and loneliness, waiting for his turn in the barrel.

As expected, Forester plopped down beside Ben. He got a "No Comment" for his trouble.

"I didn't come over for a comment. Just a seat. And to see if a friend needed anything."

"Do me a favor, huh?" Ben grumbled. "Cut that 'friend' crap. It's wearing out."

Forester nodded, set his jaw without comment, rose, and walked away.

Much later, to Ben's complete shock, the meeting broke up without his having been called. The police and fire chiefs, all but holding hands as usual, left together. The reporters poked at them but got nothing. Musselwhite was reserved. Castronovo looked madder than a wet hen but said nothing. Ben had no reason to hope for good news; still he hoped.

Two of the commissioners came out, with their Human Resources fourth, and the city attorney. Behind them came an elderly man, the same old man (with the spectacles hogging his face) that had appeared at the police station the night of Ben's almost-arrest. Crossbinder, that was it. Llewellyn Crossbinder, the river museum curator. There he was again. He paused, looked at Ben as he had that night, and groaned as he had that night. Then he joined the commissioners. They left en masse without a word or second glance at the paramedic.

Ben's lawyer called him into the chamber where only the mayor and chairman remained. Both gave speeches, neither worth reporting in detail, that amounted to the same thing: the museum curator had not wanted to press charges earlier in the week and did not want Ben disciplined now. Any discipline would be reported, giving Forester another opportunity to squawk and Ben a chance for rebuttal. The museum, the town, and tourism might not survive the scandal. The matter would be swept under the rug. The police had, from the start, been unable to supply a motive for Ben's prank. They no longer wanted to know. The community had too much to lose by recognizing Ben's nonsense publicly.

"On a personal note," Light said, "the curator hopes you will get counseling for whatever is troubling you. I concur. Officially, there is no record and this... sordid affair... never happened."

"Unofficially," the chairman added, "the Commission will have its eye on you, Mr. Court."

"I forgot to mention," the mayor said. "You are suspended for another three days. It has nothing to do with... the matter that never happened. It is for your general 'insubordination'. Chief Castronovo is within his rights and I agree. The suspension begins… well, whenever your last suspension ends."

"We find it impossible to fathom," the chairman said. "But we're told, Court, you are an excellent firefighter and paramedic. Keep your nose clean, son."

Waving good-bye to his attorney on the City Hall steps, Ben thought he was alone. Still he wasn't surprised when he turned to find Forester leaning on a column. "You wasted the wait," Ben told him. "There's no headline for you. Just another dull suspension."

"Will you fight it?"

"No." Ben laughed and shook his head. "I'm told I should be grateful, so I am."

"Then what?" Forester asked.

"Then nothing. I've had enough, I'm going home." Ben started down the sidewalk.

"What? Suddenly gutless?" Forester chased him. "There's still a killer out there, isn't there?"

"I haven't the slightest goddamn clue anymore." Ben pointed at the gold dome. "They think I'm nuts. For all I know they're right. I jumped from a cozy frying pan into a fire. And why? Because of promises made to a suicidal man, who belonged on a psych unit as much as he did a burn ward, and to a friend who *is* on a psych unit. Now I'm supposed to jump in again because you still need a story? They've suggested I see a counselor. Who the hell are you? What meds are you on?"

"This situation is too important," Forester said, digging into his wallet. "You're one of the only people who understands it."

"I don't understand it," Ben insisted. "I don't understand it at all!"

The reporter handed Ben a card.

"What's that?"

Forester shook it at him. "It's my psychiatrist. He's off on Mondays."

"I knew it," Ben said, tucking the card away. "You're nuts too. Everyone I know is certifiable."

Erin stared at the case board, the pictures of each victim, the dates, and details of their deaths; human lives reduced to push pins on a city map. She thought of each for the thousandth time: Linnea Keddy, an estranged wife inexplicably found on the Opera House roof; her ex with an airtight alibi. Crystal Evers, a hooker killed on the Fourth Street Elevator. Repeatedly rattling her pimp and johns had produced nothing. Both pregnant, both with the same wound on their stomachs. Catherine Herrera, pregnant but without the wound, alive but with no memory of her attack. Detectives Shane and Chandler, the only reasons, perhaps, Herrera survived? Shane's wounds, unlike any up to that point. A different weapon? A different killer? Chandler, MIA from the Clock Tower Plaza. Angelina Pena, pregnant, attacked at home, with the same wounds as the first two victims. Mother and child dead; Nestor locked up on the funny farm.

Erin stared at Ben's photo of Angelina and Nestor. Despite a neighbor's insistence, there had never been any concrete evidence Nestor was responsible. Ben had been right. She'd never told him, had never admitted it, but she knew it now. She grabbed a red pin denoting victims, a pin for Nestor to go with Angelina's already on the board. Her hand shook as she reached for the map.

Duncan Memorial already had nine pins in place. How many more could it take? How many more could the city map take? She'd lost Angelina, Traer, and Chandler. Her tears again threatened to flow as Erin wondered if she'd lost Ben too. She had to stop. She had to get it together.

Erin stared at the board, wondering what questions she'd forgotten to ask. The attacks had taken place… where? Was location a factor? Downtown, mostly. Historic downtown. Historic sites? Were the attacks the work of an aggrieved tourist? It sounded ridiculous. Then again, hadn't they all taken place near historic sites? Coincidence. Duncan was mostly historic sites; it was their bread and butter. You couldn't twirl a cat without hitting one. Try something else, she told herself.

If history wasn't the answer, why downtown? What else was downtown? The hospital. The hospital? The attackers, the exotic lady and her pets, had made mincemeat of the Obstetrics Ward. Many of the victims had been pregnant. Could it be as simple as that? Were the killers looking for pregnant women near the hospital? What kind of freak killed pregnant women? What kind of woman killed pregnant women? She scanned the faces of the victims, wondering what they'd say, given the chance? Could the dead tell her anything? The living weren't helping a bit.

The phone rang and Erin jumped. She saw it was her private line and her heart jumped too. It was Ben calling, she knew. He'd had his Commission hearing and would be calling to tell her the results. She wanted to know, needed to know, and wanted so much to talk to him. But she couldn't, not now. She couldn't deal with any more disappointments. She wouldn't hear any more about Philippine ghosts. She needed every ounce of strength to face this case. The phone rang a dozen times before it stopped, before Erin could breathe again.

Maybe she was being stupid. But Ben had been nothing but ridiculous lately. They would have to talk, have to have it out. She loved him. She did love him, but there was more than that to think about. She had her baby to consider. If the child's father was a loser, she'd have to deal with that. If he was off his rocker, she would have to deal with that. But she couldn't deal with it now. Other things demanded her attention. She looked at the board again, to the facts. The killers were downtown, near the hospital, the Port District, the casino, the river museum, in historic Duncan.

Her phone rang again. Erin grabbed her jacket and left.

Thirty - Two

Rickie Savage poked his head out from the opening in the thatched teepee, just like an American Indian. With the moonlight peeking through the clouds he had to squint to see across the water, the 'wetland' the museum people called it, to the big deck on the other side. Sneaking into the museum's back yard to play was not for kids. It took a smart guy. It took an American Indian.

The guard had been there, looking out the glass doors, a few minutes before, but was gone now. *Good,* Rickie thought. With the coast clear, he crawled across the grass to the edge of the American Indian Island, that's what Rickie called it, on the grounds at the back of the museum. There was a steamboat engine on display over there, a big one from a Mississippi paddle boat, and a steam powered boat, a dredger, called the William T. Greene in the museum part of the harbor down there, and a boat racing game in a pool right there, and a boardwalk that let you cross a bridge to where Rickie was. A yellow sign nearby called the teepee a 'wigwam' and the Indians, 'Native Americans'. Wigwam was an Indian word; Rickie didn't speak Indian. To him, it was a teepee. And if evolution was true, like the schools said, the first people really walked here from Africa, before it was Africa, across the Bering Strait, before it was the Bering Strait, then nobody was a Native American. But they didn't really know and neither did he. There were lots of things Rickie didn't know, but he'd admit it. He had no bone to pick, as his daddy said, he was just an American Indian sneaking out of his teepee.

He crawled out onto the bridge and stared into the money pond. That's what Rickie called the water that visitors, when they crossed, sometimes threw money into – dimes, nickels, pennies and, once in a while, quarters. Rickie didn't know why. Sometimes on his night visits Rickie collected them. Not all, and not too many, just some. He liked coins. He needed money like everybody, but more than that, he liked coins. He liked the way the moonlight made them shine. That night there weren't many. He fished them out (not all, just some) without getting too wet, shook them dry, and put them in his pocket. He was done being an American Indian, and wasn't crouched anymore as he followed the boardwalk from the museum to the harbor, headed for the William T. Greene. It was time to be a boat captain.

Captain Rickie Savage stepped over the chain and started down the long gangplank, over the harbor water, under the sign reading: *William T. Greene – Welcome Aboard*, to the dredger's foredeck. He paused in the bow under the derrick. It rose into the sky past the top deck like the skeleton of a great bird and he couldn't help but stop to stare.

There weren't any lights on the dredger at night, but Rickie knew what to expect. Even when the moon disappeared behind the clouds like it did then. "You got good eyes." That's what his mama used to say. Then his daddy would add, "Good eye, Rickie," though he meant both of them. He used his good eyes as he made his way aft, down the starboard side of the main deck, up the metal stairs to the boiler deck (a silly name, as it was above the boilers), forward, then up more stairs to the hurricane deck. There was the box they called the pilothouse, with big square windows to the front and wings on each side (a silly name too; they couldn't fly), and three doors, all reached by eight-step stairs.

Rickie liked playing Captain because he loved the lights of Duncan at night from the bridge of the dredger. Excited at the thought, he hurried across the top deck, up the stairs, and through the stern door into the dark pilothouse. In his excitement, Rickie tripped, stumbled forward, and fell on his face. He threw his hands out to catch himself. His left hand landed on the cold brass of the binnacle. His right landed on something cold too, but it wasn't part of the ship. It was soft and silky, some kind of fancy cloth. He let go. When he set his hand down again, it landed on something altogether different, soft too, and familiar... with toes. Rickie shouted and let loose, backing away on his knees. Someone was standing by the boat's controls in the dark.

"I'm playing Boat Captain," Rickie told the dark. "I didn't break nothing or take nothing."

Moonlight, peeking again, stole through the pilothouse windows. Rickie stared. He ran a hand over his gray crew cut, then across his dry lips, trying to understand what he saw. What he saw was nothing. Nothing, that is, above the waist. A shadowy pair of legs stood alone beside the controls. By the shape, and by what wasn't there, Rickie knew they were the legs of a naked lady. On the deck near one of the feet lay the silky thing he'd touched. It looked like a dress. But there was nothing else there; the legs stopped at the waist with nothing above!

Rickie tripped again, getting out into the fresh air and onto the deck. He hurried down both sets of stairs to the main deck. He stumbled again on the gang plank, getting off the dredger, and almost fell into the water. That would have been bad because Rickie couldn't swim. He caught himself in time and scrambled to dry land. He ran for the American Indian Island, and safely across the bridge, hid in the high grass behind the teepee.

Shaking and gasping, Rickie just got hunkered down when the dark thing appeared in the cloudy sky. Flapping powerfully, it landed atop the dredger's pilothouse. It folded its great wings in, swung down and through the door Rickie had left open and disappeared. Confused, unsure what he ought to do, Rickie merely stared.

He was still staring, a moment later, when a lady walked out of the pilothouse. She was a long way away, backlit by the moonlight over the harbor, and mostly in shadow. But it was a lady in a thin dress. She stared at the museum grounds from the bridge of the William T.

Greene and Rickie had never been so afraid. But she didn't seem to see him. She left the hurricane deck and wound her way down to the lower level. She left the boat and crossed the gangplank to the grounds. Rickie held his breath. But, instead of taking the boardwalk past his hiding place and to the museum, she headed in the opposite direction to where the walkway ended at one of the closed outbuildings.

There was a sudden flash and out of thin air, like a magic trick at a birthday party, a big red bird appeared, perched on the edge of the outbuilding roof. It looked like an eagle; Rickie had seen many on the river. Looked just like an eagle, only bright red, with a mean-looking black head and a long beak. It stared down at the lady and sang her a song as she came: *Tik. Tik. Tik-tik. Tik-tik. Tik-tik.*

The lady reached the building, not a hundred feet from Rickie's hiding spot, and looked up at the ticky bird. Then the lady jumped into the air, higher than a person should be able to jump, and onto the roof beside the bird. The bird sang again, then it vanished. It didn't fly away; it just disappeared. The lady jumped again, from the top of the outbuilding roof, six feet high and eight feet across, over the wall of the enclosure. Two impossible leaps and she also disappeared.

Terrified, Rickie scrambled up from the grass at the pond's edge and around the teepee, glancing repeatedly at the rooftop from which the lady had vanished. He raced across the grass, across the boardwalk, around the boat pool and, as fast as his legs could carry him, across the blacktopped yard. At the steam engine garage, he paused to pull his bicycle out of hiding. Pushing it, he hurried to a spot in the wooden fence with three loose boards. Since discovering this secret, the museum grounds had been his private night time play area. But Rickie wasn't playing now. He lifted a slat and scratched his knuckles shoving his bike through. The board slammed shut behind him. It didn't matter. Rickie wasn't coming back there, ever again.

He jumped onto his bike and started across the empty parking lot, riding like the wind. He put a full block behind him without once looking back. So frightened was he, thinking about the naked legs, the dark flying thing, the ticky bird, and the jumping lady, Rickie couldn't think about anything else. A block further on, he raced his bike through an unlit intersection without even slowing to look or listen. Before anything could prevent it, Rickie was caught in the lights of a moving car on the side street. An instant later, he and his bike were hit broadside by Erin Vanderjagt's new, unmarked squad.

Thirty - Three

"Oh, God! Oh, God, oh, God, oh, God, oh, God!"

Erin threw her replacement cruiser into Park. She hustled out and around the busted front grill to find Rickie Savage knocked on his rear, on a bed of shattered glass and broken plastic, in the street. He was dazed and crying in pain and fear. "Are you all right?"

"My bike."

"Don't worry about your bike. Are you all right?"

"My bike!" he wailed.

She spotted his pride and joy, the bicycle that carried the child-man from one end of the city to the other, lying twisted and ignobly thrown over the curb, on the grass eight feet away.

"It's right there. Don't worry, honey."

"I'm not honey. I'm Richard Savage the third. People call me Rickie."

"Of course they do. I'm sorry, Rickie. I didn't mean to speak to you as if you were a child."

"That's okay."

"I'm so sorry, Rickie. I didn't see you. Did you stop at the sign? You were just… Why are you riding in the dark? Why didn't you stop?"

"I had to ride away," he cried. "I had to ride away… from the big bat and the ticky bird." He gasped, tears racing down his face, trying to catch a breath. "She put her legs back on and jumped the fence."

"The big bat?" Erin repeated. "She put her legs back on?"

"The lady put her legs back on!"

"The lady put her legs on?" Erin asked. "And you were riding away from the big bat?" Rickie nodded. Erin frowned. She had it right, but what *it* was, she had no clue.

"My bike is broke."

"We'll take care of your bike. But we have to take care of you first. You need an ambulance."

That did it; Rickie began to shriek. "They take you away," he cried. "You never come back. They took mama away. She never came back!"

Erin tried to calm him. She changed the subject and asked again why he was riding at night without a light. Rickie returned to his rambling story of the big bat, the ticky bird, and the lady who reclaimed her legs and jumped the fence. Then, switching from one terror to another, he begged again that she not call an ambulance. Erin tried to reassure him. Shaken and shaking, she grabbed her phone.

Moons ago, in Ben's lonely days, he could be found on a bar stool. That had changed after he and Erin hooked up; more so, when they'd grown serious. He'd found better things to do than hang out in an old dive. Then trouble came to Duncan. Soon after, he'd started an acquaintance with Forester the reporter, renewed his acquaintance with The Well, and returned to being one of its better customers. Now he and Erin had fallen out, and he and Forester had fallen out, Ben was back on his old stool, lonely again. He hadn't started yet, but he had every intention of getting drunk.

He brushed his pocket looking for cash and found the card Forester had given him; his shrink's phone number. Amazing how something could be amusing and, at the same time, not at all funny. What would he tell a psychiatrist? What could he tell the guy about the recent trouble? The museum incident? His visits to both of the late demon experts? What confession might appease everybody, get him back to work, without a reprogramming session in a nut house? He'd skip any talk of monsters and murder, of course, blame it all on alcohol; that'd be the way to go. He'd done all he could to help Nestor. He couldn't do a thing, no matter what, to help Ruzicki.

Buried in thought, Ben paid no attention when the woman sat down beside him. Had she been stark naked, he wouldn't have given a damn. But she wasn't naked, merely exotic. He wasn't even paying attention to the island accent when she said, "I am almost finished."

Ben stirred. "What?"

"I am almost finished."

He frowned. A caveman by nature, he'd never gotten used to the idea of women hitting on guys. With opening lines like hers, he never would. "Congrats," he said, staring at his glass. "Good luck."

She wasn't taking the hint. "I am a creature of habit."

Ben sighed. Whatever she was after, he didn't feel like providing it. He didn't like riddles. Just then, he didn't like anything. "Look, sweetheart," he said. "I'm not a social drinker; I'm a drunk. I don't know what you're talking about. And I don't care. Try another stool."

She grabbed his forearm like the snap of an iron trap. Gasping at the violence and pressure, Ben tried uselessly to pull away. He almost cried out when her nails grew to claws before his eyes and dug into his flesh. He clenched his teeth as his hand went numb, and envisioned crushed bones. He looked up, giving the stranger the attention she wanted. As quickly as she'd snatched him, she released her grip. Ben grabbed the bar to keep from falling. Then he grabbed napkins to tamp the bleeding.

She was exactly as described by witnesses; dark, beautiful, exotic. No one had mentioned 'damned scary'. "As I said, I am a creature of habit." She lowered her sunglasses, staring. Ben started again. Her eyes were a brilliant yellow-green with veins of blood shot all around. His reflection in them glinted upside down. All doubts vanished; this was Ruzicki's Vong, Poni's legendary monster, an aswang in human form. He gulped air. She smiled, amused, and slipped her glasses back on.

"I've been watching you," she said. "From early on. Watching you pick up after me. Watching you squirm. Watching you dig for answers like a mutt for a bone. It seems pointless. You are a slow learner, so I will tell you plainly. I eliminate those in my way. You saw what happened to the soldier's wife and child." She licked her luscious lips. "You know what happened to the women in their junk shop. Yet you and your friends try to make trouble for me."

She ran a fingernail along his arm. Ben jerked it back. Vong laughed. "Someone visited me tonight. Was it you?"

Ben stared without answering. Vong grabbed her sunglasses to remove them again. "No!" he said, too loudly. He had no desire to see her eyes again. He cleared his throat and quietly said, "I wouldn't know where to visit you."

"No matter. When I find him, he'll die. For now, you need to know that I know many things. I know you have committed yourself to my destruction. I know you should reconsider. Because I also know your little bitch cop has a bun in the oven." She laughed. "I'll be finished here soon. In the meanwhile, mind your own business and maybe – maybe – I'll leave your brat alone."

She paused as a young couple, the woman coincidentally and obviously pregnant, passed behind them. Vong ogled her and loudly exclaimed, "Yummy."

Instantly livid, the man turned back, and despite the woman's attempt to stop him, came at Ben and Vong. "You freaks got a fucking problem?" he demanded.

"No," Ben said.

Vong snatched the man by the throat with the same grip Ben had felt. She jerked him up against the bar like a rag doll. Ben jumped up. Tightening her grip, Vong hissed, "Sit down." The man was turning blue. "Sit back down," she demanded.

Ben did as he was told.

Ignoring the woman's cries, and those of the staring patrons around the bar, Vong asked, "What should I do with him?"

"Why not let him go?"

Vong smiled. "Why not?" She opened her fingers and the man fell, gasping, grabbing his throat as he hit the floor. The terrified woman was still shouting as she helped her man to his feet. Vong laughed.

The couple backed away and beat it for the door. The others in the bar continued to stare, but now that her hands were free, nobody said a word. The bartender downed a shot then, decided, marched toward them. "You," he said, addressing Vong. "You need to go too."

She rose, ran her hands down her dress, and offered the bartender an unsettling smile he would remember for a lifetime. "Remember what I said," she told Ben. She started to leave, but turned back. "I forgot to mention. I left your lady cop a little something… somewhere… Tell her I said, 'Happy Easter'." She smiled again and left the bar.

"A friend of yours, Ben?" the bartender asked.

"No. The opposite."

"She's gorgeous but…" He rubbed the gooseflesh on his arms. "She gave me the fucking willies."

Ben couldn't have agreed more. He was still there, holding a Coke in trembling hands, trying to comprehend the threatening visit, wishing he could talk to Erin, when his cell phone vibrated in his pocket. When he saw Erin's name he couldn't flip it open fast enough. He nervously croaked a hello.

"Ben! I need you. I need your help."

Dating a cop had its ups and downs. He'd been thinking about the 'downs' for days. A definite 'up' was her ability to give directions. Ben found Erin where she said she'd be, a dark intersection in the Port District. He saw her unmarked car nosed to the curb with its rear tires a foot too far into the street. He slowed and parked. Then he saw a familiar bike and the picture came into focus.

Rickie Savage sat on his prat, on the sparse grass, his feet dangling over the curb beneath Erin's headlights. She was crouched, comforting him. He held his arm, then his knee, touched his lip, then his swollen brow, and rubbed his elbow, tearfully visiting each and every "Owwee" before starting over. Ben grabbed the First Aid kit from his trunk.

"I think he's all right," Ben said, after a quick assessment. "But the body hides injuries. He needs X-rays." He hesitated. "The best way to get him to the hospital is to call an a-m-b-u-l—"

That was as far as he got before Rickie went ape. He started to bleat, then tried to stand and would have made it, had Erin not been there to corral him. She scowled at Ben. "He's afraid of ambulances."

"I know. I've had him in mine. Okay."

"Don't worry, Rickie," Erin said. "No ambulance. You come with me. We'll go together in a police car. How would that be?"

That, apparently, was fine. He sat back down while Ben finished with his patch job. Then he happily allowed the detective and the firefighter to help him into Erin's squad and off to the hospital they went. Ben followed in his car.

Thirty – Four

Rickie Savage didn't mind at all being seen by the Emergency Room doctor. He had all kinds of great things to touch, play with, and talk about. Above all, Rickie wanted to know what each item cost, including the bandages being wrapped around his head.

Outside of the room and down the hall, Erin apologized to Ben, who didn't catch it all because he was apologizing to Erin. Emergency responders, they agreed, could handle any emergencies but their own. They further agreed they needed each other, and that their baby needed them together. It might have been old-fashioned, but there it was. Not only was it time to get together, it was time to tell their families and friends they were a couple.

The one area where their minds didn't meet was on the cause of their city's traumas. Erin was still looking for a perpetrator. Ben, with a bandaged arm for proof, no longer had any doubts; he knew the enemy to be a demon. The easiest way to convince Erin, he realized, was to empty the bag, including a confession. "One weapon used against aswang is the tail of a manta ray. With it you whip the demon into submission."

"That's what you were doing in the aquarium tank? You were going to cut the tail off the manta?"

"I did not, out of the blue, decide to maim an exotic sea creature. People are being killed all over town. My best friend's wife and baby were killed. Everyone that's tried to help me has been killed. Now you and I are being threatened. I'm not crazy. And I'm not an animal hater. I'm trying to do the best I can with a lot of people insisting they're depending on me. God knows what you've been thinking."

"I don't know what I think. My job has gotten crazy. My boyfriend is out of his mind; no offense."

"None taken."

"Morning sickness is killing me. My hormones are shot to hell. And in my hometown of Duncan, Iowa, I'm asked to believe some creature from Hell—"

"The Philippines, actually."

"Have it your way. Is committing serial murder."

"Do you think we can get the tail of a manta?"

"Benjamin Court, are you out of your damned mind?"

"I thought you believed me? I thought you were going to help me?"

"I am going to help you. I don't know yet if I believe, but I'm going to help. I'll risk life and limb to help you. But you can forget the manta tail, Ben, or I'll kill you myself. Think of something else."

"That's twice you've threatened to kill me."

"I know and I'm sorry. I'm going to be sad if you make me do it." She looked at the waiting area clock, then looked at her watch as if she couldn't believe her eyes. She kissed Ben on the forehead. "I've got to get to work." She kissed him on the lips. The surroundings prevented passion, but when it ended, Ben had no doubt about her restored affection. "Promise me you'll stay with Rickie. And get him home safe."

"I will. If you promise not to take any crazy chances."

She held up three fingers. "Scout's honor."

He grinned. "You weren't a scout." His face grew grim. "Promise me you will not search for this killer, for Vong, alone."

"I promise." She kissed him hard, clutching his shirt front with her left hand. She couldn't use both; the fingers of her right hand were crossed behind her back.

Erin was not a belligerent and she didn't have a death wish. She would not break a promise made to Ben. But the crossed fingers kept it from being made, didn't they? She had no desire to hunt Ben's monster on her own. But it was her duty to find and stop the killer. She couldn't tell her co-workers they were hunting a demon. That meant she had to hunt alone. As she had no notion what the night would bring, she had no choice but to punt her promise to Ben.

Perhaps he sensed her equivocation. As they walked to the door, he said, "Erin, let's blow this pop stand."

"You mean leave?"

"Just pick up and go."

"I can't," she said.

"I know. Neither can I." He took her hand. "But if we do ever need to escape; remember the plan."

Erin kissed him, took his waist and started to slow dance, singing, "My kind of town, Chicago is. My kind of town, Chicago is." Ben joined her. "My kind of razzmatazz. And it has, all that jazz…"

"Hey," he whispered. "Do me a favor. Pray to the virgin when the tik-tik sings."

Erin grimaced. "I'm a Baptist."

"Yeah. I know. Well… Be careful when the tik-tik sings."

"I can do that."

Rickie was in good hands. That was one worry down but there were plenty left. She still couldn't swallow Ben's theories whole, no matter what he'd seen at The Well, no matter what she'd seen at the hospital. She had no choice, she figured, but to return to the Port District and see what she could see. She also had no choice, she figured, but to turn her squad radio off. Erin wanted nothing to do with the mayor's next press conference and couldn't explain her mission in the Port, if the chief asked. So why give him the chance to ask? She was all-in now and bound to do the one thing she'd promised Ben she wouldn't. She had to search for signs of this Vong, the one Ben insisted committed these murders.

She started her search from her lookout on the world, the point of Eagle Point Park. Erin climbed from her car, thinking again about Ben's story. If Vong was what Ben thought she was, she was also the lady Rickie had seen; the lady who'd put her legs back on and jumped the fence, whatever that meant. She passed the Duncan Memorial tower and thought about the scare she'd received during her jog the morning of the Garfield explosion; the morning all this had started. She remembered the fright, the flight, and the 'tick, tick, tick'. What of the big bat? And the ticky bird? What did bats and birds do? Where did they go? Where could they be found? A cave? A nest? An aerie? A perch? She reached the bluff and leaned on the fence overlooking the city. She asked herself the ridiculous question: If I was a bird, where would I build my nest? A tree? A pole? And if a bat? Did bats nests? High like a bird? What in Duncan came close to a skyscraper? Nothing at all. The hotel downtown? The old brewery where Ben lived? The Ulysses Grant Bridge? The Wisconsin and Iowa bridge? The golden dome on the City Hall? Several there had bats in their belfries, but bats in their dome?

A big bat and a ticky bird. That's what Rickie had said. Erin's cynical mind tried to insist it was just Rickie. Tried to insist she forget it and solve the murders the old fashioned way. But that wasn't fair. It wasn't smart either. Rickie was mentally challenged, he wasn't an idiot and he wasn't crazy. He got around as much as the police. He saw and remembered. He had the mind of a twelve-year-old, yes, but a sharp twelve-year-old all the same. Now, if a sharp twelve-year-old saw something he called a big bat or something he called a ticky bird? What had he seen? And where did he see it?

She thought of Linnea Keddy atop the Opera House. Nothing about the scene indicated anything unnatural lived there, the body had just been left. By a big bat? By a bird? Or, if Ben was right, by a Philippine demon? If not the Opera House, perhaps another roof? Maybe, but if so, Erin was screwed. It would take the department days, weeks, to search every roof in town. Alone, it would take her a year. Where could a bird hide a big nest without being seen? When the answer dawned,

Erin could have kicked herself. She jumped back in her car, headed down the bluff, and toward the north end of the Port District. She followed Seventh Street out, turned onto Commercial, and eased her cruiser along the railroad tracks toward one of the lonely Mississippi points where the Shot Tower stood sentinel by the river.

One of the last of its kind, the Shot Tower was built in 1856 to produce cheap round lead ball (shot) ammunition for the military. A 120-foot-tall tapered column, the tower was nineteen feet square at the base, thirteen at the cap, with a hollow interior thirteen feet square top to bottom. Lead was melted, hoisted to the top, and poured through screens of differing gauges. The liquid metal drops rounded as they fell and splashed into water vats below to cool instantly as round shot. The death of the musket spelled the death of the facility, but in a city all about history, the Duncan Shot Tower lived on.

Erin stared up at the landmark; a perfect home for a nest. And, just then, no one would have known. A major renovation had been started and the tower closed to tourists for weeks. The work was half-finished, but problems with grant funds had developed, and the site stood temporarily abandoned. It's normally tapered shadow was deformed by scaffolding to its full height on two sides, and in the moonlight, the tower looked a misshapen parody of itself. Flashlight in hand, Erin slipped under the yellow warning tape around the perimeter. The door was locked but that meant nothing. A big bat could fly. Erin couldn't, but she could climb. She slid the light into her belt and started up the scaffolding.

As she climbed, Erin was suddenly reminded of Horatio Shane and the late detective's fear of heights. How he would have hated this. Then again, given the choice of being where she was or being where he was… Erin told herself to knock it off. A philosopher she wasn't. Besides, thinking of Shane had returned her to thoughts of Peter Chandler. Where was her friend and mentor?

Eighty feet in the air, where the gray Galena Dolomite of the tower base met the soft red brick of the uppermost stories, Erin found a window broken in. It was more than the result of a vandal's rock. From the shattered and missing glass, and marks on the frame, someone – or something – had made entry. It was a textbook situation for backup. But she wasn't there, officially, and Chief Musselwhite wouldn't recognize chasing monsters as part of her job. She was on her own. Erin flashed her light inside and found the wood stairs she knew switch backed up from the base. She climbed through.

The cool of night grew cold within. A draft rose up the ancient column past Erin. She flashed the light down to the entrance, eighty feet below, to the working floor with the shot bath cordoned off to keep tourists from turning it into a wishing well. The depth, the darkness, and her recent nausea met. Erin gripped the wall and concentrated on her breathing. The dizziness passed in time for the so-near square walls to close around her like a tomb. *Come on,* she thought, *vertigo and claustrophobia?* Everything about being pregnant was a bed of roses! She turned her thoughts back to her mission, and turned her light, following the stairs into the darkness above. She stopped suddenly, gasped, and caught the rail. Something was hanging from the grate in the top of the tower.

Terror welled up as the ridiculous phrases *big bat* and *ticky bird* suddenly found life in her world. A moan escaped the detective's lips. She willed a quick recovery, and training the light on the hanging object, strained to see. Then Erin's hopes vanished. It was not a bat, or a bird, or a monster hanging in the tower. It was a man, suspended by his feet; it was Detective Peter Chandler.

Numb with the realization, on instinct alone, Erin raced up the stairs. But as she drew near, her training kicked in. She stopped, drew her weapon, and passed the light over the scene scanning for dangers. Convinced she was alone, Erin reached the grate, Chandler, and a sobering conclusion at the same time. Ben was right, this was the work of a monster. More than that, Vong had been telling the truth when she'd delivered her Easter greeting to Ben in The Well. She had left a little something... somewhere. Erin had just found it.

Thirty – Five

Love was a pain in the ass. Respecting the rules for cell phone use in the Emergency exam rooms, Ben had picked up the in-house phone, lied to the hospital operator (to Rickie's giggles) about a phony affiliation with the police, and got an outside line. He'd been trying to call Erin since, without success. It had happened a hundred times, before their relationship bloomed, and he hadn't given it a second thought. Now he and Erin were in love, and she was pregnant with his child, and she was out there in the streets with whatever else was out there – not being able to reach her was making him crazy. So, like a crazy person, he added both her apartment and his to the list of numbers she wasn't answering. He slammed the phone down with a snarl.

Rickie lay comfortably on his wheeled cot, watching cartoons and waiting on the doctor.

Ben joined him but couldn't concentrate. Soon he was back on the phone, trying Erin's office again. No answer. He called the PD front desk and got a repeat of, "Detective Vanderjagt is unavailable. If you'll leave your name and number." *Yada. Yada.* When they transferred him to the chief's office, Ben really started to worry. A voice, not Musselwhite's, demanded his name. Something was wrong. Either something had happened they were not telling or they had no clue where Erin was. Ben gently hung up, controlling his panic by muttering, "Erin, where are you?"

"Pro-ly looking for the big bat," Rickie said.

"What?"

"Pro-ly looking for the big bat. Or the ticky bird," Rickie repeated matter-of-factly. He returned to staring at cartoons.

Ben scowled, annoyed. Then he gave the matter an instant of thought and felt guilty as hell. Rickie was a middle-aged man with a child's mind. He had no part in Erin's silence, whatever the cause. He was just talking or, Ben realized, maybe trying to help. "Do you mean from the cartoon, Rickie?"

He turned from the television to look at Ben as if he were crazy. "No."

Ben grimaced and tried not to laugh. "You know about the big bat and bird?"

"Yes."

"You saw them?"

"Yes."

"Did you tell Erin about them?"

Before he got his answer, the doctor, lantern jaw and lab coat, entered eying an x-ray film against the ceiling lights. He switched to another, and another, then turned his Hollywood smile on Ben. "I don't see any fractures. Looks like he's good to go."

Ben was helping Rickie dress, when his cell phone rang. He nearly dropped it answering. But the nervous excitement was wasted. It wasn't Erin. It was Nestor, from his room upstairs. Ben filled his partner in, complaining, "Erin isn't answering anywhere."

"She's looking for the big bat," Rickie shouted, pulling on his shoes. "I told you. The big bat. The ticky bird. Pro-ly, the lady who takes off her legs."

"What's that?" Nestor asked on the phone.

"Rickie has seen it… them," Ben said, anxious again. "He saw them. And he apparently told Erin all about them. But she didn't tell me."

"She believes it?" Nestor asked. "She's looking for the creature?"

"I don't know if she believes it. I believe it. I met the damned thing and believe me, I believe it. Erin still sounded skeptical. But your answer is, no. She promised she wouldn't go after it alone."

"My God, Ben," Nestor squawked on the other end of the line. "I told you before I know more about you than you do. Apparently I know more about your girlfriend than you do. She's the lead investigator. She'd go after it in a heartbeat."

"What do I do? Damn, Nestor, what do I do?"

"What do you think? You go find her. We both go find her."

Ben glared at the phone. "How are you going to get out?"

"Jesus, Ben," Nestor yelled. "Come get me!"

Erin was in tears. Her attempts to free Chandler's body and get it off the tower grate had failed. It remained dangling a hundred feet above the floor. The last thing she wanted was to accidentally drop it, and alone, she had neither the leverage nor the strength to get it loose and onto the stairs. Worse, she couldn't call for help. To raise an alarm would be to end her search. No one would believe an aswang had killed him. And no other explanation could touch the facts. Ben was right. Nestor was right. She knew it now. A supernatural creature, a demon, was killing people in the Port District.

"I'm so sorry, Peter," she said, choking off the tears. "I have to leave you here right now. I'll get you down, I promise. I'll get you out of here. But I've got to find the thing that did this. I've got to stop it. You taught me the importance of duty and priority; that nothing means more to a cop. You taught me people can understand or get the hell out of the way. I know you understand."

She made her way down to the window, slipped out, and onto the scaffolding. "Okay, you bitch," she told the night sky. "Ready or not, here I come." She started down.

The psych unit was no prison, by any stretch, but patients' peace and safety were jealously guarded and visitors strictly regulated. Ben's 'upsetting' phone call several days earlier had already made him *persona non grata* in the mind, and chart, of Nestor's charge nurse. Getting onto the floor to see him would be difficult. Getting him out of the hospital would be impossible. They needed a plan.

The unit was shaped like a great 'T', a long wing of patients', community, and consultation rooms stretching from the west, intersecting shorter north and south wings at a nurses' station (Four East). The south door, to a fire stairwell, and west doors, to the hospital proper, had keyed locks. The hospital's visitor elevators by-passed the floor. All Four East visitors came and went through an electrically locked door leading to a second set of elevators at the far end of the north wing. Each arriving visitor rang a bell and, once they were seen through a wire-reinforced Lexan panel in the door, were *buzzed* in via a nurses' station control panel. Green and red lights on the panel indicated when the door was secure and a clerk watched it like a hawk. Strike that. According to Nestor, she watched the panel like a humorless three-hundred-pound ogre. Any hope of freeing Nestor meant diverting her attention. Ben needed help.

"What the hell do you want?"

He hadn't expected hugs and kisses when he called Forester's number, but Ben hadn't expected to get his head bitten off either. "Is that any way to talk to a good source?"

"A good source of what? All you've ever brought me is grief. Come to think of it, all you've ever brought anyone is grief."

Ben ignored it. "You've been pestering me for weeks. Now I've got it and I'm offering it to you; the biggest story of your life."

"Please." If he looked like he sounded, Forester's disbelief had become disgust. "One, if you really had anything you wouldn't give it to me. You've proved that. Two, you've got nothing. You're out of the loop, suspended, which means you know nothing, which means you've got nothing."

"How do you ever get a story when you talk so goddamned much?"

"I can fix that."

"Don't hang up," Ben shouted.

"All right. I'm listening. What's your story?"

"You'll get it. But first, I need a favor."

"How are you in a position to ask a favor? Your own mother wouldn't do you a favor."

"I'm not asking, Mark. I've got the story that's going to make you the big reporter you've dreamed of being. Yours, exclusively. Not from the front row; from the stage. You're in the show. For this story, you will do one huge, easy favor without negotiation. I'm counting three, then I'm hanging up and calling Jamie 'Bigmouth' Watts and making her famous instead. One. Two—"

"All right. What's the favor?"

Ben told him.

Outside of the movies, complex covert plans usually collapsed under their own weight. When telling lies or pulling fast ones, simple was always better. So too, when sneaking a friend out of a psych ward.

One quick, three-way conference call arranged it. Ben and Rickie waited, Rickie wrapped in a blanket, in a borrowed wheelchair, between the electric north door and the visitors' elevators. Nestor waited, on the opposite side of the same door, in his room twenty feet down the hall. Forester waited, in the center stairwell, outside the keyed door nearest the nurses' station. When a legitimate visitor was buzzed out, they all went to work.

Ben smiled, said hello, and grabbed the door as the visitor passed, preventing its closing. He spoke into his cell phone, "See you." Forester took his cue, hung up, and started banging the hell out of the stairwell door. Nestor, loitering in his doorway and holding a small wooden chest, watched the nurses vacate their station for the hubbub. The ogre didn't move. Thanks to Nestor, they hadn't expected she would. But, in what for her was an explosion of frenzied activity, she turned her head from the panel to the to-do. A nurse unlocked the stairwell door and Forester, a professional question asker, started in, spreading manure and raising enough cane to get everyone's attention. Everyone but Nestor, who walked calmly and quickly out the open north door. He traded places with Rickie, and Ben and Rickie rolled him into the elevator and down. They didn't stop until they reached Ben's car. Forester joined them in the lot a few minutes later, chewed out, but none the worse for wear. He climbed into the rear, beside Nestor, with Rickie and Ben gawking back from the front seat.

"I promised you a story," Ben said.

"What story?"

"It's coming. We had to get our team together first."

"What team?" Forester said, with a laugh. "A washed-up reporter conspires with a suspended firefighter, and a coin-slot checker to help a second out-of-work fireman escape a psych unit. Okay, we're the Justice League. Where's my Pulitzer? You owe me a story. Give!"

Ben started the car. "I'll empty the bag on the way. We've got to get to the Port District now."

"Not yet," Nestor exclaimed.

"We have no time to lose."

"Ben, Erin's after that thing. When we find her, we're going to find that thing. It's not going to do us or Erin any good if we're unprepared," Nestor insisted. "We won't be helping the city, or Angelina, or any of the other victims, for that matter. We'll only have one shot. We have to be ready."

"What are you guys talking about?" Forester asked.

Ben ignored the reporter, asking Nestor, "What do you recommend?"

"I know where we can get a manta tail."

"That's not funny, you son of a bitch."

"Sorry. Forget it. But we need the stuff on that list. As much of it as we can come up with quickly."

"Fine," Ben said. "Where do we start?"

Nestor held up the small chest he'd carried with him. He handed it forward to Rickie. "Here."

Ben nodded and Rickie opened it. The chest was full of gray ashes.

"Ashes?" Ben asked.

"Blessed by a priest," Nestor said. "They were on the list, weren't they?"

"Yes. But... where did you get them?"

"I called my priest; told him I needed something tangible to help me through my difficulty. I asked him to bless some ashes and bring them to me."

"Didn't he think you were nuts?"

"I called him from a psych unit, Ben. Of course he thought I was nuts. He wanted to bring me a rosary. I told him I was afraid the humanist staff members would make it difficult for me if they knew I was religious; that I felt awash in a sea of evil. That got him on my side. Nobody resists a conspiracy. You were too cheap to spring for them when you had your chance. There you go, blessed ash."

"Great," Ben said. "But I was too cheap to buy a copper stake too. So we're still screwed."

"Make one."

Everyone stared at Rickie.

"That's a fine idea, Rickie, but we don't have any copper."

"A penny has copper," Rickie said. "A penny's got copper. Nickel's got nickel. Dime's got tin."

"Tin?"

"Dime's got tin. Quarter's got—"

"Got it," Ben said. "There's metal in coins." He turned to Nestor. "Is there still copper in pennies?"

"He knows there's tin in dimes and you're asking me? What do I know?"

"Doesn't matter." Ben put the car in gear and pulled out of the stall. "There aren't any banks open. There's no way to get pennies."

"I got pennies," Rickie said.

"I don't think there's much copper in a penny anymore."

Undeterred, Rickie said, "Got lots of pennies."

Ben checked the rear view mirror for help. Nestor and Forester stared, refusing to throw a bone from the peanut gallery. "Rickie, to make a stake… You'd need to melt a thousand pennies. Heck, who knows, you might need to melt ten thousand pennies!"

"I got sixty-two thousand, eight hundred, twelve pennies."

Ben hit the brakes, skidding. Like animatronic dummies, all three turned to Rickie, the child-like, middle-aged man who'd spent five decades riding from phone booth, to soda box, to candy machine, apparently scoring like a Vegas shark. "Sixty-two thousand, eight hundred?" Ben asked.

"Sixty-two thousand, eight hundred, twelve pennies," Rickie repeated matter-of-factly.

The toys turned in Ben's head. "We'll need a torch," he declared. "Cast iron pots, conduit, a sturdy ladle. Coconut oil. Garlic. We need gas cans."

"Walmart!" Nestor shouted.

Ben hit the gas.

With images of Peter Chandler hanging lifeless in the Shot Tower flashing in her splitting head, Erin returned to the Port District intersection where she'd knocked Rickie from his bike. He'd been scared into a panic and she wondered, by what? With no other starting place, she would track him backwards, go where he'd been. She eased her cruiser down the dark street in the direction from which Rickie had come. Two blocks later, she drove under the bypass and into the Port's tourist playground. She passed the hotel and water park, Diamond Ed's tiny inland casino and, nearing the harbor, the river museum.

She thought of Ben making a horse's ass of himself, swimming with the fishes, and shook her head. Then she thought of him responding, the instant she'd called, to help her get Rickie to the hospital, and even now, seeing Rickie safely home. He was a sweetheart, and God, she loved him. But, geez, the guy was nuts. She returned her attention to the Port and her search, pulled up on the quiet street between the museum and the harbor, and climbed from her squad.

What had frightened Rickie so? Where had he been? He saw the big bat. He saw the ticky bird. He saw the lady put her legs on and jump the fence. The fence? Her eyes fell on the tall wooden fence at the back of the river museum. Behind it lay the native displays, wetlands, and the entrance to the dredger steamboat. He saw the lady jump the fence, Erin thought, and he ran off. From where or what? At the hospital, Rickie had said something about the boat or a boat. It was a harbor; boats were hardly in short supply. What boat could Rickie – and the legs – have been aboard? The William T. Greene? What else had he given her? Nothing else. She sighed and scanned the night sky.

Erin worked down the fence line, kicking the slats. Three-quarters of the way down, one popped up. The next two in line did the same. They looked secure but were free at the base. Rickie, it seemed, had a secret entrance. She'd have to remember to give him hell. In the meantime, though she didn't want her brothers and sisters in police and fire there with her, she knew it wouldn't hurt to have them near. She flipped her cell phone, dialed 9-1-1, and when dispatch answered, said, "There is a body in the Shot Tower. There is a body in the Shot Tower." And snapped the phone closed.

Erin pushed the boards to Rickie's secret access and slipped into the museum property.

Thirty - Six

They were the living definition of a *Motley Crew*; Ben, Nestor, and Forester hurrying around Rickie's apartment like decapitated chickens readying themselves to face aswang. The reporter sorted their purchases. Nestor heated one cast iron pan overturned atop another. Copper melted at just under 2,000 degrees, he knew. His propane torch reached 3,600. Rickie scurried about, through a trove of coins, cans, bottles, metals, and rock treasures collected over decades, searching for squirreled away items that matched, or might stand in for, those on their list. Bitching a blue streak, Ben carried bags of pennies to Nestor's workplace in the kitchen.

"He's charging us a penny apiece!"

"Us?" Nestor asked. "You got a mouse in your pocket? They're pennies. They're worth a penny apiece, aren't they?"

"There you go again, giving away my money. I thought we were in this together?"

"We are. Rickie gave us a headquarters, didn't he? After Erin ran him over? Show some gratitude, he could charge two pennies apiece."

"Do you have any idea how much sixty-two thousand, eight hundred pennies comes to?"

Rickie entered carrying a cardboard box. "Sixty-two thousand, eight hundred, twelve pennies," he said, correcting Ben. "Six hundred, twenty-eight dollars, twelve cents."

"See." Ben pouted. "Like it's nothing." He scowled at Nestor. "All that crap compassion you were selling. Poor Rickie. Have you looked around? Televisions, plural. Stereos, CD players, video games, metal detectors. He's richer than Julius Caesar!"

"I haven't looked around," Nestor said. "I've been busy. We're all busy. What the matter with you?"

"I'm worried about Erin!"

"Me too," Nestor said.

"Me too," Rickie said.

"And me," Forester shouted. "One for all and all for Erin."

"I'm sorry," Ben said. "I appreciate you all."

Rickie unloaded his box; a collection of crucifixes, empty glass bottles that had once held perfume, and several fat rolls of stripped Romex wire.

Ben gawked. "Is that copper?"

"Yes," Rickie said. "If you don't want the pennies."

"Forget the pennies." Ben examined a roll. "This will melt faster with no slag. It's just copper."

"Yes." Rickie pulled a scale from the box. "Copper. Seventeen cents an ounce. Two dollars, seventy-eight cents a pound."

For a tourist attraction, the scene was grim. Flickering red and blue lights rupturing the night on a lonely point beside the Mississippi as squad cars, fire apparatus, and the stoic figures who operated each moved somberly about the Duncan Shot Tower. A generator howled on the scaffolding. Cords hung from the broken window and the interior of the civil war relic glowed with floodlight. Shadows danced as Tucker, Arbuckle, and even Pontius, struggled with their burden.

On the ground, Castronovo stepped from the entrance to his brother-in-law nearby. "It's him," the fire chief said. "Chandler. He's long gone. Any ideas?"

"None," Musselwhite replied. "The 9-1-1 call lasted less than five seconds. The dispatchers had to play it back just to get it. All that was said was, 'There is a body in the Shot Tower' twice."

"Now what?"

"Add another file to the pile; begin a new murder investigation. And start by searching for our lead investigator, again." Castronovo looked a question. "Erin Vanderjagt's disappeared. She isn't answering her phone or radio. No one's heard from her."

"Where do you start?"

"We're in the Port District," Musselwhite and Castronovo stepped aside as Pierce and the 'B' Shift gang carried Chandler's covered body past on a stretcher. "It's as good a place to start as any."

Erin thought the same. The murder events, the Garfield explosion, the Opera House, the Fourth Street Elevator, the hospital attacks, the Clock Plaza, the Shot Tower – all had happened in and around the Port District. Rickie's trail led there too, and to the river museum. Hadn't Ben seen it; a shadow on the museum dredger? Hadn't he seen it again recently, the same moving shadow? She'd ignored him and mocked him. Now Erin stood at the river museum, beside the dredger.

The USACOE William T. Greene was a national landmark vessel, the last side-wheel working dredge, used on the Missouri River by the Army Corps of Engineers during World War Two. Tourists could walk the decks and visit the engine room when the museum was open. But it wasn't open now. The dredger sat moored in darkness, with a pilothouse on top looking like a great place for a bird's nest and an engine room below, that Erin felt, might well make a cold black bat cave.

A strange sensation came over Erin as she moved up the gang plank. It wasn't that she felt it move. The boat was 280 feet long, held a crew of forty-nine, and could dredge 80,000 cubic yards of river bottom a day; a one hundred and fifteen-pound woman stepping aboard barely registered. Still, Erin knew she'd left the land, and more, she felt the awe of the unknown in the air and around her. Moonlight glistened on the water but vanished on the flat gray deck as if it was absorbed. She stepped aboard, and with effort, made out the biggest objects, thick bulkheads with heavy inset doors, ladders (stairs to landlubbers) , and as her eyes adjusted to the dark, the smaller, nearer objects; winch cables, piped rails, and signs warning tourists away from roped-off non-public areas.

Where to start, she wondered? Up or down? Nest or cave? Big bat? Ticky bird? Or was she hunting nothing but a wild goose? She'd found Chandler in the highest spot in the river valley, so Erin opted for the nest. She took a deep breath, grasped the rail, and on cat's feet, started up the first starboard stairs. She thought of the crib notes version of island mythology Ben had given her at the hospital, what little she'd committed to memory. She regretted doubting, regretted not taking it more seriously. If it was true, she was unprepared and knew it. But she was there and had a job to do. One stealthy lap around the second deck, seeing and hearing nothing, and she headed up again. She eased her head above the top deck, saw nothing moving, and hurried to the aft stairs of the pilothouse. The large square windows to the fore and sides of the wheelhouse glinted moonlight. The dark window in the aft door reflected her image like a polished mirror. She took a quiet breath and slipped inside. She looked out to see the moon on the still harbor water in the otherwise black port. She saw the scant lights in the Port District and the town beyond. She saw the emergency lights at the Shot Tower and silently rejoiced. Chandler had been found. She pulled her flashlight, trained it low, and flicked it to life. She saw the binnacle, the compass, the tiller controls, but nothing else. Then Erin stiffened as she heard:

Tik. Tik. Tik. Tik. Tik, tik, tik. Tik, tik, tik.

"Great rhythm, but hard to dance to."

Erin spun around, lifting her light to the figure in the doorway; green eyes glinted back. She caught her breath and made out the features of a dark-skinned beauty with long black hair. This was, Erin knew, the long-sought exotic woman. Like an eerie musical score, the ticking continued outside. The woman stepped onto the bridge, and like a runway model, circled slowly around Erin, displaying her wares. She stopped behind the binnacle, said, "I'm Vong," and, reaching to her shoulders, slipped her thumbs beneath the straps of her dress. "You're Erin, Ben's girl. Ben's pretty little girl." She pulled the straps free and let her dress fall to the deck. The cool April breeze hardened Vong's nipples. "You're carrying Ben's baby." Vong inhaled deeply, exhaled with exaggerated satisfaction, and ran a hand across her naked stomach. "Shall I say something pithy like a villain in your American films?" Vong smiled viciously, then pursed her lips. "How about; '*Oohh*. The take-out has arrived'." She laughed. "Or perhaps, 'I think I'll try the soul'."

"That's a good one," Erin said. She drew her Glock and squeezed the trigger.

The semi-automatic barked thirteen times in eight and a half seconds. Thirteen times the slide dissipated the recoil, chambered a new .40 caliber round, and ejected a spent case. A hot casing hit her on the fly leaving a half-moon burn on her cheek. Erin kept firing. The muzzle flashed like lightning, blinding her in the darkness. Vong screamed once, and grunted twelve times more, as her body received Erin's answer. At that range, the bullets that didn't hit bone passed through Vong and shattered the windows behind her. Glass fell like rain.

The shooting stopped. Erin's blindness passed quickly, but in the gun smoke, she still couldn't see. Burnt powder, and the musky scent of a wild animal filled her nostrils. The ringing in her ears ebbed and was replaced by guttural breathing. The smoke began to clear.

Thirty - Seven

Vong lived. A dark fluid, blood-like but not blood, poured from nine bullet wounds in her chest and abdomen, six of them impressively grouped above her left breast. Moaning in pain, reeling, she reached above her head, clutched the metal cage protecting the light bulb, and steadied herself. She gritted her teeth with a wild look in her green eyes.

Then reality vanished as Erin was dragged into a world of foreign legend and superstition.

Vong flexed her arm and howled as she seemed suddenly to grow taller. A moment passed and the stunned detective saw it for the illusion it was. Vong wasn't growing, her abdomen was stretching, stretching, then tearing. In seconds, beyond all reason, she had ripped herself in two at the waist. The screaming head and bullet-ridden torso dangled by her arm like a chimp in a zoo cage, dripping black blood on the still-standing legs she'd left behind.

Erin was so appalled, other changes took place without her noticing. Vong's nails became claws that *clicked* menacingly on the light cover. The flesh on her head and torso turned from exotic brown to sickly green-black, as if she'd been consumed by gangrene. The strands of her straight hair began to undulate like snakes on the Medusa. Coarse hair appeared in patches between the gunshot wounds, on her stomach, breasts, and shoulders. And, even more unbelievably, her torso sprouted wings; foul leathery wings that exploded and grew from her back until, even half-folded on a single-hinged joint, each extended five feet, to the overhead on the left, to the deck on the right as the creature hung cock-eyed from the fixture. The wings shuttered, *thwacked* on the walls, in a space too cramped for flight.

Doubt now was stupid; aswang existed. To say it was to mouth a punch line: There wasn't a lady *and* a big bat. The lady *was* a big bat! To see it was to experience terror. Whatever artist in Hell had designed this beast had done so with infinite care.

The creature's face was worse. The pointed tips of green-black ears jutted from the riot of hair on either side. Her slim nose had blossomed, pugged and flared, into the wet snout of an animal. Her odd top lip stood even more pronounced between green eyes glowing with hatred and a mouth of dingy fangs issuing a growl… that became a shriek… as a long tongue unrolled toward Erin.

Gyrations that should have been death throes became something else entirely. The creature's breasts rose and fell as her chest muscles flexed. Her grip on the light tightened. Her wings flapped a frantic beat on the bulkhead. The tongue rolled in and out like a ludicrous party favor. She gurgled and the same fluid that poured from her wounds bubbled from her lips. She sucked air, she snorted, she hissed. Her muscles rippled up her chest. One of the wounds swelled monstrously, the black blood gushed and the surrounding tissue tore. From beneath the skin, a mushroom-shaped object appeared in the wound, glinted in the stray moonlight, then fell and hit the deck with a dull *clink*. Erin stared in horrified awe.

It happened again. Aswang grunted and flexed. Another wound bloated. An object was ejected to hit the deck. Erin watched wide-eyed as, again and again, the bullets she'd fired into the creature were spit out by muscle contractions. Behind each, the wounds began to heal. The ninth and last projectile hit the deck. The final wound sealed itself. The dark thing leapt for Erin, slapped the gun from her hand, and latched onto her hair. It propelled the detective against an intact port window and smashed the glass out with its shoulder and Erin's head.

Erin was knocked out. And aswang looked out. Beyond the deck, the harbor, outside the museum fence, a junk Impala pulled up. The creature didn't know the others intimately, but it knew Ben and saw him and his companions piling out. It levered itself into the window and pulled Erin up with it. It lifted her, flapped its wings, and took to the air above the deck. Then it descended and landed with its burden on the paddle-box below. Another stroke of its wings and aswang lit on the main deck. It dropped Erin, opened a hatchway door, then dragged her into the darkness.

Barely had the creature vanished with Erin, when Rickie's secret door opened. Ben, Nestor, and Forester slipped through the fence wearing nā lei of garlic bulbs like escapees from an idiots' luau. Forester toted five-gallon gas cans in each hand. Nestor carried gas and his chest of ashes. Both wore civilian clothes with pockets stuffed with accoutrement. Ben wore his turnout coat and a loaded and sagging truck belt with equipment pouches, hand ax, and flashlight dangling. Nestor had teased him about going to a fire. "Fire, hell," Ben replied. "We're going to war."

Rickie waited outside. One meeting with aswang had been enough and he refused to enter the museum again. Everybody understood, Ben assured him, then asked him to guard the fence. Forester told him it was a very important job.

They'd seen the top of the Shot Tower reflecting emergency lights but none of the monster hunters knew why. They'd heard fire and police sirens echoing through the port. What they hadn't heard was Erin emptying her gun into aswang. The sirens prevented it. They heard Erin's scream, breaking glass, and aswang's shrieks after, as they were about to enter the grounds. But they pushed through to silence, no sight or sound of the creature, Erin, or any living thing.

From the bank, they were stunned to see the dredger's pilothouse shot to hell. And all three were frozen in place as they heard the awful song. *Tik. Tik. Tik. Tik-tik. Tik-tik.*

"What did you say?" Nestor muttered. "Pray to the virgin when the tik-tik sings."

Ben pulled his ax. "Come on."

They hurried to the entrance to the William T. Greene, jumped the chain, and ran up the gangway. Ben led, in a crouch, with Nestor and Forester on his heels. They stepped onto the foredeck beneath the towering derrick and advanced less than a dozen steps before Forester pulled up, whispering, "Wait, I'm vibrating." The reporter reached for his pocket.

"You're taking a call now?" Ben growled.

Forester paused at the realization. "No," he said. "I didn't bring my phone." He touched the pocket and looked nervously at the others. He reached in, removed one of Rickie's perfume bottles, and held it up in the moonlight. The coconut oil inside was bubbling. "It works!" he whispered.

"It shouldn't," Ben said. "We never got it blessed."

"I stirred ashes into it," Nestor said. "They were blessed."

The trio stared at the bottle of boiling oil then, as one, turned to stare at the decks above.

"Mark," Ben said. "Nestor and I are going up to the pilothouse. Stay here, will you?"

"Hell no! This is the story you promised me."

"The story comes later. We've got to check the bridge for Erin; you saw the windows. But we don't know she's there. I'm not taking you out of the action. I'm warning you, you may be facing something alone. Watch our backs; shout up a warning if need be. And shout out if you need us."

"It's a very important job," Nestor told him with a wink.

Forester didn't appreciate the humor, but did appreciate the danger. "Fine. But I want my story."

Ben and Nestor hurried quietly aft, carrying lights but not using them. They passed the winch for the derrick, passed the double doors to the engine room, and moved down the walk between the main deck bulkheads and the outboard safety fence (to prevent tourists falling into the harbor). Black windows, reflecting moonlight, watched them pass; both sincerely hoped nothing else did the same.

As they neared the paddle box, Ben and Nestor realized aswang wasn't the only monster aboard. The paddlewheels were monsters too, giants of wood and steel. The dredger originally had two, starboard and port, aft of amidships, each twenty feet in diameter with eighteen gigantic push planks spaced along the shaft. The boxes were steel fenders, supposedly covering the wheels. Supposedly as only the port wheel was there. The paddle box before Ben and Nestor was empty, the starboard wheel removed to the museum's entrance, a sentinel to awe the tourists before they bought their tickets. Ben and Nestor, oil boiling in their pockets, were in awe without it. They found a ladder and started up.

A covered walkway ran round the dark second deck from the pilothouse to an open area aft. The deck had twelve staterooms for the officers and six cabins housing four ranking crewmen each. Each cabin had a door onto the outside deck and another opening into a central passageway. There was an officers' mess, a galley, pantry, crews' mess, crews' bunk room with seventeen bunks and, aft, the crews' head. Anything could have lurked in any one of them. Opting not to search now but to risk the evil behind them, they turned back to the bow and headed up again to the top. There was the pilothouse, forward, the starboard wing and deck covered in shattered glass. Ben stepped up. Nestor grabbed him, signaling caution. It was a lesson learned in Fire Academy: Safety first. You can't help if you're dead. Observe, make a plan, then put your ass into it. Ben nodded. He pulled out his bottle. The coconut oil inside was boiling like a teapot ready to sing. Ben started forward again, slowly, this time with his partner.

They inched up to the aft door together, heard nothing, then flashed their lights inside. The bridge was a shambles, broken glass, spent casings, and black splashes of... something, on the floor. "Damn, what's that smell?" They entered and flashed their lights forward, saw Erin's gun on the deck in front of the binnacle and, behind it, deliciously golden brown from bare feet, to a neatly-trimmed triangle of pubic hair, to gorgeously flared hips, stood an absolutely inviting pair of legs. There... the invitation ended. From the waist up, the body was missing. Across the waist, viscera oozed beneath a gelling surface of pink muscle, white bone and fat tissue, and maroon, yellow and brown internal organs, all bathed in the inky muck the creature used for blood.

"What the hell is that?"

Ben and Nestor both spun to the voice. Forester stood gawping in the doorway behind them.

"Don't do that!" Nestor barked.

"That," Ben said, pointing, "is your story."

Nestor wasn't through. "Why are you up here?"

"I heard—" Forester hesitated, swallowed his spit. "There's something below. I don't know what. But there's something down there... on the main deck. Inside the ship."

"I'm going," Ben said. "You know what to do here."

"Wait." Nestor opened his chest of blessed ash. "Take a handful."

Ben emptied a pouch on his belt, dropped a rope and spanner to the deck, and refilled it with ashes. He took a crucifix offered by Forester, tucked it behind his Saint Christopher pin in an inside pocket of his coat, and started for the door again.

"Ben..." Nestor began.

Ben turned back. "It's okay, Paco. You guys take care of those disgusting things." He pointed at the legs. "Then come find us. We'll go for coffee. Erin can buy." He left.

Nestor and Forester turned to Vong's lower half, bubbling and stinking with evil life. "What do we do with them?" the reporter asked.

Nestor scooped a handful of ash and stepped forward. "Make it so the bitch can't use them." He sifted the ash across the pulsing table top of Vong's waist. The viscera began to boil and smoke, and though he wouldn't have thought it possible, stink more than before. Forester dropped another crucifix in the center of the bubbling mess and backed away.

Nestor nodded. "Let her sit on that."

The William T. Greene had no below decks. As the boat was a dredger, often requiring operation in shallow water, it was a massive flat bottom boat with no external keel. The engine and boiler room were on the main deck. The engine room was entered by way of two sliding doors in the forward face of the superstructure, to port and starboard; and in the rear bulkhead, to port and starboard. The boiler room, aft, was entered through the engine room.

Back on the main deck, Ben stood at the forward, starboard doors, listening. Forester was right. From the depths of the black engine room, Ben could hear movement and, he was certain, a sickening occluded breathing. With one hand on his ax and the other on his light, Ben slipped inside.

Thirty - Eight

The engine room extended from the front of the superstructure to aft of the middle of the boat and looked as dark and felt as deep as Poe's famous pit. A finger of moonlight stealing in behind him, and a thin sliver of the same stealing in from the windows in the port doors opposite, were all Ben had by which to see. He had his flashlight but still he hesitated using it. The sounds of breathing, of movement had stopped. Stealthily he veered left, around the volute centrifugal dredge pump, and slowly, moved aft around the triple-expansion steam engine that powered the pump. He paused by the control banks, beside the rows of colored handles, beneath the maze of steam, water, and oil gauges and the pilothouse bells, used in their day to inform the engineer of the captain's desires for speed and direction. Slow breathing himself, straining ears for sound and eyes for sight of anything – Erin or aswang – to the port, then the starboard propulsion engines atop their massive steel cylinder timbers. Each powered one of the sidewheels, independent of the other, making the dredger maneuverable but giving the monster twice as many places to crouch. The cylinders, twenty and forty inches in diameter, pushed pistons and moved the pitman rod with an eighty-four-inch stroke to turn cranks and paddlewheels. More, spaced throughout the dark beyond the engines were the auxiliary machines, steam turbine generating sets, a water distilling plant, and a wastewater filter. All surrounded by an overhead crane system for maintenance. Point was, there were a million places to hide. To Ben's shock, aswang wasn't hiding.

He heard it first, the guttural breathing again, then turned past the starboard engine to see the glint of its damnable eyes. Even in the dark, it saw him too, for it hissed its annoyance. For all Ben knew, with the reflective stripes on his turnout coat, he might look like neon in the demon's eyes. Whatever it saw, the creature wasn't afraid. Wanting the same, Ben clicked his flashlight on.

The monster lay atop Erin on the floor, wings stroking the air with delight. It hissed again at the firefighter, extended its revolting tongue, then turned back and pointed the tongue at Erin's belly, ready to strike. Ben screamed like a madman and ran at them. The creature raised a defensive claw as he drew near. Ben raised a handful of ash and hurled a gray cloud into the creature's face.

Aswang shrieked and rolled off Erin. Howling in anguish, it scurried into the dark to port. Ben pulled out Forester's crucifix, aimed it to where the creature vanished. Low growls answered. With the crucifix extended, watching the depths of the engine room with one eye, Ben bent over Erin, tapped her cheeks and called her name. Instead of coming round, Erin burst awake, screaming, struggling, and startling the life out of him. He grabbed her, told her who he was, held her until she quieted, all the time shielding them both, or hoping he was, with the crucifix.

They heard the irregular flapping of wings. They heard the periodic click of claws on the steel plate. They heard the low growl and guttural breathing. They saw black move against black in the depths, and a flash of leather and hair, as aswang scuttled from its old hiding place behind one machine to a new hiding place behind another.

"Erin!"

The cry was Rickie's. Ben looked back to see him, breathless, just inside the engine room doors in the starboard bow. He'd evidently heard Erin's cries, had overcome his own fear and come to her rescue. Ben found himself surprised by a sudden feeling of pride. Still watching the depths, crucifix aloft, he lifted Erin to her feet and walked her back toward the doors.

"Rickie. Rickie, it's Ben." The creature growled. Crucifix poised, Ben kept moving. "I'm coming your way. Meet me. Help Erin. Help her out of here."

Rickie met them by the control panel.

"Good man," Ben said, handing Erin off. "Help her off the boat." With a nod, supporting Erin's weight, Rickie started slowly away.

Ben turned back to the darkness. Holding his flashlight with two fingers, brandishing the crucifix with the same hand, the other gripping his truck belt between his ax and his pouch of ash, Ben found an odd clash of culture and religion in his head. There he was, like some kind of half-assed exorcist, chasing a Philippine demon in the dark, wishing he was Kali, the Hindu goddess of death, that he might have six hands, and six weapons, and dreaming – though he'd never confess it – that he'd gotten that manta tail. Sue him. Now that Erin was on her way out, he could admit it, he was scared shitless. Time for a little wet on red.

"Vong," he called out. He had no idea what he intended to say. Had no clue if talking to a demon was a wise move. He had to do something to steady himself. "Vong."

Aswang replied with a hiss and a beating of wings. Unsatisfied, Ben called "Vong!" and began seeding handfuls of ash into the dark. That brought a shriek and tumultuous movement. He turned in time to see the wretched thing half-scuttling, half-flying just above the deck into the boiler room. Ben studied the door, looking like a cave entrance, double-checked the homemade copper rod in his pocket, and followed aswang in.

Rickie had just reached the doors with Erin, headed out, when she saw Ben disappear into the dark. She tried to go back. Rickie refused, ordering Erin out. "Ben said."

Erin called to Ben, tried to argue. Having none of it, Rickie held her in place. "No," he cried. He shook his head like a dog shedding water.

"You got a baby in you. Ben said you got to get away. Ben said. Ben said. Ben said."

"All right, Rickie. It's all right. We'll do what Ben said." She let him lead her out onto the deck.

Nestor and Forester had returned to the main deck, and having heard the commotion in the engine room, and hoping to get in on Ben's 'war', had reclaimed their gas cans and hustled them around the paddle box to the engine room's aft starboard doors. They weren't sure how they could join in but wanted to be ready when the opportunity arrived.

Tik. Tik. Tik-tik. Tik-tik.

They heard it at the same instant. Nestor and Forester stared at each other, then turned together to the starboard bridge wing above. Perched on the rail, backlit by the moon, watching them with glowing eyes as if they were crippled rabbits, sat a great bird of prey, unlike anything either had ever seen. It had the proud breast of a Bald Eagle, but blazing in red feathers with black streaks, and the naked slanted head of a Black Vulture, giving it the look of a hooded executioner. The tip of its otherwise long black beak glinted silver like the keen edge of a blade. *Tik. Tik. Tik. Tik-tik. Tik-tik.*

"Pray to the virgin," Nestor whispered.

Forester started to complete it for him. "When the tik-tik—" The reporter cut himself off with a shout. The bird had spread its wings and was diving.

Stalking, and no doubt being stalked, Ben stabbed the darkness with his flashlight, moving through the metal maze of oil tanks, boiler drums, fire boxes, the bases of the boat's two huge smokestacks and, high and low, water and steam pipes. State of the art genius in 1934 but, after eighty years, a plumber's nightmare. Somewhere in the depths of the boiler room another nightmare waited. It didn't wait long.

As Ben eased past an oil tank that had once fed the furnace, aswang leapt from the dark behind him. Hissing and growling, it lashed with keenly sharp claws, slashing Ben's face and severing his lei before he knew it was there. Shouting, in a shower of garlic bulbs, eyes shut against the spritz of blood, Ben tripped backwards. He lost his crucifix on the way down, heard it bounce off metal and slide away, and landed with his ax beneath him. Aswang, crazy with rage and bloodlust, came after him.

On his back, kicking like a child to hold the demon off, Ben knew he'd reached the point of no return. The list of things that mattered more than he had grown too large; Erin, their baby, his ragtag crew of monster hunters, the people and property of the city of Duncan, not to mention his stupid promises. If he had to go, the Philippine bitch from Hell was going with him. Ben dug into a pocket of his coat and pulled out the hand grenade he'd stolen from Erin's office. Of course, he'd swiped it on an urge, without reason. Hell, he hadn't even believed in the monster then. It was not the first urge he'd followed that had gotten him into hot water. He just hoped Erin would remember, he'd never denied taking it.

Ben held it up, giving the aswang slashing at his boots an eyeful. The demon halted its attack. It even backed up. Ben loved Erin. He loved life and had no desire to leave it. He wasn't hero material. But he had promises to keep. And he'd damn well had enough. With a white-knuckled grip on the grenade's handle, he pulled the pin.

Following their escape to the main deck, Rickie was making a bee-line for the gangway when Erin heard an odd series of noises and pulled up. She looked to the stern and caught a flash in the moonlight. Rickie kept trying to drag her toward the bow, but Erin was regaining her senses and wasn't having it. She snatched Rickie's hands to stop him pulling and pointed to the sky. Above the paddle box was the bright red tik-tik, flapping its wings madly, with a body clutched in its talons.

Panicked, without thinking, Erin screamed, "Ben!" and pulled a backup weapon from a holster on her ankle. She took off aft, down the companionway, around the empty paddle box. On the stern side of the fender, she slid to a shooting stance, and drew a bead – as best she could in the gloom – on the head and breast of the giant bird. She didn't want to hit Ben; if it was Ben. She didn't want to hit anyone. But whoever it was, the creature had one talon clutching his throat, the other his chest. It had to be stopped and she couldn't wait. Erin started shooting.

The tik-tik bucked in the air, squawked, and dropped the body. It fell like a rock, hit the deck like a sack of sand, and from the attitude of its landing could be nothing but a corpse. Crying, Erin ran to the crumpled form, rolled it to the scant light, and saw Nestor with his throat torn out. Horror then – forgive her – relief, hit Erin. It was a dizzying shock, but her heart sang because it wasn't Ben. But it was Nestor. Erin wanted to cry, to break down. Angelina, the baby, now Nestor, a family destroyed. Overwhelmed, Erin didn't see the tik-tik, despite being full of her lead, descending on her.

Screaming, incoherent but loud, Rickie arrived on the run and jumped between the tik-tik and Erin. He pulled off his necklace of garlic bulbs and, using them like a whip, slapped at the monster's talons. He pulled out a coil of wire, exposed the end, and when the creature fluttered down, repeatedly stabbed it with copper. Rickie shouted the whole while, giving the tik-tik hell.

Dazed, Erin looked the deck over. Nestor was dead. Forester lay, maybe dead, against the engine room bulkhead. In the door, gas cans lay ripped open with a river of fuel running into the dark. Erin saw it all and smelled the heavy odor of gas but none of it seemed to register.

The tik-tik shoved Rickie aside with a swipe of its talon, and flapping madly, dove at Erin. The detective, out of instinct rather than thought, hit the deck beneath the monster's grasp. The tik-tik flew over, past Forester and through the double doors, into the engine room.

Bleeding, Rickie lifted Erin out of the pool of gas. Stifling in the fumes wafting from the engine room, he helped her to her feet. Neither of them remained standing long.

The explosion shattered every window on the main deck and most on the deck above. The tik-tik, still flapping madly on its way out of the engine room, was caught in the eruption. A bright orange ball of flame chased it out through the double doors, and overtook the creature over the top of Erin and Rickie. The bird shrieked and burst into flames. Frantically flapping, the tik-tik rose to the top of the smokestacks, then plunged into the harbor.

Erin found a reserve of strength she didn't know she possessed. Between the last flight of the tik-tik and a second equally impressive mushroom of rolling fire, the detective changed places and lifted the stunned and burned Rickie. She hurried him to the fence at the edge of the deck and shoved him over. She dove in after him as the wood frame of the William T. Greene went up in flames.

Rickie popped to the surface slapping the water and shouting for help. "I've got you! I've got you," Erin cried, slipping an arm around his shoulders and dog-paddling to shore. Still in the museum enclosure, she dragged Rickie onto the heavily-weeded bank of the wetlands display. She took a breath then dragged him, sputtering, away from the water. She propped Rickie against the fence. "It's all right. Don't be afraid."

"The boat gone?"

"It is Rickie. The boat's gone."

"Nestor okay? Mark okay?"

Erin shook her head, fighting back tears. "They're gone too, Rickie. Nestor is with Angelina and their baby."

"A family again?" Rickie asked. Erin nodded. "Where's Ben? Ben okay?"

Now there was no holding back the tears. But she fought it as best she could to calm Rickie. "It's all right. Everything will be all right." She pointed to the top of the street fence, lit brightly from outside by approaching emergency vehicles. She turned to the glass doors, beyond the boardwalk, to see the first police and fire personnel just coming through the museum. She turned to the harbor where the William T. Greene burned like a lightning-struck forest. "You stay here, Rickie. My friends are coming to help you. Don't be afraid."

Erin had never been so afraid in all her life.

She left Rickie, slipped back into the harbor, and swam out past the dredger and the debris burning on the surface. She trod water, searching for a sign of Ben. She swam in a circle, saw nothing and no one. Hope had kept her going, but hope was fading. From the shore, she heard Rickie crying over and over again, "Your friends are coming. My friends are gone away."

Pain and fear crept in. Ben wasn't in the water; the boat was burning like Hell. Common sense told her Ben was dead. Terror told her aswang was still alive.

Few things are as dark as a country night. But that night, at the confluence of Iowa, Wisconsin, and Illinois, the Mississippi River valley glowed. The golden dome of the City Hall glistened. The red and blue lights of the squad cars, ambulances, and fire apparatus stabbed the dark and dissected the shadows of the old Port District. Helicopters, one operated by the county sheriff, the other the familiar ship of Duncan-by-Air, hovered and swooped blinking pinpoints of green and red while their white searchlights carved trails through the sky. And the William T. Greene burned brilliantly in flickering shades of orange, red, yellow, white, and blue. It was Easter, but in the little town of Duncan, Iowa, and for miles around, you'd have sworn it was the Fourth of July.

Thirty – Nine

Only a few weeks before, Erin Vanderjagt had been a successful police sergeant, a Training Officer, a rising star. Then a nightmare came to Duncan. Since then, she'd been up to her ears in conflict and death. But she had the work she loved, the man she loved, their unborn child, and the future. Then the William T. Greene exploded. Traumatized, confused, angry, guilty, unsure if Ben was alive, but fearing he was not, unsure if the demon was destroyed, but fearing it was not, out of weapons with which to fight, out of courage, or perhaps, with nothing left but courage, Erin followed the plan.

It was crazy. It had been a joke, a romantic fancy at best. But she'd been well trained, conditioned, to take orders and follow them, to give orders and expect they be carried out. When horror had consumed everything around her, what could Erin do but follow the plan?

After pulling Rickie from the harbor, after searching and being unable to find Ben, convinced that nothing inside the dredger could have survived, nothing but a demon, Erin swam to the other side of the harbor, away from the destroyed steamer, away from the police and fire personnel flooding the grounds of the museum, away from the questions she could not answer alone, away from aswang. For want of a better term, she 'borrowed' a boat, and in the dark, rowed across the Mississippi. At an East Duncan, Illinois gas station she hitched a ride to Galena. At Galena, she caught a bus for Chicago. In a controlled panic, she did these things because all Erin had left was the plan.

That was the reason, simple or insane, the nightmare ended in a low-end hotel in the Chicago Loop, a place so seedy, no self-respecting civil servant would be caught there dead. What better place, Ben had asked when suggesting it, to hide and wait? It was a huge city, a couple of hundred miles away from the terror. As the first to arrive, Erin checked in as Julie Duncan, in honor of their town, and had the clerk make a note of the group name, the Court Reunion, in case they were hinky about giving out guests' names. Ben, if he was alive, would follow as soon as he could.

The twelve story Travel Inn Hotel – Downtown Chicago had everything their plan demanded, an uninterested staff, cheap accommodations, and a South Loop location (on east Hardigan), between Wabash and Michigan, a half block west of Grant Park, two blocks south of the Public Library on the Congress Parkway, around the corner from the Museum of Contemporary Art. It was an easy walk to shops, theaters, museums, restaurants and the famous tourist attractions, McCormick Place, the Sears Tower (regardless of its current name), Millennium Park, Navy Pier, and Lake Michigan. It wasn't a palace, the carpet was worn, the towels thin, the low-pressure water took forever to get hot, and the sink took forever and a day to drain. The thin walls let in outside noises; the El red line, the traffic five floors below, the elevator bells down the hall, and her transient neighbors. But the room was relatively clean and the bed comfortable. She hadn't slept; but it was comfortable for crying on, crying and waiting.

The room had cable television and free HBO, neither of which she'd watched. She had caught the news and an odd story from Duncan, Iowa about an inexplicable explosion aboard a museum display. A police detective, two firefighters, and a reporter were missing. No further information was available. An investigation was ongoing. A minor item buried on a back page of Chicago's leading newspaper offered even less information.

On her sole excursion, to get the paper, Erin noted a Thai restaurant off the main lobby. She hadn't stopped. She did pop in and out of the donut shop across the street. She was a cop after all; at least she was once upon a time. But she wasn't a cop anymore, merely a nervous wreck. In the heart of a city where nobody needed a car, Erin had refused to take so much as a short walk. She'd considered a pre-dawn run through Grant Park and around Buckingham Fountain, but only for an instant. Fear got the better of her – make that blind terror. She put running on hold, as she had her life, in favor of waiting.

Between bouts of emotion, Erin stood beside the window, watching through the curtain, like she was then. From that vantage point, most would have looked out to the excitement of the nighttime bustle, the lights, the skyline, the crescent moon reflecting off the wide black sheet of Lake Michigan beyond the park. All Erin saw was Hardigan Street five stories below, the hotel's massive marquee above the entrance, and at the curb, a white and black checkered cab idling. She'd been watching for Ben, night and day for days, watching and waiting. At the same time, praying she'd never again see...

She found herself concentrating on the roof of the parked cab, on the glowing roof light amid the painted checks. The light could be a target, a point to keep her eyes on while she wrestled the sash up, ducked under and through, and let herself fall. Erin blinked, and 'came to', with no clue where the thought had come from. She'd never had a suicidal thought in her life. She released the curtain and leaned against the wall. The phone rang, and Erin's heart stopped.

She stared at the instrument on the bedside table, ringing like a singing monster. It couldn't be for her; nobody knew she was there. The only one who might guess was Ben. But Ben was... Erin started to shake. It rang again. She knew she had to pull herself together. It was a terrible world out there and, no, she wasn't thinking of crime and poverty and overpopulation. She was thinking of darkness and evil, real evil, at a level no one could know until they'd seen what she'd seen. Even then how could they believe? She didn't answer it; she couldn't. The silence, when the phone stopped ringing, was numbing.

And the sound, when something heavy hit the window beside her, made Erin all but jump out of her skin. Amplified, it might be the sound of a bird hitting a windshield. A bright red tik-tik smashing her car outside of Duncan Memorial. Erin gasped, grabbed the curtain, and yanked it down. There pressed against the spidered glass, dark wings feverishly flapping, viscera dangling from its torn lower half, hung aswang suspended in air. Save for a few pathetic strands, its wild hair was gone, singed to brown, brittle curls. Its rotten green-black face, horrible before, was now horribly scarred with pink and oozing burned flesh. Its tongue, the hated tongue, poked past the fangs in its blistered red mouth, *tap, tap, tapping* at the window. The glass gave way, rained on the carpet, as the creature tucked in its wings and crawled through.

Erin couldn't back away fast enough, couldn't scream loud enough. Aswang was upon her. Its ice cold claws clamped her wrists, pulled her hair, ripped her shirt, and scratched her breasts, as its wings fluttered and drove her back. The stink of burned and rotting flesh overwhelmed the room. In an instant, Erin was on the bed and aswang on her. Its green eyes bored a hole into her mind. Its tongue unrolled...

Erin stretched... She'd moved the coffeemaker – on the bureau when she'd checked in – beside the bed for her convenience. Now it was. Erin grabbed the pot and smashed it on aswang's pointed ear. The coffee burned like hell. She didn't care as it burned the creature too, with glass shards. She jammed the broken edge home and the monster let loose. Erin slid from under it and rolled off the bed.

Aswang lashed out again, knocking the lamp off the bedside table. The table cartwheeled. Erin backed away, avoiding the claws. Wings stuttering, the monster pulled itself off the bed and digging into the worn carpet, started toward her. Erin took advantage of another of the few amenities afforded Travel Inn customers; with all her might she planted the microwave into aswang's scalp.

Erin leapt over the downed creature, or tried. Like the slap of a cane, one of the ever-flapping wings caught her foot. She went down hard, hitting her already bruised head. She regained her senses to find the monster crouched over her. Its face hovered above hers, green almond eyes blinking in pain and lust, fangs dripping saliva. Its hot acrid breath seared Erin's nose and eyes. Revulsion hit. Her stomach turned, and she gulped air, fighting not to vomit. The creature threw a claw over her face, stifling her, pinning her head to the floor, and turned to stare at Erin's bare stomach and barely-showing baby bump. With the wet sound of an old pervert smacking his lips, aswang unrolled its tongue and leveled the tip at Erin's belly. Erin couldn't see it, but she heard and knew what aswang was about to do. Straining, she grabbed the ears of the demon bitch and pulled for her life. She pulled for the life and soul of her baby.

From a thousand miles away – or just across the room, Erin couldn't tell – came a thunderous crash of flesh, wood, metal, and plastic. Pinned down, she couldn't see the cause. Aswang, intent on its feast, paid no attention. After the collision came a startling series of events. The creature halted its tug. The grip on Erin's face let loose. A splash of hot liquid hit Erin's belly. She screamed; aswang shrieked.

The creature jerked up, into Erin's line of vision, howling and spitting the disgusting oil it called blood. Erin saw a glint of gold against the dead green-black of the back of aswang's neck. It took her an instant to realize the creature had been stabbed – by a stake of copper. It took an instant more to wrap her mind around who had done the stabbing.

Ben reached between the creature's frantically beating wings, grabbed the demon beneath the chin, lifted it gurgling and choking on its own blood, and yanked it off of Erin. She rolled away in disgust, jumped to her feet, and grabbed the bed sheet. Half blinded by the blood spat in her eyes, Erin used the sheet to wipe the gore away. Beyond her face, she was drenched. Trying to wipe the rest off would have been pointless. Besides, the party wasn't over.

Ben Court – *her* Ben – was alive and there, grappling with that thing! His clothes, the same ones she'd last seen him in, were filthy and scorched. He had a black eye, swollen shut, but was otherwise pale as a ghost, exhausted, and even from across the room Erin could see his face and arms were burned and several red gouges marred his cheek. He was hurt, but he'd survived. And he'd remembered their plan.

From the corner of her eye, Erin saw Mark Forester as well, standing in the doorway, wearing a big bandage on his face and looking as grungy and used as Ben. The crash she'd heard had been Ben and the reporter breaking down the door. Forester stared wide-eyed, taking in the scene, searching for a way to help.

It was a battle of mythological proportions, the winged griffin and the cyclops, an unbelievable jumble of arms, legs, claws, and slapping wings; the whole affair decorated in oozing red and spattered black blood. Ben shouted and swore. Aswang screeched and sputtered. The creature flexed and flitted, grabbing for Ben's face and eyes. Ben ducked the claws and thumping wings. Then a claw got through, reopening his cheek. Ben returned the sting, grabbing one of its few remaining locks of hair with one hand and its tongue with the other. They smashed into the wall, the window frame, and against the broken window. The creature's wings whipped wildly; neither Erin nor Forester could get close.

The struggle rattled the window frame. The broken glass cut the creature's hide, tore Ben's skin. Gore painted the woodwork and walls. Ben wrestled the monster into the opening and nearly pushed it out. The flailing demon shrieked, gurgled, and fought to pull itself back. The positions were reversed and Ben held on for dear life. The sidewalk and pavement waited five floors below. The unthinkable happened. Ben and aswang toppled out the window together.

Erin went berserk. Forester, freaking himself, had to restrain her.

For Ben, time stood still. A hundred thoughts flashed through his mind, all merging into this reality. Distantly, he heard Erin scream as he and the creature fell through space. Aswang, still choking on the copper rod in its throat, tried to grab the building but couldn't get a hold. It tried to fly, but Ben locked onto its wings. Screw it, Ben thought. At least I'm taking this bitch with me.

The marquee above the Travel Inn entrance hung in place from anchors outside the building's third floor. To end their thirty-foot plunge, the pair hit one of the tension cables. Like a cheese wire, it sliced off the creature's left wing, missing Ben's arm and head by inches. The force of the blow rolled them. Ben was riding on top and landed that way when aswang hit the edge of the marquee. Aswang broke Ben's fall, broke its back, and broke the tension cable. The marquee gave way.

Erin didn't wait on an elevator. She hit the stairs running, with Forester on her heels. Both burst from the stairwell five floors below as if on fire. They raced across the lobby, shouting, "Move!" and "Make a path!" and pushed through a crowd of gapers gathered at the front windows and doors. Erin reached the sidewalk, gasping, with Forester behind, expecting… neither knew what.

From the anchor cables to the sidewalk was another twenty-foot fall for the marquee, Ben, and the demon. Aswang landed and lay struggling in the concrete parking space in front of the hotel doors. A yellow taxi skidded, trying to avoid hitting its flopping wing. The alarmed hack jumped out, mouth gaping, hands on his head. An instant later, and whatever it was, would have landed on his cab. Horns honked, tires squealed, and metal crunched up and down Hardigan Street as drivers tried, some more successfully than others, to avoid hitting the stopped cab and each other.

Ben lay on the sidewalk, to the north of the entrance and the collapsed marquee, unmoving. Aswang had broken his fall above, but the last twenty feet had been all his. He stirred on the ground, alive but gasping like a landed fish, trying to refill his lungs. Erin ran to him, crying. He stopped her with a raised hand. He wanted her embrace, of course, but needed a breath worse. Erin helped him to his feet, then released him to resume his struggle for air. Ben got his breath back, as over the shouts of the stunned crowd, sirens rose and filled the night air.

Erin shouted, "Ben, look!"

There was plenty at which to look and Ben and Forester saw what Erin saw at the same time.

The copper stake, previously lodged in aswang's throat, lay shining in the gutter. And the demon, now on its stomach, raising itself on flexed arms, was sprouting a new wing.

Ben pushed Forester down going for the stake. Copper rod in hand, the paramedic dove for the creature. Up again in seconds, Forester got hell slapped out of him as he grabbed the monster's wings. Ben stabbed aswang's neck, again, and shoved until the point of the rod popped through the flesh beneath its chin. "Roll it!" he shouted.

They flipped the demon. Erin was there to add a headlock. The cop and the reporter held aswang fast while Ben stuffed its mouth with ash from a pouch on his belt. The creature coughed a gray cloud. Its shriek became a choked gurgle, then stopped altogether. The trio released the demon and watched as a pool of black ink grew on the pavement around it.

Erin, Ben, and Forester, oblivious of the alarmed crowd swarming, limped their way back to the sidewalk. There they stood staring at their handiwork until a Chicago cop shouted, "Hey!" for the third time. "You got a lot of explaining to do."

Ben stared blankly. "How do you figure?"

"With that laying in the street," the cop said, pointing. "You got the nerve to ask—?"

"I stop to visit a friend," Ben said, cutting him off, pointing himself. "And that comes through the window. What the hell kind of town are you running here?"

The cop stared at Ben, then the thing on the sidewalk, then Erin and Forester, and finally, at Ben again. "What is that?" he asked, with an adjusted attitude.

"I don't know," Ben said. "But do yourself a favor. Burn it as quick you can. And whatever you do, leave that stake alone until you do."

The cop looked again, to see the glinting copper rod protruding from the gore. For a minute, he seemed as if he might ask another question, then decided against it. "Right," he said. "Right."

Ben took Erin in his burned arms. "Don't you answer your phone?"

"I was busy."

Neither Erin nor Ben lost their jobs, but the details of their return to Duncan… would take another book. Their first steps on the road back were slow and limping ones as they returned to the hotel. The night manager lost his mind, screaming at them, but the trio barely heard him. Erin was too busy holding Ben up. Ben was too busy reminding Forester, "I kept my promise. There's your story."

"Story? It's the record of a nightmare. Nobody will believe a word of it!"

Turned out, the reporter was worried for nothing. Nobody would even print it.

About the Author

Doug Lamoreux is a father of three, a grandfather, a writer, and actor. A former professional fire fighter, he is the author of five novels and a contributor to anthologies and non-fiction works including the Rondo Award nominated Horror 101, and its companion, the Rondo Award winning Hidden Horror. He has been nominated for a Rondo, a Lord Ruthven Award, a Pushcart Prize, and is the first-ever recipient of The Horror Society's Igor Award for fiction. Lamoreux starred in the 2006 Peter O'Keefe film, Infidel, and appeared in the Mark Anthony Vadik horror films The Thirsting (aka Lilith) and Hag.

Other Books by the Author

The Devil's Bed
Dracula's Demeter
The Melting Dead
Corpses Say the Darndest Things: A Nod Blake Mystery
Apparition Lake (with Daniel D. Lamoreux)
Obsidian Tears (with Daniel D. Lamoreux)

Made in United States
Orlando, FL
29 February 2024